P9-DJV-049

THE

**REAL
BOY**

THE REAL BOY

Anne Ursu

Drawings by Erin McGuire

WALDEN POND PRESS

An Imprint of HarperCollins*Publishers*

Walden Pond Press is an imprint of HarperCollins Publishers.

The Real Boy
Text copyright © 2013 by Anne Ursu
Illustrations copyright © 2013 by Erin McGuire
All rights reserved. Printed in the United States of America. No part of this
book may be used or reproduced in any manner whatsoever without written
permission except in the case of brief quotations embodied in critical articles
and reviews. For information address HarperCollins Children's Books,
a division of HarperCollins Publishers, 10 East 53rd Street,
New York, NY 10022.
www.harpercollinschildrens.com

ISBN 978-0-06-201507-5 (trade bdg.)

Typography by Carla Weise
13 14 15 16 17 CG/RRDH 10 9 8 7 6 5 4 3 2 1
❖
First Edition

For Dash

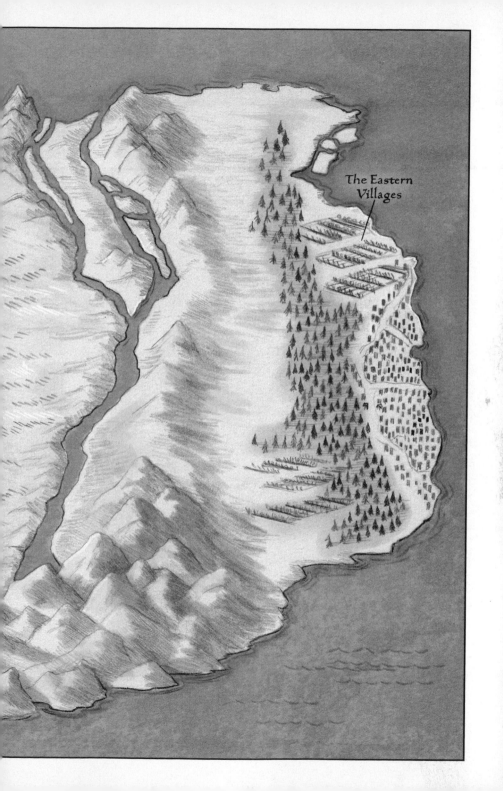

The Eastern
Villages

CHAPTER ONE

The Cellar Boy

The residents of the gleaming hilltop town of Asteri called their home, simply, the City. The residents of the Barrow—the tangle of forest and darkness that encircled the bottom of Asteri's hill like a shadowy moat—called Asteri the Shining City, and those who lived there the shining people. The Asterians didn't call themselves anything special, because when everyone else refers to you as the shining people, you really don't have to do it yourself.

Massive stone walls towered around the City, almost as tall as the great trees in the forest. And, though you could not tell by looking at them, the walls writhed with enchantments.

For protection, the people of the City said.

For show, the magic smiths of the Barrow said. After all, it was in the dark of the Barrow where the real magic lay.

And indeed, the people of Asteri streamed through the walls and down the tall hill to the shops of the Barrow marketplace, buying potions and salves, charms and wards, spells and pretty little enchanted things. They could not do any magic themselves, but they had magic smiths to do it for them. And really, wasn't that better anyway?

The Barrow even had one magic worker so skilled he called himself a magician. Master Caleb was the first magician in a generation, and he helped the Asterians shine even more brightly. He had an apprentice, like most magic smiths. But like the wizards of old, he also took on a hand—a young boy from the Children's Home—to do work too menial for a magician's apprentice.

The boy, who was called Oscar, spent most of his time underneath Caleb's shop, tucked in a small room in the cellar, grinding leaves into powders, extracting oils from plants, pouring tinctures into small vials—kept company by the quiet, the dark, the cocoon of a room, and a steady rotation of murmuring cats. It was a good fate for an orphan.

"Hey, Mouse!"

Except for one thing.

"Come out, come out, Mouse! Are you there?"

At the sound of the apprentice's voice calling down the cellar stairs, a large gray cat picked herself up from the corner and brushed softly against Oscar. "It's all right," Oscar whispered. "I'll be fine." The cat sprang up and disappeared into the dark.

The apprentice's name was Wolf, because sometimes the universe is an unsubtle place. And even now Oscar sometimes found himself expecting an actual wolf to appear in place of the boy, as if the boy were just a lie they were all telling themselves.

"Where are you, little rodent?"

Oscar put down his pestle. He was not a rodent, but that never seemed to stop Wolf from calling him one. "I'm here," he called back. Stupid Wolf. As if one could be anywhere else but *here*.

Wolf appeared in the pantry door. He was only four years older than Oscar but almost twice as tall. With his elongated frame, the apprentice seemed all bones and hollows in the lantern light. He looked around the room, dark eyes flicking across the floor.

"Where are your little cat friends, Mouse?"

"Not here," Oscar said.

Like he would tell Wolf. Only Oscar knew the cats' secrets, and he guarded them closely. He knew all their names, he knew the sound of their footfalls, he knew where each of them slept, hid, stalked, he knew which one would visit him at what time of day. The gray cat with the lantern-bright green eyes was Crow, and she liked to come into the pantry in the mornings and nestle in the parchment envelopes.

"I don't actually care," Wolf said. He turned his gaze to the towering wall of shelves behind him. "We need some raspberry leaf for a Shiner. Now."

Oscar didn't even have to look. He could see the jars on the pantry shelves just as clearly in his head. "There's none left."

Wolf narrowed his eyes but did not question Oscar. A couple of years ago the apprentice would have stalked over to the shelves himself to make sure. Except every time he did, he'd discover that Oscar was right. Then he'd get angry and kick Oscar. It worked out better for both of them this way.

Wolf scanned the room. "Well, what about that?" He pointed at a jar at Oscar's feet filled with dry, crumbled green leaves.

"That's walnut leaves!" Oscar said.

"It looks the same. Give me four packets."

"But . . . ," Oscar sputtered, chest tightening. How could Wolf think they looked the same? "That's not what they want. It won't work." In fact, the herbs were opposite—raspberry leaf was to protect a relationship and walnut leaf was to break one up. But Wolf did not like it when Oscar knew such things.

"Oh, it won't work!" Wolf exclaimed, slapping his hands on his forehead. "I had no idea! What would *I*, apprentice to the Barrow's only true magician, do if it weren't for the cellar mouse to tell me that it won't work!"

"Well," Oscar said, "you could always look it up in the library."

Wolf's eyes flared. Oscar flinched. He hadn't even been trying to make Wolf angry; all he'd done was answer his question.

Wolf took a step closer to Oscar. "Do you even know what a freak you are?" he asked. "There's a reason Caleb keeps you in the basement." His eyes flicked from Oscar to the doorway and back. "Anyway, who cares about the herbs? It's a Shiner. She won't know the difference."

"But . . . what if she does?" The words popped out of Oscar's mouth before he could stop them. He could not help it—they were fluttering around in his head and needed to get out.

Wolf drew himself up. "Look, Mouse," he said, voice carnivorous. "She won't. Shiners want magic to work, and so it works. If you weren't dumb as a goat, you'd know that."

Oscar smashed his lips together. If that was true, it was no magic he understood.

"You let Caleb and me worry about the customers," Wolf continued. "You can worry about the cats, and your little plants, and—"

But whatever else Oscar had to worry about would remain a mystery, for just then the magician's voice came echoing down into the cellar, calling for Wolf.

The apprentice turned, collecting his bones and hollows. "Bring the walnut leaves up as soon as you have them ready," he said as he moved out the door. "And for the love of the wizards," he added, "don't come out into the shop. We want the customers to come back."

Five minutes later Oscar was creeping into the shop's kitchen, four packets of herbs in his hands. They were not walnut leaves. He hadn't had much time, so he'd put together a package of passionflower and verbena, which at least would not cause active harm.

From his position in the doorway he could see Master Caleb leaning across the shop counter, his tree-dark eyes focused on the lady before him as if they existed for nothing but to behold her.

The shining people didn't actually shine, not like a lantern or a firefly or a crystal in the light. But they might as well have. The young lady in front of Caleb looked like all the City people did—perfectly smooth olive-touched skin, cheeks with color and flesh, hair done up in some elaborate sculpture of braids and bejeweled pins,

a gleaming amulet around her neck, wearing a dress of such intricately detailed fabric it made Oscar's hands hurt just to look at it.

Wolf appeared in the kitchen and immediately grabbed the packets out of Oscar's hand. Oscar gazed steadily at Wolf's chest. *The passionflower looks like walnut leaves,* he whispered in his mind—though whether to convince himself or Wolf he was not sure.

Wolf eyed the contents and sniffed, then turned and went back into the shop. His whole body seemed to change as he walked through the door, as if he were transforming from beast to human.

Oscar let out a breath and then suddenly caught it again. Wolf was handing the packets not to the customer, but to Master Caleb. Who was expecting raspberry leaves. Oscar had never made a mistake, not with herbs anyway, not in five years.

Caleb took the packets in his hand. Oscar's heart thudded. But Caleb just smiled at the customer, his mouth spreading widely across his face the way it always did when there was a woman on the other side of the counter. He looked as though nothing had ever made him so happy as giving her what she wanted.

The lady smiled back. And her cheeks flushed, just a little.

"Four envelopes of raspberry leaves, my lady," said

Caleb. "Though"—he leaned even closer—"I don't see how a lady like you would need such a thing."

"Oh," she said, laughing like a chime, "you can never be too careful."

Caleb straightened and ran a hand slowly through his dark hair. The lady's hand flew to hers.

"I agree," Caleb said. "And that's why we're here. We in the Barrow serve at your pleasure." He leaned again, and his face grew serious. "Whatever you need."

The woman opened the package and inhaled deeply. Oscar froze. He hadn't had time to mask the smell, and surely the verbena—

"I just love the smell of raspberry," she said.

"We'll mix up some perfume for you if you want. You have such natural beauty—we could put in things that would . . . enhance it."

The lady's smile grew. "I'll come back next week," she said, and then gave a little laugh. "It's true what they say, isn't it? Everything is better here than anywhere else in the world." For a moment her eyes dropped on Oscar in the doorway and then moved away, as if they had seen nothing at all.

Wolf appeared next to Oscar and leaned in. "He's quite a master, isn't he?" the apprentice whispered, nodding in Caleb's direction.

Oscar could only nod back. Of course he was.

Wasn't that the entire point?

Just before she got to the door, the lady stopped and smelled her envelopes again. And then she turned, gave Caleb one last raspberry smile, and left.

"I don't understand," Oscar muttered.

"You don't understand anything," Wolf said. "Caleb is a genius. He makes all the old wizards look like little cellar boys."

Oscar inwardly winced. No one talked about the wizards that way. He half expected a shelf to fall on Wolf's head.

It didn't. Shelves never fell on Wolf's head when Oscar wanted them to.

"Caleb can do things no one's ever done before, incredible things." Wolf looked down at Oscar, his eyes sparkling. "I know. While you're in the cellar filling envelopes, he's teaching me everything. He's going to make magic great again, greater than it ever was in the era of the wizards, and I'm helping him. You—"

In a flash Wolf shut his mouth, turned around, and transformed into Nice Wolf. It was his best feat of magic. Master Caleb was hanging on the door frame, leaning in. Caleb was taller than Wolf, and there were no bones and hollows to him. Caleb filled everything.

"Ah, you're both here," Caleb said. "Oscar, why don't

you go to the gardens this afternoon? I believe we are low on supplies . . . particularly raspberry leaves."

Oscar's stomach dropped to his feet.

Caleb turned his gaze to Wolf. "And, Wolf, why don't you stay in the kitchen the rest of the day and sort the dried herbs. It seems like the time with them would do you some good."

Wolf stiffened. Oscar gulped.

Turning back to Oscar, Caleb added, "Not bad, my boy. But next time, add some rose hips or another berry leaf for scent."

The magician raised his eyebrows slightly. Oscar's mouth hung open. Then Caleb winked, ever so quickly, before heading back into the shop.

Oscar exhaled. He could feel his mouth twitching into a smile. Caleb's words perched on his shoulders: *Not bad, my boy.*

And then the smile fled, and the words, too. Wolf turned on him, all beast. "You think you're Caleb's little pet, eh?" he snarled. "I don't know what you did, Mouse, but you will regret it."

Oscar stepped back. He didn't know what he had done, either, but Wolf was definitely right: Whatever it was, he would certainly regret it.

◆ ◆ ◆

Oscar was out the back door of the shop and into the forest before Wolf got a chance to pounce. Some presence followed him, something soft and stealthy and entirely un-Wolflike. Oscar turned around and a smile spread across his face. "Are you going to keep me company, Crow?" he whispered.

The smoke-gray cat's eyes danced, and she slipped next to Oscar, as close as a shadow.

Oscar had been to every part of the forest, including the thin strips in the southwest and northwest that wrapped around Asteri's hill like fingers, buffering the City from the plaguelands and the sea beyond. Though hundreds of people lived in the forest's villages, and though the forest was miles wide and even more miles across, it felt as secure and familiar as Oscar's own pantry. Better, because there were only wolves, and no Wolf.

The rest of the villagers had their gardens and pastures just outside the northeast of the forest, in the swath of fertile land that separated the eastern Barrow from the plaguelands. And their barns and stables, too. No farm animals liked being in the Barrow—except for Madame Catherine's Most Spectacular Goat.

But Caleb's gardens were in the southeast. And though everyone knew of their majesty, no one would ever find them. Caleb had hidden them behind an illusion spell, so anyone who did not know what was actually there would see only a meadow. The secret belonged to Caleb, Oscar, Wolf, and the trees.

The magic of the Barrow came from its soil, and the soil birthed a half a world's worth of plants and countless species of trees—from black cherry to red mulberry, quaking aspen to weeping willow, silver maple to golden rain, persimmon to pawpaw. Plants and shrubs and flowers grew everywhere; purplish-greenish moss crawled on the rocks; improbable mushrooms sprang from the soil in tiny little groves of their own.

But nothing compared to the wizard trees. The great oak trees grew to the sky like ladders for giants or gods, and spread their twisting branches as far out over the soil below as they could.

Once upon a time, magic flourished on all of Aletheia. And for centuries, legendary wizards worked the island's magic. The wizards were so powerful that they never died—when it was time for their human life to end, they would make their way into the Barrow forest, plant their feet in the hungry soil, and transform. Their body and spirit would go, but their essence would live on forever in a majestic, thriving monument. It was the only fitting end for a wizard of Aletheia. This was the island's gift to the wizards who tended to its magic and made the island thrive. Everyone knew the story.

And the wizards had never stopped serving Aletheia. When they became trees, their magic spread down through their roots, infusing the forest earth. And that was why the Barrow was a place like no other.

At some point the last wizard of Aletheia became a tree, and some time after that the island brought forth sorcerers—not nearly as powerful, but still with the ability to work the magic for the good of the people. Gradually the sorcerers faded, too, and were replaced by magicians, and then the magicians by magic smiths. Until Caleb, that is.

The forest had exactly one hundred wizard trees, and Oscar knew every one of them. He could close his eyes and see the map of them covering the forest, watching over it, feeding it with magic. Whenever Oscar touched one, he could feel some warmth humming just beneath the surface. And whenever he passed one, anything that was buzzing or roiling inside him stilled.

When he reached the edge of the forest, Oscar stopped. He had crossed through the line of trees into the gardens countless times, and each time he had to will himself to do it. Because maybe this would be the time Oscar would step through and the gardens would be gone, and Oscar would fall into the sky.

He looked at Crow, who trilled at him. He took a deep breath. He stepped forward. The trees released him, and the ground caught him; *It's all right.*

The gardens stretched along the edge of the forest, over an area three times as big as the main courtyard in the marketplace, a small orchard, rows of bushes, and plants of all kinds spreading out everywhere. *Angelica, anise, arrowroot.* It was all perfectly organized, logical—you didn't even need to think to find what you wanted. *Basil, bay leaf, bergamot, borage.*

In the back stood Caleb's towering achievement, the greatest man-made thing in the forest. And probably the entire world.

When Caleb had begun to import plants from far-off countries, things that didn't even grow in the Barrow (*eucalyptus, wolfberry, saffron, bellflower*), he'd announced he was going to design a house to hold them all, someplace bright and lush and moist to trick the plants into thinking they were somewhere warm and wet.

The result was a great steam house—the biggest building Oscar had ever seen. Panels of glass as tall as Caleb's shop and just as wide stood proudly next to one another, embraced all around by iron. A peaked glass roof sat on top, catching the sun and cradling the plants, giving them a place that was even better than home.

Walking into the house felt like stepping into an enchantment. It was a completely different world, warmer than the real world ever was, and the air had texture and moisture and life. The flowers burst forth in colors no illustration in a book had ever been able to reproduce— they looked like birds, like bells, like butterflies. They made even the clothes of the shining people seem dull. Oscar always stepped quietly through the glass house, trying to make as little disturbance as he could. He was trespassing; this house belonged to the flowers.

Oscar took a cart from the side of the glass house and began moving it through the gardens. He scanned the pantry shelves in his mind, making a list of jars that needed filling. He worked for two hours among the green and thriving things, picking plants, trimming off leaves and flowers, plucking berries, until his cart was full. He found Crow curled up near the raspberry bushes, as if to remind him not to forget the leaves.

"It's time to go," Oscar whispered. "It will be dark soon."

Crow blinked up at him sleepily.

Oscar sighed. "You're not going to walk, are you?" The cat eyed him, as if that was a very stupid question. "All right," Oscar said, picking Crow up in his arms and putting her in a corner of the cart. She crawled onto a pile of meadowsweet and immediately curled up again. "Well," Oscar murmured, "those needed to be crushed anyway."

• • •

It was near dark when Oscar got home. He opened the back door of the shop carefully—maybe if the door moved slowly enough Wolf would not notice a thing. But Wolf was not there. Crow jumped out of the cart, and Oscar unloaded everything into the kitchen and crept back down to his pantry.

As soon as his hands were working the mortar and pestle, everything else was gone. It was just his hands, the plants, the cool brass, the steady crushing and grinding, as soothing and steadfast as a cat's purr.

He made dough with anise and slippery-elm powder, picked off small pieces, and rolled them in his hands so they were the size of tiny pellets, small enough that people could swallow them. You had to roll them for a hundred counts, one at a time—*one, two, three, four*—all the way up to a hundred. Your hands became infused with the sharp, sweet smell, as if you yourself had absorbed some little bit of magic. He fed mugwort leaves into his small mill and turned the crank—fifty times, for mugwort, as fast as your hands could go, and faster still. He peeled white bark off pieces of birch and then smoothed out the wood so it was prepared for Caleb to carve charms. He cleaned and polished some of the strangely colored stones that had come in with the last boat shipments, until they were as shiny as they were smooth. He could not help but hold them in his palm for a moment when he was done, fold his hand around them, and squeeze—each one seemed like such a fixed, true thing.

And soon it was time for Oscar to go into his room. It was one of the rules Caleb was strict about: Oscar must be in his room at nine and not come out again until morning.

Oscar's room—down the hallway from the main cellar—was just big enough to hold a narrow mattress, a little table for a lantern, a washbasin, and a small cabinet for Oscar's things, of which there were not very many. Tonight, just like every night, a small orange kitten named Pebble lay on the bed, licking her paws. Oscar scratched her in between her two shoulder blades, washed up, and got into bed.

One hour. Two. Pebble got up and began to pace. Three.

After he heard everyone go to bed, and an hour after that, Oscar finally left his room, shushing a protesting Pebble. He moved whisper soft through the cellar hallway, passing by Caleb's workshop on his way to the library like nothing more than a breath. These are the things you learn when you spend your days underground, when your body spends so much time in shadow you can't always tell where you end and the shadow begins, when all your friends are cats.

It was impossible that he could read. It was not the

sort of thing they taught in the Children's Home. Reading was for apprentices. Oscar wasn't even supposed to be out of his room.

But, somehow, he could read. And ever since he'd come to serve Caleb, he could not resist the library and the whole world of things in there.

Without the books, Oscar would not know about the herbs, about their properties and powers—could never have combined passionflower and verbena to make something that looked like raspberry leaves and did not work like walnut leaves and could cause the greatest magician in the Barrow to wink at him and say, *Not bad, my boy.*

It was worth a small disobedience.

As long as he did not get caught.

The library, like everything in Caleb's underground complex, was impossibly large—the size of the entire footprint of the aboveground shop. All the walls were covered with shelves. It looked like a room made of books, with a floor and a ceiling attached for propriety's sake. There was a desk tucked into one end and, next to that, a large red upholstered chair on which slept a skinny cat with black spots that spread across a base of shining white fur like islands on an ocean. His name was Map.

So Oscar settled in the library as he did many nights,

pulling out books while the cats slept on shelves. Since Caleb had started importing from beyond the boundaries of the island of Aletheia, there'd been much to learn. And more books to learn it from, too—*Gardens of Babylon* and *The Bounty of the East*. Oscar flipped through the pages, collecting images in his mind and filing them away.

Suddenly he felt a nip at his ankles. The brown tomcat, Cat, was staring at him, thumping his tail.

"What is it?" Oscar whispered.

It was a noise in the hallway. Footsteps. Coming toward the library. Slowly.

Oscar's heart sped up. He leaned over and turned down his lantern. The footsteps stopped for a moment. Silence. Cat blinked. And then again—heading back toward the bedrooms.

Oscar gulped. Caleb or Wolf?

He sat in darkness in the library, counting to two hundred, his heart pounding like footsteps. He should not be here, should not be reading, should not be out of bed, should not do anything to jeopardize his place in Caleb's house.

He picked himself up and tiptoed back to his room.

Once, Oscar had lived in the Children's Home— across the plaguelands, across the river, on the eastern side of Aletheia where no magic lived. He did not remember much about the Home; whenever he tried to remember, his head filled with noise, some heavy pressing feeling, and flickering shadows that were the color of an old bruise. It was not a place he wanted to think too much about.

Now he served the only true magician in the Barrow. He spent his days tucked safely in the quiet and dark, with his hands and the plants and the cocoon of the pantry and the steady company of cats. His days had been like this as far back as his memory chose to reach— and they would be like this as far forward as he could imagine.

If it weren't for Wolf, everything would be perfect.

CHAPTER TWO

Wolf's Revenge

Oscar awoke in the morning with the feeling of dread twitching in his body, as if mice had been skittering along the inside of his skin all night. With a deep breath, he counted the things around him that were real. There was the ceiling; there were his walls; here was his bed, his blanket, his Pebble.

Whenever he woke up from a dream, he had to talk himself slowly back into this world, counting its structures and boundaries and steady, sure things. Whatever great gaping world his mind had taken him to the night before, the one he lived in was made of small closed-in spaces. It was all right. It was all right.

He sat up in bed and Pebble brushed against his

side. The structures and boundaries of the day laid themselves out before him, and he counted them: get the water; sweep the shop; go pick up the washing from Mister Albert (for it was Tuesday); go to the pantry; sort yesterday's haul into things that needed to be dried, pressed, and pulped; dry, press, and pulp them; and go back to bed after nightfall.

And try to avoid Wolf the best he could.

Oscar got up and washed, then put on his white shirt and brown pants and black boots. The footsteps of the night before echoed in his head. But maybe it was nothing, he told himself. Maybe his secret was safe.

His secret was not safe. When Oscar opened the door to his room, a small stack of books from the library waited for him in the hallway. *Orphans: Boon or Bane?* read one. *Misfits and Madmen: Common Disorders of the Mind* read another. *The Plight of the Idiot* read the last.

Not Caleb's footsteps, then.

Checking carefully up and down the hallway, Oscar picked up the books and put them under his bed. "You can read these while I'm working," he muttered to Pebble. If Oscar was lucky, Wolf would just decide to torment him rather than tell Caleb that Oscar had been in the library at night.

It was a bad day when Wolf's torment was the better choice.

Oscar was sweeping the shop when Wolf strode in, wearing the red cloak and the small leaf pin that marked him as an apprentice. His face was split with a smile, the sort that said Wolf was about to enjoy himself and Oscar was not.

"So you can read now?" Wolf said, his voice bouncing off the walls. "That's marvelous! The idiot can do tricks!" He thumped the counter emphatically, making Oscar jump.

Oscar's eyes went to Wolf's shoulder. "It's not a trick," he said through clenched teeth.

"You think you can make me look bad in front of Master Caleb? You think you're so special because he lets you grind herbs? That's not real magic; that's just plants. There's a whole wide world outside of your little pantry." Wolf leaned in and grinned. "He needs me for the important things."

Oscar's grip around the broom tightened. "I do not think I'm so special," he said. "I like plants."

"Oh, do you?" Wolf drew himself up, his thick eyebrows knotting together. "I'm the apprentice. I have magic. I was certified by the duke. Were you?'

No, Oscar was not.

"You think Caleb likes you. But you're useful to him. That's all. You would be smart not to forget it. Because when you stop being useful . . ." Wolf threw out his wide arms as if there were a world of possibilities of what might happen to Oscar when he stopped being useful to Caleb. At the moment Oscar could think of only two: back to the Children's Home, or stepping out of the forest and falling into the void.

"I am useful," Oscar whispered. But whether for his benefit or for Wolf's he wasn't sure.

Wolf let out a noise and then shook his head slowly. "You don't even know where you came from," Wolf said.

Before Oscar could ask him what he was talking about, Caleb strode in from the back room, and in a blink of an eye Nice Wolf appeared.

"Are we ready?" the apprentice asked.

Caleb eyed him. "Ah. No," he said, adjusting his gray cloak. "That is, I have urgent business to attend to on the continent. I will be gone for a couple of days."

Oscar swallowed. This happened sometimes: Caleb often locked himself in his workroom for a day, or all night. And more and more lately Caleb left altogether— sometimes for an afternoon or a day, sometimes for days. Wolf ran the shop and acted like he was the only true magician in the Barrow, and Oscar did his best to stay out of his way.

But that worked best when Wolf wasn't actively out to punish him.

"I know you'll both keep everything running

smoothly," Caleb added. He glanced at them and then nodded, as if that were all there was to be said.

"But Master," Wolf said after a moment, "I thought we had that . . . errand."

"Mmm?" Caleb blinked. "Oh, yes. We do. We'll do it when I get back."

Wolf tilted his head. "If it's important, I could do it on my own."

Caleb frowned. "That will not be necessary. We do not close the shop during marketplace hours." He motioned to the framed piece of paper that hung next to the door—his license from the duke to sell magical goods to the Asterians. "You will run the shop, and Oscar will keep you in supplies." Caleb looked from Wolf to Oscar. "I trust everything will be in order when I return."

Wolf glanced at Oscar and smiled so that only Oscar could see his fangs. "Certainly, Master Caleb," he said. "You can count on us."

Oscar blinked. "It's Tuesday," he said. And then he slipped out the door to head to Mister Albert's to get the washing.

An hour later, Oscar was back in his pantry. It was the first time he'd ever wanted to stay in the marketplace for longer than he needed to. As much as he shrank from the noise and bustle, it was much better than whatever

Wolf had in store for him.

The shop would not open for another half hour, and Oscar could hear nothing from upstairs. Caleb was certainly gone already—the magician did not waste time—and Wolf was probably outside somewhere sharpening his claws.

The only sound came from the white puffball in the corner—the very fluffy cat Bear, who made little grunting noises when she slept. The company was nice; Caleb's complex felt eerily hollow when there were no people in it.

And then—footsteps walking in the shop overhead. Two pairs: Wolf's assertive footfalls followed by someone else's lighter tread. Then, three big stomps right above him. The ceiling trembled, the glass jars shook, and Bear started awake with a cranky meow.

Oscar was being summoned.

He took a deep breath, rubbed his arm, and headed upstairs, trying to put some identity to the second pair of footsteps so he could prepare himself. His heart was pounding—whether out of fear of Wolf or fear of a stranger he wasn't sure.

And, indeed, there was a stranger: Wolf was standing near the front door next to a tall girl with straight black hair and angles for cheeks. She, too, wore a red cloak joined with an apprentice pin. Oscar felt himself shrink, as if he could disappear entirely.

Wolf grinned at Oscar. "Hello, Oscar," he said, drawing out the name like a purr. "This is Bonnie. She's Master Robin's new apprentice, just certified." Master Robin was the Barrow guardian, and his former apprentice had had an unfortunate incident involving a warding spell and a tree.

Oscar swallowed.

"Why doesn't he look at me?" the girl asked.

"I'm sorry," Wolf said. "The boy has no manners. He's an orphan and he's not quite right in the head. Caleb and I have taken him under our care."

Oscar gritted his teeth. "You have not—"

"Anyway, Oscar," Wolf interrupted, voice puffed out like a cloud, "something urgent has come up. Bonnie and I have very important business deep in the forest."

The new apprentice grinned and flipped her hair.

"Now?" Oscar said.

"Yes, now." Wolf held up a hand. "With Caleb gone it is my job to act in the magician's stead. I'm afraid we will be out all day."

Oscar's breath caught. "You can't close the shop! Master Caleb said—"

"I know what Master Caleb said. We can't close the shop." Wolf waved an arm toward the shop's license. "But I have very important business, you see. Magician business. So you'll have to mind the shop."

"I'll . . . what?"

Wolf stretched a long arm out and put it around Oscar's shoulder. "There's nothing to fear, my lad. Remember how special you are? You can read; you can even grind up plants into tiny bits. I'm sure you'll have no trouble running the shop for a day."

"But—"

"And I'll talk to the customers and tell Master Caleb all about how well you did." Wolf's bony hand squeezed Oscar's shoulder. "Then he'll see how capable you really are."

"You can't—"

Wolf squeezed his hand, tight enough to make Oscar yelp. "Have fun!" he said. And then in a swirl of cloaks the two apprentices were gone.

Oscar stood. And stared. The red of the cloaks flashed behind his eyes. His gaze went from the shop license to the clock. His heart sped up.

And then the front door opened.

Oscar took a step back, gripping the counter tightly with one hand.

A woman and a girl walked in, both dressed in loose white shirts, long brown skirts, and cloaks: gray for the woman, red for the girl. The woman—Madame Mariel, the Barrow healer—stood in the middle of the shop and squinted at Oscar. The girl, who was made of vines of curly black hair and darting eyes, was her apprentice, Callie. Callie was a couple years older than Oscar and never seemed to speak much. Though even Caleb did not speak much around Madame Mariel.

Madame Mariel cleared her throat and looked around the room. "Where is everyone?"

Oscar froze. She seemed to be asking him. His eyes darted to Mariel's left boot. "Um," he began carefully, "Master Caleb had to go to the continent, and Wolf had very important business deep in the forest with Master Robin's new apprentice, and everyone else . . . is somewhere else."

He winced. He could feel Madame Mariel's eyes on him.

"What are you doing here? Who are you?"

"I am minding the shop today," he said, keeping his eyes on her left boot. "I am Oscar."

"Oh," Madame Mariel said, "you're that odd little hand Caleb has." Oscar blinked and dared a glance up as high as Madame Mariel's stomach. Why did she ask who he was if she already knew?

Out of the corner of his eye he saw Callie, who was standing right behind the healer, raise her eyebrows at him. It probably meant something. It would've been nice to know what.

For the last five years, most of Oscar's non-cat interactions had been with Master Caleb and Wolf. And so he had learned them, learned the ways their faces moved around, learned how their voices rose and fell, thickened and thinned, learned the way their bodies spoke. But when he went out into the marketplace and tried to apply what he'd learned to other people, their faces all moved in different ways and their voices did all different things, their bodies were all over the place, and nothing meant anything from one person to the next. They said words they did not mean, and their conversations seemed to follow all kinds of rules—rules that no one had ever explained to Oscar. And if that weren't enough, people talked in other ways, too, ways that had nothing to do with the things coming out of their mouths.

Like raising their eyebrows.

"Look me in the eye, boy," Madame Mariel snapped.

Oscar flinched. Her words echoed in his mind, multiplied like shadows. The shadows stretched back through the years, took on the color of an old bruise. Bodiless hands grabbed his chin and forced it up: *Look me in the eye, boy.*

Oscar swallowed and looked down at the counter.

Madame Mariel let out a Wolflike laugh. "If Caleb is such a master magician, why didn't he get a normal boy for his hand?"

Callie was still standing in the corner, arms folded, watching Madame Mariel. Her gaze shifted to Oscar, and she rolled her eyes.

Flushing, Oscar looked quickly back at the healer, who seemed to have grown several inches in the last minute. He was not doing this right. What was it Wolf said to customers when he was working the shop and pretending to be a mere pup?

"What . . . what do you want?"

No, that wasn't it.

"I need Caleb," said the healer.

"He's not here," Oscar said.

"But I need him," she said.

"But he's not here," Oscar repeated.

"But I *need* him."

"But . . . he's not here." Oscar frowned. This seemed like it could go on for some time.

"You—" The healer raised her hand.

"Madame," Callie said suddenly. "Do we need more rue?"

The healer turned. "Of course we don't. We have rue coming out of our nostrils. What's wrong with you?"

There was a flash of something on the girl's face, but before Oscar could identify it, it was gone, and she simply shrugged and tightened her cloak around her shoulders.

Madame Mariel turned back to Oscar, and Oscar's gaze darted away. "Would you tell Caleb to come see me as soon as he gets back?" the healer said, each word a sigh. "And really, little hand, if you're going to be out with the people, you should go to Master Julian's and have him do something with your hair. He is quite gifted, and I think even that"—she pointed to Oscar's thicket of black hair—"is within his power to control."

Oscar opened his mouth. Nothing came out.

Madame Mariel plucked two packets of chamomile from their places on the shelves and slid four gold coins across the counter at Oscar. On the way out, Callie looked back at him, eyes wide, eyebrows up. Her cheeks puffed out and she blew air from them. This apparently meant something, too.

Oscar missed the cats.

He squeezed his eyes shut. One customer was plenty; Wolf could come back now, and then Oscar could dive back into his pantry and never come out.

The shop door opened again, and it was not Wolf, but rather Master Julian himself, followed soon after by two villagers Oscar did not recognize. Three customers at once—it felt like the shop was being invaded. The villagers bowed their heads slightly at Master Julian and stepped back. The magic smiths wore cloak pins with trees on them (courtesy of Mistress Alma, the silversmith), but no one from the Barrow villages needed a pin to identify them. Even the small children of the Barrow could recite all thirty names like a song—*Madame Alexandra, tanner; Madame Aphra, cloth maker; Master Barnabus, butcher;* all the way down to *Master Thomas, blacksmith*—and would whisper and point whenever one was near.

The customers poked around the shop—Master Julian in front of the tinctures, the villagers by the small wooden charms Caleb carved. Some invisible nagging presence was poking Oscar in the side, tugging at his sleeve, telling him he should be doing something now.

But he had no idea what that might be.

After a few minutes, Master Julian approached the counter.

Look him in the eye, Oscar told himself. He lifted his gaze up to Master Julian's face, and then suddenly his whole body rebelled. His eyes snapped away, his heart pounded, his throat went dry. He gripped the counter harder.

Master Julian cleared his throat. "Are you Caleb today?" he asked.

"What?" Oscar started. "No! I'm Oscar!"

"Now, now," Master Julian said, lifting up a hand. "It was just a joke. Easy."

Oscar exhaled. He could feel the magic smith's eyes on him. He rubbed his arm. The other villagers murmured to each other by the potions. Master Julian made a small "Hmmm" sound and then handed him a tincture of lavender and three gold coins.

It was a good thing the customers knew how much things cost.

Villagers kept coming into the shop, looking for things to help them polish their magical blades, keep their fires burning longer, protect their homes against thieves. They said the strangest things, and the words jumbled up in Oscar's head and he couldn't put them in the right order. They asked for things, and Oscar dropped vials and tore the packets he'd so carefully prepared. His hands had turned into bread loaves.

The cats kept peeking their heads out of the back room. First Crow, then Bear, then Pebble, one after the other. They were expecting him downstairs. He was expecting himself downstairs.

"How much are these?" called a woman, motioning to the cleansing powders.

"Four coins?" Oscar asked.

"That's absurd," she said. "How about one coin?"

Oscar chewed on his lip. "All right?"

She smiled. Another customer turned and held up one of Caleb's own special herbal decoctions—Prosperity Powder. "How about one coin for these?"

"All right?"

Soon everyone was naming prices and taking things off the shelves, things that Caleb usually sold to only the shining people—special decoctions and potions, charms for luck, gleaming amulets, and carefully carved cameos that changed to suit the tastes of the beholder. They bought enchanted dice, remarkably accurate arrows, mirrors that showed you your allies, mirrors that showed you your enemies, mirrors that revealed your true love, crystals that could show you all three. They bought glass globes with little china figures inside that danced whenever you played music, little figurines of napping cats that actually purred, even little glass houses with tiny plants inside—miniatures of the real thing, since people could not see it for themselves.

They bought all these things and more, handing Oscar coins while he stared at their hands, and leaving, with the shop door banging loudly behind them.

Where was Wolf?

And then the City people came, with their glowing skin and perfect hair and preternatural eyes. They came in their clothes made from magic cloth that would never fray or fade and leather boots that would never wear and jewels that kept fortune smiling upon them. They wanted things to sprinkle on their money to make it grow; they wanted things to curse their neighbors, things to protect them from their neighbor's curses. They wanted magic to get other people to do them favors, to win disputes, to slow aging, to ensure success in financial endeavors. They wanted pretty little enchanted things, better ones than everyone else had. But Oscar could not help; he could not even look at them. They left and took their coins with them, the shop door banging behind them.

There's a reason Caleb keeps you in the basement, Wolf had said.

One lord lingered in front of the jewelry for some time—an impeccably coiffed man in a green cloak. He had a little girl with him, a perfect little girl with black ringlets and full cheeks and impossibly big eyes. As Oscar fumbled around, the lord kept stealing glances at him. Oscar could feel each one like a poke.

"I am Lord Cooper," he said finally, approaching Oscar. "Might I ask who you are?"

Oscar's mouth opened. "Uh . . . Oscar?" He kept his eyes on the lord's shoulder.

"Do you work for Master Caleb?"

"Y-yes."

"How old are you?"

"Eleven."

The answers were right—yes, he was all those things—but they still felt wrong.

Something pressed against Oscar's cheek. His eyes flicked over to the little girl and then darted right back.

She was standing perfectly still, inhuman eyes fixed directly on him. And though he looked away, the pressure did not waver.

"I see," the lord said. "That's very interesting. Thank you. Might I ask, how long do you remember being here?"

Oscar frowned. "Since this morning?"

"No, I meant—well, never mind. Thank you, Oscar." Lord Cooper turned to the girl and smiled. "I want to pick out an amulet for Sophie," he pronounced, gesturing at her. The wall of amulets that Caleb fashioned for the City people glittered behind the girl. *They're infused with the magic of the Barrow,* Caleb would tell the shining people as they handed over their coins. *You are a blessed people, after all.*

Lord Cooper's voice suddenly filled the room. "My girl is five now. I want to get her the best one. Which is your finest amulet?"

"I—they're all the same," Oscar said. The little girl's brow wrinkled.

The lord frowned. "Ah. Well. Thank you, young man. We'll come back another time." He whispered something to his daughter, and they left.

Oscar did not understand. He did not understand the questions people asked or the way they looked at him or why every time he tried to look them in the eye he felt like he was being chased by seventeen angry Wolfs.

Maybe Wolf had been right. Maybe Oscar really was all wrong, somehow.

Oscar was buzzing. His mind felt like a lantern turned too bright. Yes, Wolf had been correct. He could not do this, he was not made for this. He was a fool, a freak. Oscar needed the apprentice to come back now, so he could go back into his pantry and never come out.

But where was Wolf?

And then, just as night was falling, the door burst open. Master Robin, the guardian, came rushing in carrying a sack with what looked like a bundle of logs inside.

"Where's Caleb?" he said.

"He's not here!" Oscar said. "What is that?" he added, pointing to the bag.

Robin dropped the sack. It made a slight splurching sound when it hit the floor. "That," he said, motioning to the sack, "is Wolf."

CHAPTER THREE

The Sack

R obin stared. Oscar stared. The sack was still.

"Is he all right?" Oscar said.

"No," Robin said.

Oscar turned his head and looked as far away as he could.

"I have a new apprentice," Master Robin said softly. "She did not come back when I was expecting her. After the last . . . incident, I developed ways of tracking my apprentices. And so I found the two of them in the north of the forest. Or at least . . ." He motioned to the sack.

"Your apprentice?" Oscar whispered. "Is she all right?"

"No."

Oscar swallowed. Behind his eyes, a flash of red capes.

"Where's Caleb?" Robin said.

"He's not here," Oscar said, for the thousandth and worst time that day. "He went to the continent. He said he would be back in a couple of days. I don't know anything more. I don't know anything more. I don't know anything."

A hand on his shoulder. A hard squeeze. Robin, staring down at him. Robin was so big, the biggest man in the Barrow, his hands were the size of Oscar's head, he was the biggest man Oscar had ever seen. Oscar closed his mouth so the words stopped coming. But his mind did not stop speaking them: *I don't know anything.*

The cats had gathered. Oscar could feel them in the back room, eyes moving in and out of the shadows.

"Why don't you go downstairs," Robin said. He put his hand on Oscar's shoulder again, but now it felt very soft.

"I don't know anything," Oscar said.

"I know. It's all right. I can send him a message. Just"—he looked down at the sack at his feet—"tell him to find me when he comes back."

"Do you . . ." Oscar's eyes darted to the sack and then quickly away again. "Do you know what happened?"

Master Robin shook his head. "Not yet. But I will find out. You don't have to worry."

That night in his room Oscar sat on the bed, legs pressed against his chest, arms squeezing them even closer. He was all folded up, like an envelope.

Pebble's small orange head kept nudging him. This was what her head did sometimes when he was huddled up in bed hiding from the afterimages of a nightmare. *Come back, come back,* she said. *Whatever place you have gone to, this place is better, because there are kittens here, kittens who really wouldn't mind having their ears rubbed.* But though Oscar felt the soft pressure of her head, heard her forest-rumbling purr, it did not seem like something that was really happening to him, now, here. He soon noticed that he was rocking a little on the bed, like a boat on the waves.

Eventually, sleep reached its long tentacles out and pulled him close.

This night it was the sky's turn to haunt him. Bright and blue, it threatened to suck him in, drown him in its vastness. No, it was something more than the sky. A creature. A monster. Great and blue and bottomless. It dazed you with the sun, battered you with the wind, and then it wrapped wispy cloud fingers around you, pulled you in, and ate you up. The monster was ravenous, always, and would never be sated.

Of course. Something as big and empty as the sky must be so very hungry.

He woke up with his heart pounding, with his blanket tangled, with his hair wet. Cat was in the doorway, thumping his tail loudly against the floor, golden eyes fixed firmly on Oscar.

"Did Caleb come home?" he asked. Cat just gazed at him. But Oscar knew the answer. He could feel it in the house. He was still alone.

"What am I supposed to do now?"

He could close the shop. He could put a sign up: *Closed. Master Gone. Apprentice in Bits.* He could close the shop and then go back to his small room and sit on his small bed and be as small as possible.

He sat on his bed for the next three hours—hours he should have been spending bringing in the water, getting the bread (for it was Wednesday), preparing his work for the day. But he just sat there telling himself again and again, *I could close the shop.*

Then it was nearly time for the shop to open, just like all the shops of all the magic workers in the marketplace. Oscar unfolded himself from the bed, washed, and got dressed, and then dragged himself through the cellar toward the stairs. Pebble followed him into the back room, where they split a piece of stale bread.

As he ate, Oscar stole glances at the shop through

the kitchen door. Maybe no one would come today, he thought. Maybe news of Wolf's fate would have spread through the villages already, maybe even up to the City. People were always looking out for bad omens. What could be a worse omen than an apprentice in a sack?

And then, knocking on the door.

Customers.

Early.

"You'll stay, won't you?" Oscar whispered to Pebble.

He walked into the shop, half expecting to see the sack of Wolf still in the middle of the floor. The customers could step over him. *What's that?* they would ask, walking carefully around the bag.

Oh, just Wolf. Step around him. He won't mind.

But, no, the floor was empty. Wolf was gone. Robin must have taken him—somewhere. Maybe he dropped him off the edge of the world.

Oscar unlocked the door and then darted for the cover of the counter. A moment later, a man and woman from the village came in. The man strode up to Oscar and glared down at him. Oscar's breath caught, and he fixed his gaze on the counter.

"You know something," the man said.

A pause. He seemed to be waiting for an answer.

"No." Oscar shook his head. "I don't know anything."

"No, there is something strange about you. You look

like you're hiding something."

Wolf: *No, you are just strange.*

"Imagine that," the woman interjected. "Two apprentices killed! The girl was brand-new, of course. But you would think an apprentice of Master Caleb's would be able to defend himself!" She shook her head. "They just don't come like they used to." Her eyes landed on Oscar. They seemed to be trying to grab something from him and pull it out.

The man stepped closer to her. "He's hiding something," he half whispered, indicating Oscar. "He looks shifty. Doesn't he look shifty? He won't even look at us."

A flash of orange down below, and suddenly Pebble was there, tucked neatly in an open cupboard, crumbs on her whiskers.

"Let me try something," the woman half whispered back. She turned to Oscar, and a smile contorted its way along her face. "I am Mistress Jane," she said. "I am so sorry for your loss."

Oscar chewed on his cheek.

"So . . . do you know where the apprentices were going?" she asked. "Did they say what they were doing? Maybe trying some new spells, or boar hunting, or . . . ?"

"I . . ." Oscar could barely remember. "Very important business," he said finally.

The man and the woman exchanged a glance. "You're

right, Buford," Mistress Jane said. "Shifty."

In the meantime more villagers had come in. And Master Julian was back, along with the perfumer, Master Charles. The room was crackling—Oscar could feel it, just as he could feel the force of everyone's attention directed at the counter. The customers whispered to one another, though this time so quietly Oscar could not hear.

Oscar caught sight of a head of curly black hair near the healing potions. Callie, studying a piece of paper in her hands. He had a strange desire to wave, though he did not know if that was all right to do.

"Nothing human could have done that, you know," one woman said loudly.

"I bet it was a bear," said another. "There are some very enormous bears out there, you know."

"I don't think it was a bear," Oscar mumbled. He glanced down at Pebble. Yes, there were bears in the woods, and some of them were enormous. But they were friendly, if you knew how to talk to them.

Mistress Jane's head snapped back. "You do know something!" she said.

"No, I just—"

A villager stalked over and handed him a sachet. It was a defensive ward, to be worn next to your skin: *cockscomb, burdock, foxglove, agrimony.*

"Do you think this will be enough?" he asked.

"Enough for what?" Oscar asked.

"To protect me!" the man exclaimed. "I go into the forest all the time. I want enough magic to protect me. Should I buy two?"

"Yes," Mistress Jane said, suddenly smiling at Oscar again. "Let's just . . . *pretend* you know what killed your master's apprentice. What kind of charm would you recommend?"

Oscar's face scrunched.

"Boy?" she said. "Are you listening to me?"

"I'm trying, but you're not making any sense!" Oscar said, pressing his foot into the floor.

A dark head whipped around. Callie, now watching him.

"Excuse me, boy?" said the woman. She squinted at him. "You're not quite right, are you?"

Master Julian let out a loud "ahem." The whole room turned. "Do not harass the boy," he proclaimed. "He is an orphan and simple." Oscar's face went hot. Out of the corner of his eye he could see Callie fold her arms across her chest.

"What happened to Wolf and . . . oh . . . that girl was a tragedy," Julian continued. "It happened in the distant north of the forest, and while we cannot be sure of what befell them, I think we all are familiar with the tendency of apprentices to try magic well outside of their capabilities. You remember the incident with Master Robin's last apprentice and the tree?"

Oscar glanced around the room. The crackling emanating from the people was lessening, and they'd turned the force of their focus to Master Julian. They were all nodding, as if this was the obvious answer. Oscar shifted.

Master Charles, the perfumer, cleared his throat. "Even if it were a very enormous bear," he added, "and even if the bear did wander this far south on his very enormous legs, here in the Barrow villages we have magic to protect us."

"And magic smiths!" called Mister Buford.

The two masters smiled slightly and bowed their heads to the room and all its misters and mistresses. "Magic smiths," echoed Master Charles, "who are devoted to keeping the Barrow, and its magnificent residents, safe. And you have the bounty of the Barrow"—he opened his arms and gestured to the shelves all around—"to protect you."

It was as if a spell had been cast around the room. The air suddenly lightened. People chattered like exuberant crows and began to ask Master Charles and Master Julian about protection herbs. The customers came to the counter and handed wares to Oscar—teas made from hawthorn and heather, amber necklaces, packets of basil, little charms carved of birch—and he kept his eyes on their hands, took their offered coins, and dropped them in the box underneath the counter. His head was buzzing, and their words began to slip though his fingers like water.

Then, suddenly, quiet. Oscar looked up. A lady from the City had come in, her jewel-blue dress a violent gash of color against the white, brown, and black of the villagers. The lady stopped and looked around at the crowd, as if it were so terribly odd to find people in a store. The villagers bowed their heads. Her eyes searched the room, and she sighed heavily, fingering the green amulet around her neck.

"I need Caleb," she said. Her voice was like an arm that reached toward everyone in the room. It could pluck Caleb from the continent.

The Barrow people all moved away from her at once. The lady stood in the middle of the shop, and for the first time Oscar noticed she was not alone. She'd brought a small girl with her, a little copy of herself down to the long sapphire dress. But the girl, with her big brown eyes, sleek black hair, and shiny emerald bow, looked even more unreal. She held her mother's hand and did not move or speak. She looked like a doll come to life. The lady put her hand on the girl's shoulder and scanned the room again.

"Something's wrong with her," the lady said.

A soft murmur went through the crowd. Oscar bit his lip. She was a City girl; nothing could possibly be wrong. This girl made the City adults look dull in comparison, so bright Oscar could barely stand to look at her. Just like the girl yesterday, Sophie. Just like all the City's little kids. Like they were the best flowers in the garden, just plucked.

No one said anything. The shining lady saw Oscar behind the counter and stalked toward him, pushing the girl with her. Oscar took a step backward and bumped into the wall.

"Something's wrong with her," the lady repeated, her voice a hiss. "I need Caleb."

Oscar had been down this road before. You would think telling someone *Caleb's not here* would be enough, but it never was. "There's a healer," Oscar said. He kept his eyes away from the girl. "Madame Mariel. That's who you see when someone's sick: the healer, not the magician." From the corner of the shop, Callie cleared her throat and shot him a look.

"No," said the lady. "The healer can't help me. She's not sick. I need Caleb."

"Um . . ." Oscar's eyes caught movement. Pebble was hunched down and had started to creep in a wide circle around the counter, moving as if the floor might shatter under her at any moment. Her eyes had grown to twice their size. Carefully, carefully she moved, focus never wavering from the lady and the girl. The kitten stopped two feet away from them, crouching on the floor, and and a long, low growl emanated from her and began to spread its way across the floor like spilled oil.

The girl shrieked and grabbed on to her mother's skirt. Her mother yelled at Pebble. Pebble growled with a note of finality, then sprang up and darted out of the room.

The lady's eyes narrowed. "What is that filthy creature doing in here?" she asked.

"That's Pebble," Oscar said. "She lives here."

The lady huffed. "Caleb will hear about this. Have him call on me, as soon as he gets back. Tell him it's urgent." She tossed a card on the counter, made a sniffing noise, and grabbed her daughter by the arm. "Come on."

The door slammed—the lady was gone. But her card lay on the counter. Oscar shrank. If a City lady complained about him, it was all over.

Suddenly, Callie was by him, rolling her eyes again. "They think they're in charge of everything," she muttered.

Oscar blinked. Weren't they?

"Don't worry." Callie palmed the lady's card and

crumpled it in her hand. "He'll never know."

Oscar inhaled sharply. The smooth white card turned into a ball in front of his eyes. "You can't—"

"I just did."

"What if someone tells? You'll be in trouble!"

"It's worth it." She looked around the room and then whispered, "I have to go now. Madame is expecting me back. You'll be all right. Just . . . try to pretend."

And then she picked up her parcel of herbs from the counter, set down some coins, and left—Oscar watching her the whole time. She didn't even know Oscar, but with one squish of her hand she'd taken his troubles away.

The shop had cleared out while the lady and her daughter had been there. The remaining villagers made their purchases and left. Crow tucked herself into the cupboard underneath the counter, and more City people started to come. For them the day was just the same as the day before. No one asked Oscar about Wolf. No one speculated about bears. They just tilted their heads and eyed him, like they were trying to make the pieces fit together but couldn't quite.

Finally the last of them left; it was time to close. Oscar had work to do so they would have something to sell tomorrow—he would have to spend the night chopping and mashing and pulping and grinding. And

though he would be up all night, though he had been up all night the night before, though he felt like a tap squeezed of its last drip, some small part of his mind settled at the thought.

He moved to the door to lock it. And then, a knock.

Customers.

Late.

"Closed!" Oscar yelped, just as it opened.

"It is only I," said the man who walked in. His features blurred and then clicked into place: Mister Malcolm, the baker. Oscar went to his shop on Wednesdays and Sundays. He loved going there; it smelled so warm, and familiar, and peaceful—like how a real house might smell, if you lived in one.

Malcolm was tall and thin and at least two decades older than Caleb. His skin was like bark, his hair was the color of iron but touched with white—it was only a couple of years ago that Oscar had realized that it was not because he had flour in his hair.

"Why are you here?" Oscar asked.

"Is that the way you talk to customers?" said Malcolm. The words were hard, but his voice was not.

Oscar looked up, settling his gaze just below the baker's cheek. His shoulders collapsed. "I don't know," he said.

"A precise question requires a precise answer," Malcolm said. "I am here because you did not come by today to pick up your bread." He held up a cloth bag with several loaves in it.

"Wolf's dead."

Malcolm regarded him for a moment. "I heard. It sounds like the circumstances were . . . troubling."

"They think it was a bear. Or some spell that went awry."

"I see. What do you think?"

"I don't know," Oscar said, trying not to look shifty. "Everybody bought all the protective spells today. I don't have any left."

"I do not need any spells, my boy," Malcolm said, though that was not really why Oscar had said it.

"But," Oscar found himself saying, "I could give you something. We—Caleb has things you could use. He has things that can make bread rise faster, that can make it keep for longer. He can give you something for prosperity or for luck or to keep out thieves." Oscar could not stop himself from talking. Mister Malcolm had brought him bread, and it seemed suddenly so important to give the baker some magic, if only just a little bit. "Caleb has all kinds of things. Or I . . . I could make a decoction for you."

He stopped dead. His cheeks burned. He was a hand, not an apprentice.

Malcolm raised his iron-colored eyebrows. "I do

not need any spells, my boy. But you need bread." He handed Oscar the bag then and turned to go. "There are some extra buns in there," he added. "In case anyone else is hungry."

Oscar held the bag close, let it warm his chest. The smell pulled at him like a wish.

Malcolm left, and Oscar was alone again in the big hollow building. He sat at the kitchen table and cut himself a piece of bread, trying to push everything else away. He didn't understand. He didn't understand anything that had happened today, why people said the things they said or did the things they did. He didn't understand why everyone else seemed to understand one another and no one understood him.

Oscar took his bread downstairs with him. Though he had so much work to do, all he wanted was to go to his room and lure in as many cats as possible.

But that would not happen. For when he got to the cellar, he heard footsteps echoing down the hallway and the sound of a door closing.

Caleb was back.

CHAPTER FOUR

Scraps

Oscar ducked into his pantry, where Bear was waiting for him.

"How long has he been back?" Oscar whispered.

The big white cat didn't answer, merely rubbed herself on Oscar's legs. Oscar crouched down and petted her guiltily. It was evening; Oscar was supposed to be in the pantry keeping her company. That was the way it had always been.

"I couldn't get away," he explained. "There were so many people." He tore off a chunk of bread and fed it to her.

Hugging himself, Oscar leaned against the pantry wall. For two days all he had wanted was for Caleb to come back, and now he was back and Oscar had made a mess of things: he had angered half the customers and confused the other half, and the coin boxes did not look as they should, and shining people were complaining about him, and he couldn't look at anybody, and Wolf was dead, and Oscar was odd.

"What if he doesn't keep me?" Oscar said to Bear.

Oscar gulped. The cat twitched her nose. Oscar looked into her blue eyes, took a breath, and then walked through the main cellar and down the corridor, his heart dragging behind him.

The door to Caleb's workroom was closed, and Oscar could hear the magician moving around inside. He lifted his hand to knock, but then he stopped. He could go neither forward nor back, so he simply stayed that way—hand frozen in the air.

And that was when the workroom door opened.

"Oscar!" said Caleb, stepping into the hallway. "What are you doing?"

Caleb was so tall that Oscar always felt like he was looking up at a tree when he was standing next to him. And there was something about his face that looked sculpted and slightly weathered, like bark—though he was one of the younger shopkeepers in the market and had no flour streaks in his black hair.

Oscar's breath fluttered in his chest. He focused on

Caleb's chest. "You're back," he said, lowering his hand slowly.

"Indeed. Were you looking for me?" Caleb closed the door behind him and stared down at Oscar.

"Um . . . I . . ."

"Yes?"

"Did you just get back?"

"I returned a few hours ago," Caleb said.

"Oh," Oscar said. "All right." His hand flew to his chest and rubbed it, as if to soothe something.

"Is there anything else?"

Yes. There was a lot else. There was so much else it was going to come crushing down on top of their heads. And since Caleb was taller, all that else would hit him first, so really the magician should have been concerned, far more concerned than he was acting.

"Wolf's dead," Oscar said.

"I know," said Caleb.

"He went off into the forest and got killed."

"I know," said Caleb.

"He was very very dead when they brought him back."

"I know," Caleb said.

"He was in a bag," said Oscar.

"Yes," Caleb said. "I have a letter from Master Robin."

"Oh," said Oscar. He paused to allow Caleb to continue. Caleb did not.

Oscar rubbed his arm. "Do . . . *you* know what happened to him?" he asked quietly. It was a silly thing to ask. But Caleb was Caleb, and so he asked it anyway.

Caleb regarded him. "I have theories," he said after a moment. "Wolf had his talents, but he was reckless. I thought this quality might develop into potential. But I fear he delved into matters beyond his power. I am a magician; I should have been more careful about whom I brought into this house."

Oscar swallowed.

The magician cleared his throat. "Oscar," he said, voice suddenly formal, "you're a hand. You're no apprentice."

Oscar's eyes flicked to the floor. No, he was not.

"I did not make you my hand so you could work the shop," Caleb said. "Your uses lie elsewhere. You have not had much experience with people, and it shows in your manner. Wolf is gone. This makes things very difficult. I have much that calls me in my workshop, and urgent dealings on the continent. I have to know the shop is running smoothly."

Oscar closed his eyes. Caleb knew how to persuade people of things; Oscar had seen it countless times. People left the shop with twice as much as they'd come in to buy, and then they came back with their friends. You would think that, after years of watching, Oscar would have picked up something of this magic, just a touch—a way to smile, a word or two.

But Oscar was no magician.

"Yes, Master Caleb," said Oscar. "I understand."

"So I'm going to need you to serve in Wolf's stead for a while."

Oscar's head snapped up.

"When I am gone and you are in charge of the shop, you will have to do the best you can," Caleb went on, as if what he'd said was completely reasonable. "The situation is very delicate right now. I do not want to bring in a new person, and I do not want to bring in the wrong person. When I must be away, I need you to keep the shop open as much as you are able to. We don't need the duke poking around."

The best you can. Oscar gulped.

"You'll be fine," said Caleb. And there, there was the smile, the magic one, that warmth spreading out like an embracing cloak. "You can do this, Oscar. I know you can." Oscar could not remember a time when Caleb had spoken to him with such soft words. He felt like he was holding a basket of newly baked bread. "Later, when things calm down, I'll find a new apprentice, and you can go back to your pantry."

"I can?" said Oscar.

"Of course you can. This will all smooth over soon." He smiled his cloaking smile, and Oscar folded himself up into it. "It will be like it never happened at all. I promise. Now, I'll need you to go into the forest tomorrow and gather some items for me. It's a long list, I'm afraid."

"I'll remember," said Oscar.

"I know you will."

After Caleb gave Oscar his instructions and disappeared back into his workroom, Oscar walked slowly to his own room—the room that would still be his tomorrow. Pebble was there already, bathing herself on the bed. Oscar closed the door and she looked up, pink tongue hanging slightly out of her mouth.

Oscar leaned in, eyes wide. "He's keeping me," he whispered to the kitten.

Pebble chirped. Oscar's eyes flicked to the books underneath his bed. They called out to him: *Misfit. Orphan. Idiot.*

Oscar coughed and shifted his eyes back to Pebble. "He thinks I can work the shop," he added. Pebble cocked her head. He hadn't meant for that sentence to sound like a question. "He said he knew I could do it."

Wolf: *He didn't see you work the shop. He doesn't know. Just wait until he hears.*

"He wants me to do the best I can."

Wolf: *If only he knew how bad that was. He'll know soon.*

Oscar clenched his hands into fists and squeezed his eyes shut. Then, with a long exhale, he sat down on the edge of the bed and began to scratch Pebble on the neck. He shifted, and then shifted again, but he could not get comfortable.

"Master Caleb's not worried," Oscar told Pebble. "About Wolf. He said . . ." Oscar stopped. What had Caleb said, exactly? Not what he thought had happened, quite. There had been an answer, but not one you could hold your hand around and squeeze when you needed to.

"I'm not going to disappoint him," Oscar said. He repeated himself once more, in case the words themselves had any power. "I'm not."

Oscar and Crow were out in the forest before the shop opened the next morning. Maybe, he thought, if the customers from the last two days didn't lay eyes on him, they would forget he'd ever been there, and never say a thing to Caleb about his odd little hand.

And then maybe Caleb would go on thinking Oscar could do this. For at least a little while longer.

Oscar pushed the thoughts away. He was in the forest now; everything was exactly where it was supposed to be. As Oscar concentrated on the list of plants Caleb had asked him to gather, the map of the forest spread out in his head, and the locations of Caleb's plants lay themselves on top of the map like pins. Oscar would be in the forest for hours.

"We'll get the honey mushrooms first," he told Crow.

It wasn't the natural place to begin, but that grove of little red mushrooms grew underneath the biggest wizard tree in the forest. If you looked at the map of the trees in your head, you would see this one right in the middle of the Barrow. Most of the wizard trees had towering trunks that stood majestically straight, as high as the eye could see, but this one split off a few yards up into six thick branches that spread out from the tree like petals on a flower. If Oscar had been a little taller and a lot braver, he could have climbed up the tree and sat in the cradle the branches made, right in the heart of the forest.

Instead, he picked the mushrooms at its feet.

With the canopy of low, thick branches just above, you felt perfectly protected around this tree, like you could live underneath these outstretched arms and nothing could ever harm you. Oscar collected mushrooms, and everything buzzing and agitating inside him eased.

He worked though the morning, making his way around the forest, gathering berries and leaves and bark, trying to hold everything that had happened in the last two days in his mind at once. Crow kept him company until the baneberry bushes, where she darted off chasing her lunch.

She always had plenty to choose from. In addition to the ravens and owls and buzzards who lived in the trees, the forest was home to red-eyed white mice and red-tailed black rats and spiders the size of a man's fist that looked like miniature fanged octopuses. Wolf had gotten bitten by one once and then poured an entire packet of capsaicin down his throat. Afterward, his face turned red and his eyes popped and he sweat for three days straight.

Wolf. Oscar grimaced.

As if summoned, the Wolf in his head spoke up. *I died out here,* he said. *Shouldn't you be scared?*

"You were reckless," Oscar muttered, shifting. He rubbed his chest. The Barrow was his home, he had trees watching over him—why would he be scared out here?

It's not your home, Orphan.

Biting his lip, Oscar looked around the green world. No. He was not *from* here. Not like everyone else. Oscar had grown up across the river in the Children's Home. Eastern Aletheia had no magic, no forest—just farmland and the Eastern Villages and the sea all around.

Maybe, he thought, that was why he could not

understand anyone here. Maybe people in the Eastern Villages were just different. Oscar didn't remember—it was five years ago, and it was all so fuzzy. His life before coming to Caleb was just shadows of moments and a burning, grinding sensation that seized him whenever he thought of it.

There had been a day, once, when Caleb came across the river to the Home to pick his hand. Maybe all the young boys and girls had lined up. Maybe he asked them questions. Maybe he gave them herbs to grind. Maybe he could just tell who would be able to look at plants and know how to listen to them, who would be able to carry long lists of plants in his head. He was Caleb, after all. He would know who would be useful to him.

And on that day or one soon after, Caleb must have taken Oscar across Eastern Aletheia. Across the river. Across the plaguelands—the dead swath of land that surrounded the Barrow, where the plague had taken every last thing that grew or thrived, had killed the land so badly that now even magic could not survive crossing it.

But all Oscar could remember of that day was the sight of the front of the Home growing smaller and smaller and then disappearing. You'd think one would remember the rest, it seemed odd not to remember. Maybe all that really mattered of the Home was the leaving of it.

Wolf: *You don't even know where you came from.*

Oscar collected his last berries and headed back toward the marketplace. After a time, Crow slipped next to him. That helped. He mapped out the rest of the day—go back, sort his harvest, dry the berries, grate the bark, then work on replenishing the herbs that had been bought out the day before.

A normal day. Everything in its place.

Just as Oscar could sense the smells of the market-place working their way into the wind, his eyes flicked over an Oscar-sized rock. There, in the shadow—a flash of something that didn't seem to belong.

"Wait," he said to Crow.

Crow let out an impatient trill.

"I just want to see what it is," Oscar said, moving over to the rock to investigate. He found a small pile of wood scraps, nothing more—just discarded pieces from someone's project. Yet the arcs and blocks and triangles and angles and little scraps and bits seemed to call to him. Like if he sat down and concentrated hard enough he could put them all back together again.

"What do you think this was?" he called to Crow.

Crow sat on the ground and began licking her paw, as if she couldn't hear him. Oscar turned back to the pile of wood.

There was a piece on the side of the pile a little

bigger than Oscar's hand. He picked it up and ran his fingers over the bumpy edges, then opened his satchel and dropped it inside.

He looked at Crow and shrugged. "Because I feel like it, all right?"

The cat turned around and began to trot ahead, and Oscar followed suit.

The noises of the marketplace greeted him—doors opening and closing, people calling out to one another, and someone ranting very loudly about fish heads. Oscar carried the bag to the back of Caleb's shop. And then he stopped. In the path in front of the shop stood a girl with curtains of dark curly hair, wearing a bright red cloak.

Callie.

She had her arms wrapped around her chest and was tapping her boot against the stone. Her eyes lit on the boy standing frozen behind the shop. "Oscar," she called. "Can you come here?"

Her hand crumpled up his thoughts and threw them away. All he could do was obey.

Callie was almost a head taller than Oscar, and he was not entirely sure how to manage. To look up at her would involve craning his head awkwardly. But to look straight ahead would mean he was looking at her neck, and that was probably strange, too. Oscar compromised and looked at her chin.

"What's all that?" Callie asked, pointing to Oscar's bag.

"Oh," he said, taking a deep breath. "Well, it's bane-berry, foxglove, willow bark, red clover—"

Callie coughed.

"—white pine needles, walnuts, honey mushrooms, dragon's blood—"

"That's good enough," Callie said.

"You asked," Oscar muttered, shifting.

"So, do you know why the shop is closed?"

"What?"

"The shop," she said, motioning to the front entrance. "It's closed today. Well, to us. . . . It's open for City people."

There was a slight force to the way Callie said *City*, as if she were using the word to elbow someone.

"That's . . . weird," Oscar said.

Callie tilted her head. "Yes. It *is* weird. So . . . do you know what's going on?"

"No!" If anything had become clear over the last two days it was this: he had no idea what was going on.

She studied him, her right boot tapping harder. "So, is he going to open up for everyone at some point? Because, you know . . . we might want to buy things."

"I—I don't know."

Callie paused then, like he was supposed to say something else now. But she gave no clue as to what.

"Oscar," she said finally, "if we need something, how are we supposed to get it?"

"Oh! Do you . . . need something?" Oscar asked.

Callie exhaled. "Yes! I—that is, Madame Mariel— well, we have someone who has hives. And so Madame Mariel sent me to find some treatment. For hives. He said he touched some Barrow ivy, and . . ."

Oscar closed his mouth emphatically. Barrow ivy was unique to the forest and made people magically itchy. He could see the ingredients on his shelves, see them combine: *catclaw, licorice, yellow dock.* He could make it for her, crumple her problem away. But Callie would never believe it; she was an apprentice, and he was a hand.

Callie blinked at him. Oscar half smiled, keeping his eyes on her chin. Callie blinked some more.

"The patient's waiting. He's extremely itchy. Do you think Caleb might come out, or . . . ?"

"Look," Oscar said, feeling suddenly out of breath, "I'll go in, all right? I'll ask Master Caleb for whatever you need. And I'll bring it out for you. How's that?"

"Thank you!" Callie said. She stepped back, as if to make room for Oscar to go in the front door. Oscar's eyes went to the door, imagining the bright shining buzz of City people, with Master Caleb at the center.

"I'm just going to go around back," he said.

He ducked around the shop before she could say

anything, and slipped in the back door. In the pantry his hands reached for the right jars automatically. This was Oscar's lair, after all. A scoop here, another one there, and he was done. And a little extra, too, just in case. He might not know how to talk to Callie, but at least he knew how to help her.

When Oscar got back, he handed the pouch to Callie, hands shaking just a little. She took it and looked inside.

"It should help," Oscar said quickly. "Caleb says."

"Thank you, Oscar," Callie said. "You are very kind."

"I am?" He pressed his hand to his chest.

Just then, the door to Caleb's shop swung open. Oscar started and stepped back. He had been so nervous to go in he'd forgotten anyone might come out.

A boy from the City appeared, one not much younger than Oscar. He wore a fitted black velvet coat with a tasseled gold belt wrapped around his waist. A little white collar peeked out from underneath the coat. His black hair lay perfectly flat on his head, and he stood up so straight, like he had been posed, like his whole skeleton was made of different stuff from Oscar's.

The boy looked right at Oscar and Callie and then walked uncertainly over to them, as if that were the sort of thing that happened, as if a young City boy always stopped to talk to two Barrow kids on the marketplace

street. Oscar's skin itched. How was it possible for anyone ever to be so clean? He shifted backward, trying his
very best to look like he wasn't there at all.

"Can you help me?" the boy asked. "Do I know you?"
Even for a City child, the boy spoke strangely, as if each
word needed to be chewed on a little.

Oscar could feel Callie's eyes snap to him and
then away. "What do you mean?" she asked. Her voice
sounded different, too. Like she'd polished it.

"Do we know each other?" the boy said. He took
another step forward. Oscar glanced at his face. His eyes
had something odd behind them, something completely
out of place in a City child. Oscar looked away.

"I don't think so," Callie said, giving the boy her full
attention. "Have you ever come into the healer's?"

"I don't know. Mum says Master Caleb should help
me remember things. But it's all gone. I don't remember
anything."

Oscar watched the boy, trying to make sense of the
words on his face It was all so strange—this City boy
didn't remember where he came from, either.

"That's terrible," said Callie.

"Can you help me?" the boy said, eyes widening. "I
need help."

Callie had leaned closer to the boy, so her hair fell
around the sides of her head as if creating a space just for

her and him. "Did Master Caleb help at all?" she asked softly.

"Who is Master Caleb?"

The shop door opened again, and a City lady glided out. She had even bigger hair, bigger skirts, shinier jewels than the rest of them.

"She says she's my mother," whispered the boy.

"You've even forgotten we don't talk to wretches," muttered the lady, not very softly. "Come on, Ronald." A sweep of skirts, and then the lady had her hand on the boy's back and was pushing him ahead, back through the courtyard.

Oscar gasped. "You're not a wretch!" he said hurriedly, turning his head slightly toward Callie.

Callie glanced at him. "Well, thank you," she replied. "That's the duchess. I suppose it makes sense that she's ruder than the rest of them. Though I would have thought . . ." Callie shook her head, and with it shook the end of the sentence away. "Usually when City parents come in to Madame Mariel hysterical about something being wrong with their kids, it's because an eyelash is out of place or they forgot to use the right fork. But he . . . he seemed like he really didn't remember, didn't he?" Her eyebrows knit. "He looked so frightened!"

"He did?" Oscar asked, before he could help it. His ears went red. "Master Caleb will fix him. I know it."

"He didn't look fixed to me," Callie muttered. She fingered her apprentice pin and looked away. "I wish I knew how to help him. . . ."

Oscar studied her face. It had shifted; this was a different Callie now. He had nothing to say to make it better, he was made up entirely of a complete lack of words. Of course: he was useless to her up here.

But the cellar was tugging at him. Maybe down there, underground in the shadows, he could help.

CHAPTER FIVE

Magic and the Mind

The rest of Oscar's day went just as he'd mapped out—*sort out the harvest, dry the berries, grate the bark, work on replenishing the herbs.* But after leaving Callie he'd added another step: *go to the library.* Day turned to night, Crow turned to Bear, and Oscar could hear the sounds of Caleb closing up the shop above. Soon, Caleb was passing the pantry on the way to his workroom. His voice wandered back toward Oscar—probably murmuring something to Cat, who patrolled the hallways in the evenings.

Bear picked herself up with a yawn and slowly stretched out her long white back. Time to stop working. After meticulously putting the pantry to bed for the night, Oscar went to his room to wait.

One hour. Two. Three. He sat on his bed, one hand on Pebble, and watched the hand of the clock on his wall creep forward, one half breath at a time.

Four. Oscar picked himself off the bed, grabbed his satchel, and headed for the library.

He'd spent so much time in there, but still it contained whole universes of books he'd never visited. There were ladders that went all the way to the top of the shelves, but Oscar had never been able to climb up more than two rungs—no matter how tempting the undiscovered country of books above seemed. The shelves were so very much taller than he could even dream of being, and Oscar firmly believed people shouldn't go any higher than they already were.

The shelves were organized by subject, and Oscar had spent much of his time in one corner reading about botany, herbs, and plant magic. These hours in the library were stolen things, and he had to be as careful as a thief about how he chose to spend them.

But tonight he wandered around the library, while the cats dozed on the chairs, to see what else it had to offer. Next to the plant books there was an enormous history section. Oscar looked up as far as he could. On the high shelves were histories of the broader world, the one beyond the sea, so far out of Oscar's imagining: *The*

Mad Kings of the Meridies and *The Cold Collective: The Formation of the Northern Alliance* and *The Really Not That Great Schism*. And there, just above his eye level, an entire section on Aletheian history: *The Peculiar Isle: Discovery and Early Settlements* and *A Natural History of Magic* and *Ode to an Aletheian Duke* and *The City on the Hill: A Disquisition*. There was a small green book with no title, and Oscar started to reach for it when his hand touched a thickly bound volume—*The Chronicle of the Plague in Aletheia*.

Oscar did not know that much about the plague, except that it had come from the continent and swept across the island. Though the toll was great, Aletheia had not been ravaged like the continent, where it had killed more than half the population. It was the magic that saved Aletheia from that fate; it kept the island, protected its people, while the rest of the world was destroyed. Everyone knew that much.

What still lingered were the plaguelands. Oscar's nightmares told stories of that place, of sickly ravenous ghosts and skeletons bursting through the ground at night, of an eternal wasteland empty of everything but death.

History held no answers for him. Oscar glanced over the shelves and kept wandering around the room, traveling through the library's well-ordered countries of knowledge, shooting glances at the ladder occasionally as if it might be following him. The history shelves stretched on and on, the books as big as the world itself. Then, astronomy—books of matters even bigger than that.

There were sections on mathematics and metaphysics, natural and supernatural philosophy, anatomy and bestiaries, and theories of practically everything. There was horticulture and agriculture and climate studies and exotic zoology. The bottom few rows of Caleb's shelves contained everything you could want to know of this world, of the things you could touch, of everything sensible and effable.

But these world-bound things were not what Oscar was looking for. He needed things beyond sense. He would have to climb up.

So he approached the big wooden ladder. It was so very tall, really surprisingly tall. Ladders were not inherently dangerous, he told himself, people climbed them every day, and most of them lived. And the really high parts of this one were attached to the wall by a sliding mechanism to keep the ladder from falling backward and crushing anyone who happened to be on it at the time, and that was probably pretty secure—though Oscar had no idea when the last time was that anyone had checked.

But still. Callie said he was kind. And so he had to go up.

With a deep breath, he put his foot on the bottom rung, grabbed on to the one by his shoulders, and pulled himself up. One rung. Then two. Then three and four. He was eye level with a small book called *The Fortunate and the Fallen.* He closed his eyes for a moment and then moved up another rung. And another.

He did not look down or up, just straight ahead, watching as the subjects of the books changed from plant magic to theories of luck and fortune to small enchantments to magical creatures and beasts. The higher he looked, the fewer titles he could read—some were written in Latin, others in languages he didn't even recognize. There were even entire alphabets he'd never seen before.

If there was a book to help Callie help the boy, it would be here.

Oscar gulped and went up two more rungs, so he was now several Oscars high. His heart seemed like it was going to give up on him and leap back down to the floor. But the books called to him. This was no plant magic; this was the stuff of the heavens, of demons, of forces Oscar couldn't even imagine. This was wizard magic: *Curses and Hexes; Creating and Maintaining Illusions; Metamorphosis and Animation; Old Enchantments, New Magic; Theories of Vivification; Secrets of the Wizards.*

And this: *Magic and the Mind.*

Gripping the ladder with his right hand as tightly as anything had ever been gripped, Oscar pulled the book off the shelf and put it in his satchel, next to the block of wood he'd picked up earlier that day. And, because he couldn't resist, he took the one about the wizards, too— he could put it under his bed, where it could keep the misfit books company.

That done, he climbed back down—which did not seem at all less treacherous than going up, really, especially when you had a stolen spell book and the entire history of local wizardry in your bag.

When he got down, he settled himself in a chair and began to flip through *Magic and the Mind*.

It was nothing like a plant book, which had careful illustrations and intricate diagrams and easy explanations, the sort of thing you could study and then keep in your head to refer to whenever you needed it. Some of those books were organized by plants, some by the kind of magic—prosperity, luck, beauty, health, protection, love . . . But no matter what, the pages were so clear: when someone named a problem or Caleb told Oscar to prepare an herb, the image of the page popped into his mind unbidden. They were all there, like there was a compendium in his head, and all he had to do was sort through and find the right one.

This book was all nonsense, with still more nonsense

scribbled in the margins. The sentences stretched out and then tucked back into themselves, and then turned around again and wandered off in a different direction. There were no instructions, not that he could see—just strange scribbles and diagrams that meant nothing, and words that meant even less.

With the plants, there was a system—cultivate them, pick them, dry them, prepare them. There were rules, ritual, patterns. And there were things you could hold in your hand. If there was any system to the magic in this book, it relied on rules in languages Oscar didn't even know.

All he could make out were some of the labels of spells, and even those didn't necessarily make sense: the Black Mirror, Unbinding Powers, Blood Calling, the Breath of Life, and Living Enchantments. There were spells to make a man think he was haunted, spells to make him forget, spells to make him believe, spells to sicken his mind. Oscar could see no spell for restoring memories—but there was one for implanting them. A strange thing, to plant a memory, like a lily in a vegetable garden.

Oscar closed the book. What had he been looking for, exactly? A spell that a hand could find that the only true magician in the Barrow did not know about? A spell an apprentice could do and Master Caleb could not? He'd been pulled along by a whim, like a distant flicker in a labyrinth.

Orphan. Misfit. Idiot.

Oscar squeezed his arms around his chest and glanced over at the sleeping cats. No spell for memory. No way to help Callie. And—it was funny—a whole book on magic and the mind and there was nothing in it about fixing a boy who was not quite right.

When Oscar woke up the next morning, he laid out the map of the day in his mind. He got dressed, ate some bread, gathered water, and ran his errands in the marketplace—it was Friday, and that meant getting cheese from Madame Catherine and her Most Spectacular Goat. He spent some time dusting and sweeping in the shop, as a good hand does. The shelves looked fuller, happier than the last time Oscar had seen them. Caleb had clearly been busy the last two nights preparing potions and charms. There was even a new shelf with thick, folded blankets. Oscar snuck a peek at the information card: *Will obscure what lies beneath.*

Then he went back to the cellar and got to work. He had found no answers last night, but he was in his pantry doing the things he was good at, where the questions did not need answering. That was why he was here, why Caleb had picked him in the first place. And Caleb was in the shop, watching over it like a wizard tree in the forest. As long as it stayed that way, everything would be all right.

After a few hours in the pantry, Oscar went back up the stairs to the back room to use the still, to extract some oil from the harvest of the day before. Crow came up with him, for she had an innate sense of when it was Most Spectacular Goat Cheese Day.

As he worked, voices tumbled in from the shop, a cloud of noise. They were Barrow voices, rumbly and rough like bark. Twice, someone asked Caleb whether he planned to get a new apprentice soon. "My daughter is showing some aptitude . . . ," they each said.

Even when Wolf was alive, lots of Barrow parents would come in proclaiming their children were showing evidence of a gift, though such gifts were rare. The duke paid parents of apprentices handsomely for giving their children to the service of the magic—after charging the magic smiths an even more handsome fee. Still, Oscar did not understand why anyone would bother lying— the duke wouldn't certify an apprentice with no magic.

The voices kept floating in. Most of the people who weren't trying to sell off their children told Caleb that they were sorry about Wolf, he'd had such potential, a shame he'd had to go messing with things beyond his ability.

"Yes," Caleb said. "A shame."

"I was worried at first," one woman said. "That there might be something out there."

"I don't see how that's possible," Caleb replied.

"I am certainly relieved to hear you say that. I know you'll keep us safe."

"It is my duty and my honor," Caleb said, mouth spreading across his face in a smile that existed only for her.

Oscar could always tell without looking when the shining people entered the shop. They just sounded different, like the words cost them nothing to say, not even a thought. The air gave way for their voices—it was their land, after all—and the words glided their way to Oscar. A man wanted a charm to give him luck at cards. "I don't seem to have any of my own," he said, with a laugh.

Oscar frowned at the eucalyptus he was chopping. It was hard to believe that a City person wouldn't have luck. Why wouldn't they, when they had everything else?

Quiet for a while, some words and phrases here and there—the cloud of noise thinned into little wisps like the steam rising from the still. Caleb's boots clunked their way around the shop, his voice enchanting customers, one sale at a time. Then: "May I help you, Miss Callie?"

Oscar snapped up and peeked through the doorway.

There Callie was, in front of the envelopes of herbs, her hair in a thick long braid and her cloak wrapped tightly around her thin shoulders. He had nothing for her; he had gone looking for help for her but had come up empty.

"Yes, thank you, Master Caleb." Callie sounded so different than when she talked to Oscar. Every word sounded like it was standing up straight.

"I need more treatment for hives," Callie was saying. Oscar froze.

"What you gave me yesterday worked splendidly," she continued, "but I'm afraid the whole family has them now."

All he could do was hold his breath and watch, as Caleb arched an eyebrow and studied Callie, who was looking up at him like a cat waiting for breakfast.

"Hives, Miss Callie," Caleb said finally. "That must be a very uncomfortable family. We have many things in stock." He waved his hands over to the packaged herbs and the decoctions. "Unless you'd like me to mix something for you? Do you know the source of the hives?"

Callie's eyebrows knotted together. "Barrow ivy."

"I see. That will require something special. We'll put something together for you. And," he added, a smile creeping across his face, "where is Madame Mariel?"

Callie's hand flew to her neck. "Tending to the family," she said. "The hives, you see."

"Ah," said Caleb. "Yes, very dedicated, our Mariel. Let me see what I can make for you."

Caleb turned. Oscar watched. Callie was regarding the magician with the oddest expression, like he had words on his back she couldn't quite read. It was how Oscar felt all the time.

The front door opened then, and two City girls walked in, older girls about Wolf's age—one with tumbling black curls, the other with silky straight hair, and both with faces that seemed sculpted. If Wolf had been here, he would have started panting.

The girls parked themselves in the corner by some potions and were chirping back and forth about an appointment with Madame Lara, the soothsayer.

Caleb tossed an "I'll be back with you soon, Miss Callie" over his shoulder, then circled over to the girls. He greeted them, his voice now rich as well as enchanting. And soon both of them were gazing up at him, eyes sparkling like jewels in candlelight.

"You went to see Madame Lara, eh? Did she have good fortunes for you both?"

The girls giggled again. "Yes," said Curly Hair, "but she sent us here for some love potion. She says we'll need it to get our heart's desires."

"Madame Lara is wise," he said. "I can help you with that. But would you like something to help give you guidance in your endeavors, too? In case you need some direction when you cannot see Madame Lara?"

Both girls gasped. "Soothsaying?"

Caleb grinned. "Of a sort. Madame Lara is the one with powers. But I can help you tap into your own"—he tilted his head—"instincts."

"Yes," said Curly.

"For both of us," said Silky Hair.

"It's a very special potion," Caleb said, leaning in close, softening his voice like he was telling a marvelous secret, one only everyone else in the shop could hear. "I'll have to prepare it." He grinned again with one side of his mouth and then, without changing his gaze, called in the direction of the back room.

"Oscar, are you there?"

Oscar nodded. But nods communicate little when someone is not looking at you. He took a deep breath and stepped into the doorway. "I am," he squeaked, keeping his eyes down.

Caleb looked back. "Please bring up some cherry bark and belladonna," he called. "I have a special item to make."

Oscar smashed his lips together. That wasn't for Callie.

"This is exciting," Curly gushed. She turned toward her friend, and as she did so her velvet bag swung around and hit the shelf of dark glass vials behind her, full of carefully prepared tinctures. A whole flock of them came tumbling off, plummeting down, exploding as they hit the floor. Oscar put his hands to his ears and yelped. Crow appeared in the doorway, lantern eyes big, ears thrust forward.

Splinters of glass flew everywhere, and puddles of thick liquid spread out to meet one another. Silky screeched and picked up her deep red skirts—now dotted with splashes of tincture of camellia. She looked at her friend, aghast.

Curly Hair stepped back. "Really," she said to Caleb, jewels dimming, "you should shelve these more carefully."

Callie made some kind of small noise then, but Oscar didn't have time to parse it. He was too busy thinking that there was nothing wrong with the way the tinctures were shelved, as long as no one hit them with her purse. As he informed the girls, apparently, because they both snapped their heads to look at him.

"Oscar!" exclaimed Caleb.

Well, it was true.

The girls' eyes fell on Oscar, then darted to Crow, who was still standing as if she did not know whether to attack or flee. Oscar ached to bend down, put his hand on her back, and whisper that it was all right. But he could not move.

Curly Hair turned back to Caleb. "Master Caleb, why do you keep such creatures in your shop?"

"She's not a creature!" Oscar exclaimed. "She's a cat." Anyone could see that.

"Oh, I see!" said the girl. "You keep it because it's amusing."

Both girls laughed, so full of mirth they might burst with it and shatter all over the shop. Oscar took a step back. He wanted to turn and run, but another gaze was holding him—Callie's. She was looking at him so quizzically, like he, too, was falling off the shelf in front of her. Oscar lowered his eyes, then turned and headed back to the cellar.

Oscar spent the rest of the day in the pantry, dicing whatever dried camellia he had left into small pieces. Camellia was an exotic plant, not found even in this forest, so this would be it until Caleb could import some more. Oscar would then put the pieces in jars, fill the jars with alcohol, and seal them. He would shake them once a day, every day, for four weeks, then pour the tincture into vials and bring them up to the store. All the shining girls would have to wait until then to attract bountiful love.

Something had gone wrong today: the girls had laughed and Caleb had snapped, and a whole shelf had come tumbling down. But Oscar would remake the tinctures, and everything would be all right again—he would make it all right.

He looked down and kept chopping. There was more noise than usual coming from the shop above, or maybe Oscar's ears just hurt more now. But as the afternoon wore on, the footsteps sounded more like stomping, the talking sounded more like yelling, and the door did not so much close as slam. His whole body hurt from the noise.

Eventually night came, and with it Caleb's footsteps on the stairs. Oscar froze. *You can do it,* the magician had said. *I know you can.*

Well, now Caleb knew the truth.

In a moment, the magician was filling the doorway. There was darkness on his face. Oscar's stomach felt like he'd swallowed a whole jar of Barrow ivy.

"Oscar," Caleb said. "I want to speak to you."

"Yes, Master Caleb," Oscar whispered. He kept his eyes focused firmly on the floor.

"I am going back to the continent. My business calls me there."

Oscar sat up. "To the continent?" he repeated.

Caleb raised an eyebrow. "Yes."

"Now?" Oscar asked.

"Yes," Caleb said. "I'll be gone several days. You will mind the shop, as we discussed."

Oscar's eyes darted to the pantry shelves. They crashed to the floor behind his eyes. "But . . . what about Wolf?" Oscar asked suddenly. It hadn't been what he'd wanted to ask. Not really. He didn't know what he wanted, other than some truth Caleb could give him, something solid and smooth and sure.

Caleb put his hands on the door frame and exhaled. "Wolf's death was a tragedy. It was a terrible accident. But it has nothing to do with us."

In the distant hallway the lanterns flickered.

"The shelves were fine," Oscar said. "I didn't do anything wrong."

Caleb's gaze held him completely and would not let go. "Oscar," he said after a time, "you have worked hard for me. I knew you would."

"You did?" Oscar dared a glance up.

"Yes. I handpicked you at the Home. They recommended other children. But I picked you. Do you know why?"

Oscar's breath caught. His eyes widened and he shook his head slowly. He dared not say anything, lest Caleb change his mind and not tell him.

Caleb leaned in. "Because the wards told me you were the one who would never get picked."

Oscar's eyes darted up to his master's face for a flash, and then dropped to the floor. A snap of the fingers, and suddenly he was hollow inside.

"I needed someone who would work hard," Caleb continued. "I needed someone who would be loyal. The boy nobody wanted, that was the boy for me." The magician let go of the door frame and straightened himself up. "You are an odd little boy," he said, speaking right to Oscar's hollow places. "And it is acceptable to be an odd little boy down here in the pantry with only the cats to notice. But when you are minding my shop, you will not be odd."

As always, Caleb's words sounded sure, themselves a charm. But now they hit Oscar like a punch. There was a warning in them, too, something that called up the void at the end of the world. Oscar tried the words for himself. *You will not be odd.* He tried to wrap his hands around them and squeeze. But there was nothing there; his hands were empty.

CHAPTER SIX

The Deal

That night, the shadows of the past revealed themselves to Oscar, as the Wolf in his head laughed. The truth had been there in his memories the whole time—he just hadn't looked hard enough.

Something was wrong with him—and down deep he'd known his whole life. Maybe the wards had even said something. (*You are not right, boy.*) Maybe the other children had. (*What's wrong with you?*) Maybe it had happened while he watched one child after another walk off with a family from the Eastern Villages, with a merchant or a farmer. (*You know no one will ever take you, right?*) Maybe he'd even said it to himself.

He remembered a feeling, too—vibrations and the

sense that his whole body was charged with something, something unnatural, like his heart and brain were always spinning—and that nothing could take it away, not the sticks of the dons or the taunts of the other children or the bemused expression of the islanders who would ask him questions and then pass him by.

Look me in the eye, boy.

And another one: that grinding sensation again, deep at the core of him.

You were the one who would never get picked.

Yes, he had known.

You are not right.

A weight on Oscar's chest, a steadiness—Crow, though it was not her routine. She purred loudly, as if to overpower the voices in his head. Slowly, his mind stopped chattering at him. There was this—rhythm and softness and nothing else.

Shh, she said. *Shhh.*

She melted into his chest, and he into his bed. He was so tired.

Shh, she said.

He could not protest. Crow was right. He had nothing left. He did not care what sleep might bring, as long as there was sleep to be had.

Shhh, Shhh . . .

• • •

Caleb was gone by morning. Oscar did his chores and ate his bread and most spectacular cheese, shook the tinctures and prepared a few envelopes, and then headed up to the shop. It was all up to him: He would be loyal. He would work hard. He would not be odd.

Oscar tidied the shop; he straightened his white shirt and black pants, he smoothed his thick hair, he rubbed off all the dirt patches on his boots.

And when it was time to open for the day, Oscar walked over like a good shop boy and unlocked the door. And there, waiting outside, was Callie.

Oscar flushed and looked down, his guts burning. Callie pushed open the door, and he stepped to the side—she could just take what she needed and leave the coins and go without seeing him. His eyes darted to Caleb's obscuring blankets, as if he could will one to fly to him now.

Stillness. Oscar could see only the floor, but Callie wasn't moving; he could tell that much. The quiet lasted several heartbeats. And then, an echoing beat—the fall of Callie's boots.

"Are you all right?" she murmured.

Oscar swallowed. If only he'd found something for her in the library. He could hand her the spell, and she would know he was good for something besides making the shining girls laugh.

"Oscar," Callie said, "listen to me. Those City girls are mean. And horrible. I hope their dresses were ruined."

Oscar glanced up. "You do?"

"Yes," Callie said. "And their boots, too. Don't think about it anymore. Is Master Caleb in today?"

"No," Oscar said. He straightened and smoothed down his shirt. "He's away."

He could see Callie now—she was wearing an apron and had her hair tied back. It bounced slightly as she moved her head, like it might spring off into the air.

"Hmm," she said, glancing over at the herb packets. "All right. Well. I need some barberry."

Oscar blinked. "Barberry? Why?"

"What do you mean, *why?*"

"I mean, um, what do you need with barberry?" He leaned in. "Is someone following you?"

Callie's eyes darkened. "No."

"Oh."

"I have a patient who has a terrible headache," Callie said. "She's had it for a day. That is why I want barberry. Since you are so curious."

"Butterbur!" he exclaimed. "Not barberry," he said. "Butterbur."

Callie folded her arms and gazed at him. "That's rude, you know."

"But . . . ," Oscar started, "isn't that what you want? Butterbur? For headaches?"

"Yes! But"—Callie shifted—"you just can't come out and say that."

"Why *not?*" Oscar asked, words a plea.

"I mean, you say it *nicely*. You can't just go around telling people they're wrong. You . . . suggest that they *might* be wrong."

"I tell them . . . they *might* be wrong?"

"Like this." She cocked her head. A curl fell and dangled toward the floor. "Pardon me, Miss Callie," she began, "I don't mean to be rude, but I'm wondering if you are perhaps confusing your barberry for your butterbur."

Oscar tried it. He cocked his head to the right. It was not entirely comfortable. "P-pardon me, Miss Callie. I don't mean to be rude, but"—he looked up at her; she smiled encouragingly—"I'm wondering . . ." He shook his head. "I've said three extra things already! Isn't it quicker to just say what's right?"

"That's not the point. Keep going."

He tilted his head farther and finished: "I'm wondering if you are perhaps substituting your barberry for your butterbur . . . because they're completely different!"

He could not help it. They really were.

The left side of Callie's mouth went up. "That's better, anyway. But you don't have to . . ." She studied him.

"Well, here . . ." She put her hands on his head and moved it slightly back toward the center. "Like this."

Oscar's breath stuck in his throat. Her hands burned his skin. His neck felt like a stick of wood as she moved it, like it was not made to bend in quite that way.

"You're very stiff, you know," Callie said. "It's not natural. Just relax."

Oscar took a deep breath and willed his neck to un-stiff, to do whatever a normal neck on a normal person did.

"That's . . . better," Callie said.

Oscar jolted his head up, the way he was used to holding it, the way his wooden neck knew best. He did not look unnatural that way; at least he didn't think so.

"So," he said, breathing, "you want the butterbur, then?"

"Yes." She looked around and then added, "Madame Mariel's with the patient now."

Oscar frowned. "She usually comes in, doesn't she?"

"She's busy."

"She hasn't been here in a few days."

"She's busy."

"Is she coming soon?"

"Busy!" Callie repeated.

"Forever?"

"I can handle going to the shop," Callie said, standing

as straight as an oak. "I'm an apprentice. It's my job to take over."

"I know," said Oscar.

"I just mixed them up, that's all. It's an easy mistake."

"All right," said Oscar.

"Barberry and butterbur." She stared at him as if he were the one who had named them. "They sound just alike."

"Well . . . sort of," said Oscar.

Callie looked at him again intensely, carefully, and something in her seemed to loosen. She looked at the shop door and then leaned in to Oscar. She smelled like licorice and hazelnut oil. "Can I tell you a secret?" she whispered.

Oscar's eyes widened. "Yes!" Who was he going to tell, the cats?

"Madame is gone."

"Gone?"

"She goes to the Eastern Villages once a year for—to visit patients."

Oscar's eyes widened. The duke had made it illegal for magic smiths to practice in the east—the magic was for the Asterians. It didn't stop the magic smiths from doing it once in a while. Some years ago Caleb had invented a shield that allowed magical items to survive the trip across the plaguelands. This was the first time anything magical had left the Barrow since the time of the wizards. *And what the duke doesn't know about,* Caleb had said, *he cannot tax.*

"We have to keep it secret," Callie added, "of course. But..." She looked at Oscar, then tucked the stray strand of hair behind her ear. "She's been gone since Tuesday afternoon. Four days is a long time. I am sure there's a good reason. But I'm supposed to pretend she's just . . . out, when people call on us. Busy. It's not just the duke. She says no one will call if they know she's gone."

"But you're an apprentice!" Oscar said. It wasn't like Mariel was leaving the shop in the hands of some idiot orphan.

"Oscar, I don't have . . ." And then she stopped and shook her head.

"What?" Oscar said. "You don't have what?"

"People are sick and they come to me and they need help, and . . . Oscar . . . *I don't have magic.*"

Oscar stared. "You don't?"

She shook her head.

"But you're an apprentice! Apprentices are supposed to—"

Callie stiffened. "I know what apprentices are supposed to have! But . . . I don't. And I can't learn the remedies. Not more than the basic ones. I try to sit down and study the herbs, but it just makes me prickly and tangled and stupid, and all I want to be doing is something else. None of it makes any sense."

"I could help you," he said. The words popped out of his mouth. He hadn't even known they were there.

She blinked. "How?"

"Well, it's just that"—he coughed—"I know a little about herbs and . . . I mean . . . not just preparing them, but—"

"You do?"

Oscar's stomach churned. If this had been Wolf, he would have gotten hit already. "Actually, I . . . I know a lot about herbs," he said. "I read a lot of books, and—"

"Oh," said Callie. Her dark eyebrows knit together, and she studied him a moment. Two moments. Three. "I believe you," she said finally.

"You believe me?"

"Yes," Callie said, studying him. "That envelope Master Caleb gave me yesterday was completely different from the one you gave me the day before," she said. "Entirely different herbs. You made it yourself, didn't you?"

"I didn't—I mean, they were the right herbs," he said quickly. "I wasn't making it up."

"Oscar, I know."

"So I can show you," he said. "It's really easy once you get a feel for it. See"—he could hear himself getting louder, but could not seem to stop it; there were too many words to say—"most things work better in combination.

You want two or three things in a decoction. It's better if they flower in the same season; then they're more like each other: it's like they have the same hearts, just their bodies are different. Then they bring out the power of the other one more—"

The door opened then. Mistress Alma, the silver-smith, walked in, eyed them, and then moved over to the charms.

Callie leaned in. "You don't usually talk that much," she said in a whisper.

"Not to people."

"Why don't you?"

"Oh," Oscar said. "It's . . . better."

He flushed suddenly, intensely, like his whole face was a match someone had just lit.

Silence then. He could not look at Callie, had no idea what her face was telling him, probably could not even have understood it if it had been trying to tell him something. Mistress Alma clattered in the corner.

"In the shop yesterday," Callie said, voice hushed, "with the City girls . . . you weren't trying to be rude, were you?"

Oscar shook his head. "I was just telling them the truth." The words felt like a confession. And, under-neath, a question.

"Sometimes," Callie said slowly, "the truth is not

always the best thing to say." She tucked the errant curl
back behind her ear and studied him. "Oscar," she added,
"why don't we trade? You help me with the plant magic.
I'll help you with . . . people. Working the shop. Talking
to customers. I'll show you what to do. And how to deal
with City people. We'll just trade, that's all."

"You'll . . . help me?" Oscar said.

"Yes. A trade. A deal."

Oscar inhaled, and the breath he took in filled him
so much that he was all air. "Yes," he said, bringing his
eyes almost up to hers. "Yes."

Callie took her butterbur, with some feverfew for good
measure, and left for the healer's house, promising to
come back later, in the afternoon, when her appointments
were done. She promised, and so Oscar believed her.

He worked the shop methodically, studiously, trying to take up as little space as possible. He answered
the customers' questions in as few syllables as he could,
and every few minutes he smoothed his shirt and ran his
hand through his hair. He would do the best he could.

But he felt stiff everywhere. Even the syllables felt
stiff in his mouth. The only thing worse than being odd
was trying desperately not to be.

Then, in the afternoon, Callie walked through the
door again, now in her bright red cloak. She strode right

to the counter and stood behind it.

"Is this all right?" she whispered to Oscar, glancing at the people browsing the store. "To act like I'm working here?"

Oscar's mouth hung open. Of course it was all right. It was the most all right thing that had ever happened to him.

"I just put a sign up at Mariel's for any messages or callers to come here."

"Can you do that?" Oscar whispered.

Callie shrugged. "It's not like a shop. As long as people know where to find me, it's all right."

So for the rest of the afternoon she stood at the counter, head tilted just so, and whenever anyone came in, the perfect words came out of her mouth in the most perfect way possible: "How may I assist you?"

Oscar stepped back and watched as Callie worked the shop as if she were its madame. She never said anything like *What do you want?* or *Not barberry, butterbur*—though she meant the same things. It was like Callie covered her meaning in cushions and invited people to settle back into them. All morning Oscar had told people who wanted a special preparation that Caleb was gone and they'd have to come back when he returned. But Callie smiled and layered softness upon her words. "Perhaps you might look at the prepackaged spell kits?

I'm sure we have something that can help. Let's go see."

How could you tell someone to buy something that's not what they came in for? Why would anyone listen?

And yet they did. They took the packages, looked them over, and smiled at Callie as if she had somehow read their greatest thoughts. "Thank you, Miss Callie. This should do nicely."

Callie might not have known magic, but that didn't seem to slow her down. She directed people to the charms and the herbs and the packaged spells and the potions—where Caleb might give his Caleb smile and say he would go to the back room and whip up something *very special*, Callie would just pick a charm off the shelf and explain its wondrous properties.

Whether it had them or not.

The Barrow folk did not seem surprised to see Callie there—Caleb would want an apprentice to help mind things, and wasn't it so generous of Madame Mariel to lend hers for a time? Rather uncharacteristically generous. And the shining people did not care, as long as someone was there to give them their small magic.

Oscar worked behind the counter, sorting and cleaning and counting and listening, and tapped his foot against the floor in a steady rhythm. Whenever Callie said something to a customer, he took the words and placed them on a map in his mind. On *When a customer approaches* he put a pin that read *How may I assist you?*

No one else needed to do this. No one else needed lessons on how to be a person.

Late in the afternoon, Callie came over to him and whispered, "Do you have something to soothe animals? Mistress Margaret says something is wrong with her chickens."

"They're cranky," Mistress Margaret called from across the store, apparently putting her large ears to good use. "They're talking funny."

"Your chickens talk?" asked the villager who was standing near her, a tall man whose name Oscar did not know.

"Well, not with *words*," said Mistress Margaret. She shot the man a look and then turned back to Oscar and Callie. "But they're talking funny all the same. Like they have something to tell me. They're anxious."

"Your chickens are anxious," the man said.

Mistress Margaret turned to the man, arms folded. "Yes. My chickens are anxious. Roger, you clearly know nothing about chickens."

Oscar stiffened. Her voice had edges. The other villager in the shop turned to look at them. The City lady who was lingering near the glass figurines cocked her head to listen.

"I don't understand how you could tell that a chicken

is anxious," Roger said. "Now, goats, on the other hand—you come to my pasture, I'll show you some anxious goats. They're more than anxious; they're *agitated*." He turned toward the counter. "Do you have something for agitated goats?"

Callie's eyes slid over to Oscar.

Oscar took a deep breath. "Um, it might be . . . that they want . . . passionflower," he mumbled.

"For goats or chickens?" Callie whispered back.

"Both." His eyes shifted to her.

The other man spoke up. "Now that you mention it," he said, "my pigs have been acting funny. Not anxious, really, but—peevish, I think. Prickly."

Mistress Margaret shook her head. "I told Edmund that there was something out there," she said, her voice rattling the potions. "'Edmund,' I said, 'there's something out there. Something *unnatural*.'"

Callie cleared her throat and moved out from behind the counter. "Passionflower," she said. "You all want passionflower."

The group turned to her as one—anxious, agitated, peevish.

"I'm so sorry about your chickens, your goats, and your pigs," Callie continued, looking at them each in turn. "If you need anything else, please come back. We'll take care of you."

And at once the villagers eased, as if they'd just let go of something they'd been holding on to very tightly. Callie gave them a smile, and they all smiled back at her, like neither they nor their chickens, goats, or pigs had ever had an unpleasant thought. She gave them tinctures of passionflower; they gave her coins and left, chatting happily to one another.

As soon as the door closed, the lady from the City shook her head and exclaimed to no one at all, "Country people are so superstitious!" She laughed a pretty little laugh and then purchased three sachets of Caleb's special True Love Powder.

After the lady was gone, Callie looked at the coins she'd left on the counter and blew air out of her mouth. "Amazing," she muttered.

"It costs a lot to get good magic," Oscar said. It was something Caleb said all the time, his eyes twinkling at customers, his hand reaching for their coins—*Well, you know, you have to pay to get the best.* They smiled and handed him their money and walked away, clutching their magic close.

But Callie did not smile. She glanced at Oscar, and then looked away. "I know," she said.

A moment passed. The air thickened. It pressed upon Oscar's skin.

"I need to go," Callie said.

"The passionflower will work," he said. "I promise. I can show you in a book if you want!"

Callie gave him a whisper of a smile. "I know it will. Good night, Oscar."

Even with the shop empty, he could feel the rhythms and patterns the customers had left behind, hear the ghosts of their voices in the air. That was what happened—people came into the shop and left and went on about their days, but their echoes stayed behind, took up residence in Oscar's head, and did not leave.

He let out a breath when he got into the cellar, where the steady darkness welcomed him, took him in, wrapped him up. No unfamiliar voices lingered down here, and the only rhythms and patterns belonged to the cats. When he got to his pantry, he found Bear sleeping in a corner. So he laid himself down on the floor, placing his cheek very gently on top of the sleeping lump of cat. She rumbled softly. Her stomach rose and fell, and Oscar tried to match his breathing to hers. In and out.

Tomorrow, at least, was Sunday, and the shop would be closed. Oscar could go back to the gardens in the morning, gather some herbs, keep company with the plants. Maybe he would ask Callie along, if she didn't have appointments. There were so many herbs he could show her. Maybe if he asked her just right, she would come with him. *Pardon me, Miss Callie, I don't mean to be rude, but I'm wondering if you might perhaps . . .*

As Oscar lay with his head still resting on the accommodating cat, his eyes fell on his satchel. It was sitting underneath his bench, tucked way back against the wall. The piece of wood he'd picked up the other day nudged at his mind. His hands twitched. Oscar scooted himself over to the bench, opened the bag, and reached for it, then held it in his hands and studied it. Maybe it had come off a bigger piece of wood that had become something—a charm, a figurine, an enchanted trinket—but this was nothing, just a rough, discarded scrap, left to rot.

"I'll make you into something," Oscar whispered.

He got down his woodworking tools, shooting a glance at Bear, who was watching him curiously.

"I'm going to do some carving," he told her. "It's all right." He lined everything up on the floor and stared at the straw-colored block. "What should I make?"

Bear blinked up at Oscar, her blue eyes betraying nothing.

The wood still felt warm in his hands. He began to chip away at it, because that seemed to be the thing to do. Whenever Oscar worked, he knew exactly what his project was—gather, pluck, chop, grind, dry, sort, smooth, carve—beginning, middle, and end. Everything had its path, every process, every moment.

Until now. It should have unnerved him. Normally

it would have; normally he would have put it down and muttered something to a nearby cat and gone back to his mortar and pestle, where every system was right in front of his eyes.

But the wood, it had its own ideas. It would not let him go. And so he kept chipping away.

He could draw something first—Caleb always worked from designs. But Oscar could only draw things that were already there; how did you make a map of things that *might* be?

So he kept chipping.

Not much of the wood was left by the time he was done. But he got to the core of the thing. And he started carving, carefully, slowly. The core spoke to him and told him what to do, and for once in his life Oscar needed no map.

When he was done, he had in his palm a small wooden cat.

CHAPTER SEVEN

Glass Houses

He had the dream again. The sky, bright and blue, luring him in. The forest, empty of people, because they had all been taken already—except for Oscar, and Wolf in a sack at his feet. The wind pushed over the wizard trees, tearing the roots from the ground, leaving great mourning gashes in the soil. The roots gulped and gasped and grasped. The gashes in the ground grew under his feet; the wind battered his body. And then it was all gone—the ground, the forest, all of Aletheia—and Oscar was left with the sky and its terrible hunger. He fell into it, and kept falling, and falling some more into the blankness.

And then the dream-Oscar disappeared, expelled

by the body-Oscar, who awoke with a start. He was sitting upright in his bed, surrounded only by darkness and the feelings the dream-Oscar had left behind—and he realized suddenly that his hand was clutching something tightly. He opened it to reveal the little wooden cat. Oscar stood the cat up in his hand and stroked it with one finger.

"You need a name," he murmured.

He leaned over and lit his lantern and then lifted the cat up and appraised it. The cat gazed back with tiny etched circle eyes. "You," Oscar said, "are Block."

He gave the smooth back another stroke. Block was a good name.

Oscar looked around his room. Morning could be hours away. But he had had enough nightmares for one night.

He peered into the hallway. With his dreams still skittering around under his skin, the darkness did not feel welcoming now. Anything could be hiding there. He was in a dark underground labyrinth all alone; Caleb would not return for days, and if something happened to Oscar, no one would even know about it.

So he picked *Secrets of the Wizards* out from under his bed, slipped Block in his pocket, and headed upstairs. For the first time, the upper floor felt safer than the cellar; the moon didn't allow the darkness total reign.

After setting out some cheese for the cats, who all rushed upstairs, happily accepting this change in routine, and then setting Block out next to him, Oscar sat down at the table in the kitchen and opened the book.

"What are your secrets?" he murmured.

The first page read:

This is the official chronicle of the wizards of Aletheia. We will record our experiences here from now on, so no piece of knowledge is ever lost to time, and we entrust future generations to do the same. Our future is nothing without our history. We serve Aletheia and its magic—it is our oath and our honor.

Goose bumps tickled their way down Oscar's back—that page had been written by an actual wizard, one who lived and breathed and cared for Aletheia and performed magic far beyond Oscar's imagination. The book consisted of almost two centuries' worth of type-set entries by the great wizards who had nurtured and harnessed Aletheia's magic so the island and its people could thrive.

Oscar settled in his chair as the dread left over from the nightmare lost its hold over him. For the rest of the night, nothing existed outside the small, secret world of Oscar, the wizards, and the light of the moon.

The wizards saw magic in all kinds of things—the

movement of the planets, the tides, the behavior of animals, even the mutterings of madmen. They wrote long entries musing on the properties of turkey, tail mushrooms, or of venom from a wolf spider. Oscar began to recognize the wizards and their interests; the one named Nikola, for instance, liked animal magic, while Theodore wrote long treatises on the constellations and their movements. The generations slowly shifted over—one by one, the familiar names disappeared from the chronicle, and Oscar felt their loss as if the wizards themselves had been in front of him. But new ones always took their place, young men and women who had shown from birth some ability to bend the rules of the world. The island always replaced its wizards, one at a time. There had to have been exactly a hundred over the generations, to match the hundred wizard trees.

There was a wizard named Elia who loved plants. She discovered things that Oscar now knew as fact: *Cloves for fevers. Balm of Gilead for swelling, with alfalfa to enhance its power.* Elia wrote that everything natural had some unique element at its core, something that made the mushrooms mushroomy and the stars starry. The wizard's job was to discover that core element and coax its energy out. Magic was manipulating these energies and making them work together—creating a world not made of a jumble of discrete entities, but of balance and harmony.

She had one long entry about the wizards' orchard, about the trees that bore fruit and the great network of roots hidden underneath the soil, each almost touching the others—a secret confederacy. *The ground beneath our feet is home to more untapped wonder than the skies above our heads,* she wrote.

That was her last entry.

It's all right, Oscar told himself, rubbing his chest. *This was a long time ago.* Elia was a tree now. She got to nurture the soil in turn. She would like that. They would all like that.

Oscar read on until the presence of morning could not be denied and he shut the book, giving it a little pat. The monsters of the night had been banished. The wizards lingered on—guardian ghosts. If they watched over him, he had nothing to fear from dreams.

Oscar got up, put some water on to boil and threw chamomile in the steam basket, and tried to map out the day ahead. It was usually so easy; he could do it almost as a reflex. But the truths of the days were getting harder and harder to hold on to.

A knocking, then, at the back door. Oscar jumped and peered out through the window, but it was only Mister Malcolm, carrying a basket. Sunday, time for bread. Oscar tucked Block into his pocket, then opened the door, the non-wooden cats swarming behind him.

The smell of the bread called to Oscar, and he wanted to swarm, too.

"May I come in?" Malcolm said, as he came in.

"Yes?"

"I assumed you would not be able to make it to the bakery this morning," Malcolm said. "I was going to leave your delivery, but I saw you in the window and thought I might give you personal service."

The words did not make much sense, but Oscar moved his lips into a smile, because it seemed like the sort of thing Callie would tell him to do. He was full to bursting with the wizards, and nothing else seemed real.

"Is your master away, young hand?" Malcolm asked.

Oscar nodded. "He has business on the continent."

"Ah," said Malcolm, eyes narrowing slightly. "I see." His eyes fell on the book on the table and then traveled back to Oscar. Oscar's heart skipped, but then eased— who would see a book and think he had been reading it?

A yowl from the floor. Pebble, staring insistently at Malcolm.

"May I help you?" Malcolm asked.

Cat thumped his tail. Pebble began to crawl up Malcolm's leg.

"I think they want some bread," Oscar said, helpfully.

"I think you might be right," Malcolm said. He

reached into his bag, pulled out two rolls, and began to divide them into pieces. "Master Caleb keeps remarkable cats. I have two myself. I keep them in the cellar, as they are prone to putting teeth marks in my merchandise." He paused and looked up at Oscar. "Your master is the only magic worker I know who keeps them."

"He says they're the only animals that will stay in the forest," Oscar said. "Besides the birds and spiders and bats and rats and those kinds of things, but they're not as good to have around."

"It is true," Malcolm said, "that cats do not seem to mind the Barrow like most animals do . . . with the notable exception of the Most Spectacular Goat."

"Do you know why?" Oscar asked. "Why the farm animals and messenger horses all have to be kept outside the forest? Why the City horses need Madame Elodie to tend them when they're down here? I mean, the forest has animals, all sorts of weird ones, and they don't mind."

"I believe," said Malcolm, taking loaves of bread out of the basket and placing them on the table, "most animals do not like magic—other than the ones native to the forest, of course. But in the case of cats, I believe magic does not like them." He brushed his hands together and began to move back toward the door.

"Are you sure I can't get you anything?" Oscar asked,

squeezing the cat in his pocket. "We have things that can help you. We have—" Oscar stopped. He had told Malcolm all this already.

"You don't need magic to make bread, my boy."

"But . . . it could make things easier for you. If you tried it, you'd see . It's not anything big; it's . . . just small enchantments." He flushed, as if the wizards could hear him.

Malcolm eyed him levelly. "There is danger in small enchantments, my boy. Small enchantments make us dream of big ones."

"But . . . that's good. Isn't that good?" He bit his lip.

"Some may say so. I prefer we dream of a big world."

Oscar looked down at the cats, who were lined up happily, devouring bread. Trying to understand conversations was like trying to hear a quiet voice across the room. You strained so hard that it hurt, but it was all still just wisps in the air.

"Forgive an old man's opinions," Malcolm said. "I have been around a long time and have seen many things." Now it was Malcolm's turn to glance down at the cats. His eyes flicked back up to Oscar. "I was a magician once."

Oscar's eyes grew big. "You were a *magician*?"

"I was. A very long time ago. Now I bake bread." He adjusted his cloak.

"Wait!" Oscar gaped up at Malcolm. The baker suddenly seemed to fill the room. "Why did you stop? Why would you ever stop?"

"I chose to," Malcolm said, as if that were all there was to say. "My boy, you cannot look to magic to solve your problems. Magic is big and beautiful and terrible. The wizards understood, but no one understands anymore. People treat it like some cheap little thing, a commodity that serves at their pleasure. Magic serves at no one's pleasure but its own."

Oscar could not speak. The weathered old man who always smelled of yeast, who had a voice like the smell of baking bread, still stood in front of him. But now another presence was there, too, some mesmerizing glow just underneath the surface, as mighty and steadying as a wizard tree. Malcolm could stretch out his arms and hold the whole forest.

"Well," Malcolm said, "now I must get back; I have more bread in the oven." He picked up his basket and was just Malcolm again. But for Oscar the ghost of the magician still lingered. "Remember," he added, "if you need anything while your master is away—or even if he is here—you may come find me. Whatever you need."

"You mean if I need more bread?" Oscar asked.

"That is one possible need, yes," Malcolm said. "But you might find there are others."

"Wait!" Oscar exclaimed. "Should I call you Master Malcolm?"

A flash went over the baker's face, as if the basket in his hands were suddenly very heavy. "No," Malcolm said. "You should not."

He left, and Oscar found himself looking around the room, feeling as though he had lost something. His eyes went to the herbs steaming on the stove, and he went over and took the pot off the fire. That done, he ran the wizard chronicle back down to his room, got dressed, and a few moments later he was walking across the marketplace to Madame Mariel's.

Oscar was knocking on the door before he knew what he planned to say, exactly, or really why he had come in the first place. And there was no guarantee Callie was even there: he had no idea where she lived; many apprentices—

But the door opened, and Callie was behind it.

"Oh, you live here!" Oscar said. "I didn't know if you lived here or the village. Or somewhere else. I live in the marketplace, but I know some apprentices live in the village—"

"I live here," Callie replied simply. She leaned against the doorway.

"Good. That's good. It's Sunday. So the magic workers' shops are closed. Master Caleb's shop is closed and you're closed, unless you have appointments, but—"

"I know, Oscar," Callie said. "We are closed. I have no appointments."

"Well, you helped me in the shop yesterday. And so it's my turn to help you. We had a deal. You remember, right?"

Callie cocked her head and smiled a little. "Yes, Oscar, I do remember."

Oscar looked at her face for a half a moment "All right, good," he said, for there was nothing to do but keep talking. "So, I have to go to the gardens today. And we have all kinds of plants there. You wouldn't believe how many! And so I could show them to you. And I could tell you what they do and how you can use them. You can use them for so much." He glanced up. Callie was watching him, still with that wisp of a smile on her face.

It would be so much easier if she were a cat.

"And I could show you the glass house plants," he continued, because he could not stop. "They're from all over the world! There are really good ones for healing. There's this tree with flowers like stars. It's really good for rashes—the oil, I mean. There are these plants that look like spiders"—he made his hands into claws to demonstrate—"the leaves help with . . . well, um, bowels. They work and they're important. And the glass house is . . . it's like a palace. With . . . plants. A plant palace. You have to know it's there, though; you have to expect it. It's a spell Caleb did, so no one can see the gardens. Except the people who already can see them. I mean—"

The words kept coming and he could not stop them, not while Callie was standing there so indecipherably, and so he was going to keep talking until he used up all the words there were and then no one would be able to talk to anyone else anymore and then all anyone would have left were one another's unintelligible faces, and maybe some weird gesturing, too, and it would be all Oscar's fault.

"Yes," Callie said, saving the world with one word. "You can show me your glass palace."

Soon they were walking together through the marketplace, into the forest, each with a basket in hand. Callie's hair was wrapped up in a knot at the back of her head, and with every few steps one or two strands would break loose.

"What do you think Master Caleb does on the continent?" Callie asked, after a time.

"I don't know," Oscar said.

"It seems odd that he would leave right now. With what happened to Wolf."

Oscar glanced at her. "Well, it was an accident."

"Still," Callie said.

"If there were something to be done, Caleb would do it," Oscar said firmly.

"All right," Callie said.

"He's a magician."

"I know. It's not that. I just mean—it would be more . . . respectful to stay, I think."

Oscar squinted at her. "The magic will keep us safe," he said. "Everyone says so."

"I suppose I don't have as much faith in magic as everyone else," Callie said with a shrug. "I'm not from the Barrow. I grew up in the Eastern Villages."

Oscar stopped. "Really?"

"Really."

Most apprentices were from the Barrow village. They'd grown up on Barrow soil, the very air they breathed infused with magic, and one day they showed they had a gift and the magic smiths took them under their wings, nurturing that talent so there would be someone to take their place. So the Barrow always thrived. But occasionally an apprentice came from beyond the river. Oscar had heard the masters of these new apprentices in the shop, announcing, quite loudly, that the children had shown "exceptional promise."

"You must have shown exceptional promise!" Oscar said. Of course she could work magic. Why else would

Mariel have taken her? Why would the duke have given her her pin?

"Madame Mariel always has her reasons," Callie said quietly. Oscar opened his mouth, but Callie went on. "Anyway, I didn't grow up with magic. And we got by just fine."

Oscar's brow furrowed. "Well, I suppose, but—"

"Our healers used herbs, too. They didn't have anything like we have here, but they used the basic ones. Only they weren't magic there. Just . . . medicine." She shrugged. "Maybe it's just how you look at it."

"No, it's not!" Oscar said. Callie stared at him. He knew that expression now, the one that said, *That's rude, Oscar.*

He flushed. "You don't need magic to put herbs together. But the way they work, it's still magic!"

Callie made her mouth into a line and simply nodded.

He would just show her. It would be all right when they got to the gardens. He would have all kinds of things to say then; he could tell her about every plant, if she wanted. And she would see the glass house. If you could make a house out of glass, you could do anything. She would see that it was going to be all right.

They got to the edge of the forest, and though Oscar willed himself to walk right out of the Barrow as if it were nothing at all, his body refused to listen. He stopped.

"Are you all right?" Callie asked.

"Yes," Oscar said firmly. He shut his eyes, took a deep breath, and stepped through into the open air.

Suddenly, Callie took in a great gasp, like she was sucking in the world.

Oscar's eyes popped open.

The gardens were wrecked. A huge swath ran through them, a tumble of soil and green, all in the wrong order, like a giant scar. The swath began at the edge of the gardens closest to the forest and ran all the way to—

The glass house. Or what remained of it. The glass house had broken. Shattered. Half of it stood—one complete wall, and two half walls, great splintered shards threatening the air. The rest was in glittering piles that spread all over the gardens as if for decoration.

Oscar found himself running, tripping over plants— *angelica, anise, arrowroot*—following the scar toward the great glass building and all the treasures within.

It seemed like something had smashed into one of the walls, brought it down and half the house with it. Only a part of the roof remained—cracks and jagged edges. It looked like the sky had broken.

He ran into what was left of the house, his boots crunching bits of glass. The entire southwest corner was destroyed—glass and clay and wood and soil everywhere. And tiny bits of plants here and there, like leaves a cat had chewed up and spit out. But just bits: that was all that was left. Two years' worth of imported plants—the world's bounty, carefully cultivated, tended to, watched over, loved—were just gone. The surviving plants seemed to be withering, cowering, trying to fold back within themselves.

Oscar stood in the wreckage, trembling. He could hear the glass shattering, feel it falling on his skin, as if it were happening to him right now. It rattled his bones, troubled his blood. All he could see was the sky from his dreams, the hungry monster devouring everything in front of it.

Footsteps behind him. A presence next to him. Callie.

"What is this? What happened? Who could have done this?"

It was Callie's voice. She was right there, he knew she was right there, but her voice sounded like it was coming from across the Barrow.

"Oscar—" Callie suddenly turned and put her hand on Oscar's shoulder. He looked down, but not before catching a glimpse of her eyes. They were watery and wide, like sad moons. "Oscar," she said, her voice as firm as her hand, "say something. Can you say something?"

Wolf in bits all over again, the house in bits in front

of his eyes, Oscar in bits scattered everywhere. Everything in bits, and nothing could be put together again.

"Oscar," she said, "we need to leave. We're going to go back to the shop, and we'll figure this out. But I think we should go. I think we should go now."

She sounded so far away, but she was right there, in arm's reach, pulling him back toward her, pulling him away. He should stop, he knew he should stop, pick out every green bit and try to save it; it would take him days upon days, but he could do it—

But Callie was pulling him away, and all Oscar could do was go with her.

CHAPTER EIGHT

Secrets of the Wizards

Callie led him quickly back through the gardens, back into the arms of the forest. Oscar's feet still felt like they were crunching shards of glass, and maybe they were. Maybe the whole Barrow was covered in glass.

The echo of the house shattering hung in the air, like the forest could not let go of it. Oscar could hear it; it filled his entire head. His body was a container now, designed solely to keep the glass house's last memory.

There was pressure on his back, pressure that kept him moving forward. His legs obliged. His heart thrummed. Everything blurred. When the wind touched Oscar's face, it told him that his cheeks were wet.

At some point the force on his shoulder relaxed, and his legs stopped, and Callie appeared in front of him. She looked down at him with those sad moon eyes, and there was nothing he could say, because even the moon would mourn this.

"Oscar," she said, "I don't know how to get home." Her voice was still far away, like she did not exist in his world anymore. "Do you know how to get home?"

He nodded. Yes, he did know how to get home.

"Can you tell me?"

He shook his head. No. He could not.

"Oscar, I need you to take us home. Can you do that?"

Yes, he could do that. He walked ahead. Callie followed. The trees watched. And sometime later they were at the shop, and Callie had his key somehow—maybe he had given it to her—and then they were sitting in the back room and she was giving him tea. Passionflower.

They sat in silence for some time, Oscar huddled up inside his own mind. Every once in a while some cat or another brushed against his legs. His hand went to his pocket and wrapped around Block.

"Oscar," Callie said, voice low. "Can you talk?"

He nodded.

"Good. Say something."

Oscar stayed huddled. The cat brushed his legs

again. A flash of gray: Crow.

"All right," Callie said. "I am sorry this happened. It's awful. And I don't blame you for being scared."

No. He was not scared. He had been scared to climb a ladder. What was it that you felt when the world came crashing down?

"I'm scared, too, Oscar. But we'll make a plan, all right?"

Crow was on his lap now, heavy and warm and soft and real.

"The first thing we should do is tell Master Robin what happened. He's the Barrow guardian. He needs to know."

Some sudden sickness hit his gut, forcing him into his body. Tell someone? Oscar shook his head. What if Caleb found out? He'd left Oscar in charge.

"Oscar, someone or something attacked those gardens. I don't want to frighten you, but we need to tell someone. I think this problem is bigger than an apprentice and a hand can fix."

Fix? Oscar did not want to fix the problem. Oscar wanted the problem to go away. In fact, what he would really have liked was for the problem never to have existed in the first place.

"I don't like it, either," Callie said, reaching out and grabbing his hand. "That's why I'm going to go out and find Master Robin and I'm going to tell him what happened. As soon as I know you're going to be all right. Is there somewhere I can take you?"

It was on the tip of his tongue to say Mister Malcolm's. But this was not a problem bread could solve. And anyway, what would he care about the destruction of a garden? Mister Malcolm had made it quite clear that he was not interested in magic.

"No," Oscar said. "There's nowhere. There's just here."

"Do you want to come with me?" Callie asked. "You could come with me. We could go find him together."

"I—I don't know," Oscar said.

"All right," Callie said. "You're coming with me."

A gentle pressure on his back, a voice in his ear. "Come on, Oscar."

And so, though staying inside the shop and never leaving again was certainly the most rational thing to do, Oscar was out the door with Callie, following her through the marketplace and down the path to the main village.

The Barrow village had risen up in a series of clearings, each containing a cluster of houses. It seemed a different country from the marketplace, one Oscar could barely understand. Oscar lived below a shop.

These people lived in *homes*.

Callie led him on the path through one clearing into another—a circle of six small gray stone houses lined with thick dark beams, all covered in vines and surrounded by an overgrowth of plants, as if the forest were trying to claim the houses for its own.

"That's Robin's," she said, pointing to the second house.

Oscar looked. He'd never thought of Master Robin as having a house. He was the sort of person who was just *around*, not necessarily *there*.

Callie strode over to the door, because Callie was the kind of person who strode up to doors, and knocked. Oscar tiptoed behind her.

They waited. And waited some more. Oscar was about to step away when Callie knocked again, more firmly. For apparently she was the sort of person who did that, too.

Then, the sound of a door opening. Not in front of them, but somewhere next to them. "You're looking for Robin?" a voice called.

A short, wide-faced woman was leaning out of the doorway. She wore an apron and was holding a meat cleaver.

"Hello, Mistress Penelope," Callie said. "We are."

She straightened and suddenly looked very official. "We have something to report to the Barrow guardian."

Mistress Penelope made a sound that was something like a laugh and something like a sneeze. "Well, that's going to be difficult."

Oscar clutched Block. Callie took a step toward the woman. "What? Why? Is something wrong?"

"Master Robin went off with Master Caleb to the continent."

Callie started. "He . . . left? How could he go?"

Penelope waved the cleaver around. "Big dealings over there. Bringing magical goods to the continent! Their own marketplace! Why should we keep the magic to ourselves, Master Caleb asks, when a whole continent could benefit! Big fancy magic man, that Caleb."

"Enchanted things can't survive crossing the sea!" Callie exclaimed. "Believe me, Madame Mariel has tried."

"Oh, she's there, too. They were meeting her there."

Callie shook her head firmly. "Madame Mariel is in the Eastern Villages."

Penelope threw her hands up in the air, cleaver going along for the ride. "If you say so."

"I do say so," Callie said, eyes narrowing. "How do you know all this, anyway?"

"There are no secrets when there are open windows,"

Mistress Penelope said. "Ears are a blessing. We should use them."

"I don't understand why they would do this," Callie said flatly. "What do they need with the continent?"

"Good money in bringing enchanted wallets to people who only have regular wallets," Penelope said. "And no duke on the continent to take his share." She winked.

"And Master Robin?" Callie said, crossing her arms. "What's more important than being here?"

"Oh, well, there are stores going up now. Someone's got to guard, you know. He asked me to watch his plants. He has always been very fond of his plants."

"How could he?"

"I don't mind," said Penelope. "I like plants." She waved her cleaver around again, made some noise of finality, and disappeared into her house.

Callie gaped at Oscar, as if he had something to contribute, as if he weren't still huddled up in his head. "I don't even know how they can do that," she said, voice hushed. "It doesn't make any sense. A marketplace on the continent? There's no magic to work, and no enchantments last off the island. Even Caleb couldn't . . . could he?" She grimaced. "Don't the magic smiths have enough here?"

Oscar closed his eyes. "I would like to go back home now," he said.

• • •

Oscar told her that he would be all right, that she could go on her own, that he had a lot of work to do. And it was true—at least about the work. So much in his pantry that needed attention, so many shelves that needed filling, so many ways in which Oscar needed to work hard, be loyal. But when he walked down the familiar stairs into the cellar, he passed by the pantry without a look and went right into his room.

He sat on his bed, folded up in just the way he had when Wolf was killed. The shattered glass house filled his mind. The gap in his chest ached so badly it seemed like it might rupture. And then Oscar, too, would be in bits.

The Wolf that lived in his brain chose this moment to reemerge. He stood next to the house-in-bits and leered at Oscar. *Quite a coincidence, isn't it?*

The leering Wolf transformed into a sack of Wolf. A line drew itself between the sack and the glass house.

Do you still think my death was an accident?

Oscar pushed the thoughts away, unfolded himself, and went into the hallway, lighting every lantern in the place. He got two from the pantry and put them in his room. The lights were so bright Oscar could see the ceiling and the walls, all the structures and boundaries of his world. Cat came in and positioned himself in the doorway, like a sentry. Thus protected, Oscar picked up the wizard chronicle. As soon as he opened the book, the guardian ghosts surrounded him, filled the room, promised to let nothing else in.

He'd opened the book about three-quarters of the way through, and as he read, it didn't take him long to realize that Aletheia had changed mightily since the last entries he'd seen. They had begun exporting magical goods off the island, and getting great wealth in return. Now, the magic was disappearing from Eastern Aletheia. The wizards believed that the trade was overtaxing it; the magic was for Aletheia and had never been meant to meet the needs of an entire continent. They told the duke to stop the export, but the duke did not listen: the magic would endure; it was magic, after all.

It was funny, Oscar thought as he read. The current duke wouldn't allow magic outside of Western Aletheia, and the magic workers had to sneak any magical goods out. Back then, the duke had been sending it every-where, and it had been the wizards trying to keep it in.

Though Aletheia had changed, the wizards had not. They still cared about animal magic and the stars, mushrooms and spiders. And, Oscar realized, they never talked about things like creating spells to make luck or bring love or attract wealth. They wrote mostly about the natural world, from the roots under the soil to the plants and animals on top of it to the sky and planets overhead. One wizard wrote on and on about a cardinal that lived outside his window. They observed everything to try to understand its core.

Oscar read on into the night. The pages that marked the past grew thicker and thicker, and the future was getting very small. He stopped, eyeing the thin stack of pages he had left to look at, and suddenly his stomach was churning. The wizards had slowly died out at some point. What if the end of the book was the end of the wizards?

No, he told himself, scanning the pages. This could not be all. Surely there was another volume somewhere; surely the wizards had many pages left to live.

Chewing on his lip, he looked ahead. Many of the later entries were written by a wizard named Galen, who wrote long musings on the nature of magic and the role of the wizard as caretaker. One page had a diagram, signed by Galen. He'd sketched an oak tree with roots reaching into the ground and had drawn arrows traveling up the roots—a regular tree, whose roots took in food and water from the soil. And next to that, he'd drawn another tree—this one with the arrows going down from the tree, through the roots, into the soil.

A thrill ran up Oscar's back—this was how the wizard trees worked, had worked since the first wizard had taken his place in the Barrow. Simple, elegant, perfect.

He turned the page. The word *plague* jumped out at

him all of a sudden, and Oscar took in a sharp breath. That word did not belong in this book so filled with simple, elegant, perfect things. He flipped ahead, and the word was everywhere.

His eyes fell on the last entry of the book:

The plague is leaching every bit of magic and life from the land. The magic is all gone from the eastern regions, and the land is full of death and poison. Soon we will have nothing left. And then everyone in Aletheia will be damned.

And then, empty pages.

All the way to the end.

Oscar flipped back, and then ahead again. That could not be all. There were more words somewhere; somewhere in another volume . . . It could not end like this.

With a swallow, Oscar closed the book and leaned back against the wall. The image of Galen's entry stayed in his head, though he could not quite make sense of the words. It was not the world as he knew it.

But the world as he knew it was changing under his feet. And there was nothing he could do but light all the lanterns in the house and try to believe it made any difference at all.

CHAPTER NINE

The Shining City

On Monday, Oscar did what he could to make things right, though everything was different, everything was wrong, and all day his heart thumped and his breath thinned and his head skittered and buzzed and his insides felt like they were being pulled in entirely wrong directions.

In the morning he woke up, got dressed, laid food out for the cats, and got water. He swept the shop and dusted the shelves, in case any dirt had accumulated overnight, and then surveyed the store and set to work restocking whatever needed restocking. This was a good plan, a good routine—it was not his normal one, but it would do.

Eventually Callie came by the shop to check on Oscar. She told him she had gone to see the blacksmith about the glass house yesterday—for if your guardian has taken off to find his fortune on the continent, the man who makes the weapons is the next best choice.

And the blacksmith told her that it sounded terrible. And that the weather could do all kinds of nasty things to a garden. He said the glass house had never really been viable anyway—why else would Caleb have kept it hidden from everyone? He said you could never talk any sense into Caleb, who had dreams bigger than his magic. He said that even if there were some disturbance in the forest, nothing could touch them in the Barrow village. It was the safest place on earth.

"Except the City," Oscar interjected when Callie told him this part.

Callie scoffed. "So they all seem to think."

"Well, it's true!" Oscar said. "The City is the way it is because of the magic!"

Callie folded her arms and stared levelly at Oscar. Oscar inhaled. Callie might not have had magic, but she knew how to immobilize someone with her eyes. "Then why aren't we all like that?" she asked. "Why isn't the whole Barrow rich and . . . *sparkly?*"

"Because . . . because the City is special."

"Why?" Callie asked. "Because the shining people

own the whole island? Because there's magic around it? Did the magic *make* it? Did the City spring up fully formed from the ground, complete with excessive topiary and people who think they are better than everyone else?"

Oscar's eyes widened. "No! I mean . . . I don't know. It just *is*."

"Well, that's what they want us to believe."

"No, it's—" He stopped. Callie seemed to have crackles shooting from her everywhere. "Why are you angry at me?"

Callie's eyes popped for a second, and then she leaned backward. Her whole body rearranged itself, and the crackles fizzled out. "I'm sorry, Oscar," she said. "I'm not angry at you. I'm just . . . It's this place. I don't understand it. Everyone is so busy patting themselves on the back for having magic that no one *does* anything!"

"Master Caleb will come back! He'll do something."

Callie let out an exhale. "I hope so," she said. She had that tone in her voice, the one people had when their words didn't mean what they usually meant.

"He will!"

"Oscar." Callie looked at him carefully. "His own apprentice was killed, and he left. To bring magical goods to the continent. For money."

Oscar blinked. "He didn't know. He thought it was

an accident. When he finds out, he'll help. You'll see."

Callie opened her mouth and then closed it quickly. She tilted her head, causing a curl to tumble out of her braid. "We should open the shop," she said. "I can help for a while. I don't have appointments until the afternoon."

"Good," Oscar said. The entire conversation had left him out of breath and slightly dazed; customers might wreck him.

Callie stayed for two hours while Oscar sat back and tapped his foot on the floor and watched carefully. He concentrated on what Callie said to people and kept a map of the essential phrases in his mind. And when she left, he repeated them exactly.

How may I help you?

Caleb's not here; is there something I can assist you with?

You will find it over there.

Why don't we try some____?

Perhaps you might try this instead.

He used them whenever possible, though they didn't always fit in the places he put them. The only problem was that people tended to keep talking. He needed a better map.

At night before he went into his room he did the same thing he'd done in the morning, but in reverse, filling his mind with each task so no other thoughts could push their way in. Back in his room he read more of the wizard book until sleep grew strong enough to overcome his will. And then he slept, and dreamed, and clutched at the little wooden cat and at the assurance that the next day everything would be the same as it had been today.

That next morning, as he was dusting the shelves just in case any dirt had accumulated overnight, Callie came knocking at the door. Early. He opened it to find her standing there rod straight with her hands on her hips.

"Um," Oscar said, suddenly breathless. "Good morning?"

"Oscar," she said, her voice as firm as cherry bark, "I need your help."

"Oh!" Oscar said. "Good! Come in! Do you need me to make something, or—"

"No. I need you to come with me."

"With you? Outside with you? Where?"

"To see patients."

Oscar cocked his head. "Patients that are people?"

"Yes." She crossed her arms and glared at him. "People patients."

"I can't," Oscar said, immobilized. "I can't do that." Why was she asking? It was obvious he could not do that. He could not talk to people at all, much less patient people. Much less in front of Callie.

"Yes, you can," Callie said, her gaze unwavering. "Oscar, we had a deal. I am collecting right now." She tapped her foot.

Oscar grimaced. Callie stared. He opened his mouth to protest, and her eyebrows flew up.

"All right?" Oscar said.

"Good," said Callie. "We're going up to the City. Some of the—"

Oscar started. "What? The City? I can't go up there!"

Callie set her jaw. "Yes, you can. You can walk. I've seen you. Don't worry about the shop; you're on City business. Besides, you already agreed." She tapped her boot loudly against the floor and glared at Oscar. "That's better," she said, though he had not moved. "Let's go."

Before he could think, he'd locked the shop and was following her through the marketplace. The vendors had just starting setting up their stalls. Callie walked ahead, to the edge of the marketplace, past the court-yard where the City people parked their carriages and the stables where Madame Elodie worked to calm their spooked horses. Two brick paths led away from the marketplace—one much wider than the other. Oscar stepped on that one, but Callie whispered, "That's for City carriages and riders. We walk."

She gestured toward the narrower one and they walked ahead, through the small slip of forest that lay between the marketplace and the hill.

The western boundary of the forest was the farthest west Oscar had ever been, the western edge of his entire world. When they got there, Oscar glanced at Callie. Her face registered nothing momentous—and so Oscar took a deep breath and stepped away from the cover of the Barrow into the sunshine.

Whenever he'd stepped out of the eastern side and gone into the gardens—back before they had been destroyed by some mysterious marauding horror—he'd always known just where he was going. The garden had had boundaries, too, and though the emptiness had loomed overhead, he'd still had the forest right behind him, the familiar soil underneath his feet, and been able to count out his world, plant by plant.

Now there was just brick, a hill, the unadulterated sun, and the unfathomable sky. The air around him felt hollow, suddenly. And so did Oscar; there was no magic here.

Callie glanced at him. "Are you all right?"

Oscar sucked in his lips. "Mmm-hmmm."

They kept walking farther into the magicless void, following the path as it sloped up the hill through a meadow with grass as high as Oscar's thigh, dotted with small blue flowers. (*Bluebottle. Good for wounds and eyes.*) They couldn't see anything ahead but the path going upward.

"Can you tell me what's going to happen?" Oscar asked.

"I'm sorry, Oscar," Callie said with an exhale. "I should have explained. When I left yesterday I went up to the City and saw two children. They're really sick."

"*City* children are sick? Actually sick?" His mind flashed to Ronald, the duchess's son—though not being able to remember wasn't a sickness, really.

"Actually sick," Callie said. "And there were messengers at my door this morning with notes about two more. . . ." Her eyes grew big. "I don't know what to do!"

Oscar's cheek twitched. Of course she knew what to do. "I thought you didn't like City people."

"I don't," Callie said, glancing at him. "But I'm the healer's apprentice. And these are little kids; it's not their fault what their parents are like. Anyway, they're hurting. I don't understand what's happening." She turned her head, dark eyes wide. "They need a healer, Oscar. And all they have is me."

"But . . . that's good!" Oscar said. "Of course you can do it. I think Madame Mariel knew you had magic, and it just hasn't appeared yet. She's a magic smith; they know things about people. Magic things. And it wouldn't make any sense for her to take you otherwise. Especially from the Eastern Villages!"

"It's not . . . it's not like that." Callie grabbed her hair and began to tuck it into a bun. "It's a long story."

"Oh, well," Oscar said, "if it's too long, you can finish later."

Callie stopped for a moment. "All right," she said. "I'll tell you. You might as well know." She exhaled and started walking again. "I was the apprentice to the village healer there, from the time I was little. I was pretty young, but it kept me out of my parents' way. I had—well, have—a brother. Nico. He's five years younger than me. My parents were so happy when he was born—they'd been afraid they were going to have another girl, like me. But . . . he got sick when he was four. And he got worse and worse, always getting fevers, always sick. And I tried my best, but—" She looked off for a moment, and then continued. "I was the healer's apprentice. I should have been able to help. And our healer couldn't do anything. My parents had so little money—the Asterians make everyone pay so much rent—but they saved everything up and secretly sent for the legendary magical healer from the Barrow."

"Madame Mariel."

"Yes. They had to send her half their coins just to cover her journey over the plaguelands and the river."

"Half?" Other magic smiths sometimes asked Caleb for use of the shield he'd invented to bring magical goods across the plaguelands. He always let them use it. For a fee.

"And," Callie went on, "she said Nico had something

wrong with his body that let all that sickness in in the first place. Like we're all supposed to have these walls that keep sickness out, but he didn't. She could fix it . . . but it would cost them more than we had. And so . . ."

"So, what? What did they do?"

Callie opened up her hands widely. "They gave her me. I was the price. They gave her a free apprentice, and she agreed to cure my brother."

"But . . . but she fixed him," Oscar said quickly. "So it's all right. He's better now."

Callie gave a small shrug. "She has to keep fixing him. That's one of the reasons she goes to the east every year, to treat him. As long as I stay with her, of course."

"But then you must be gifted!" A note of pleading touched his voice.

Callie glanced at him. "Madame Mariel is quite fond of telling me how untalented I am. She says my job is to assist her, and that's all. I am supposed to keep quiet and boil water."

"But the apprentices . . . they're supposed to be able to replace the magic smiths."

"I don't think Madame Mariel wants anyone to replace her. I think that's the point."

"But—the duke must have certified you."

"Yes," Callie said. "He did." She cast him a look, then hurried on. "So that's where she is now. It just never has taken so long. Maybe she did go to the continent as well, like Mistress Penelope said." Her face tightened. "After we talked to her, I sent a message to the healer I used to apprentice with asking if Madame Mariel had arrived and if everything was all right with Nico. I'm not supposed to contact my family, but I don't think that's against the rules." Callie blinked and began to walk more quickly.

"We should hurry," she said, as if she'd said nothing else at all. "We'll go see the sick children, tell them we're going to consult with Madame Mariel, and then we'll try to figure something out. I want to help them." She turned her head to Oscar, and there was that look again, like she was stepping through the forest and wasn't sure the world would still be there. "Thank you for coming," she said. "I appreciate it. I was afraid you wouldn't."

Oscar didn't know what to say. How could Callie think there was anything he wouldn't do for her?

"We're almost there." She gestured toward the path, which had started to curve. Ahead, Oscar could see the other path leading upward. White walls peered out above the crest of the hill.

"What's it like?" Oscar said, after a moment. "The City?"

Callie thought for a moment. "Very shiny," she said finally.

And then they had come around the bend and joined the carriage path, and there ahead of them rose the towering stone walls of the Shining City.

"Oh," Oscar said.

"I know," Callie said.

People could make walls very high if they set their minds to it. These walls seemed as tall as a grove of wizard trees, and no less unearthly. They were made of thick bricks of some white stone Oscar had never seen before. He didn't know how there could be that much stone in all of Aletheia. Great red flags emblazoned with golden birds fluttered on top of the walls. An intricate and decidedly pointy iron gate awaited them at the end of the suddenly very wide path. And the path was lined with hedges that had been sculpted so they looked like great birds, one after another, standing sentry—because apparently plants could be carved just like small pieces of wood.

It was something how the path curved around the hill just so someone's first view of the City would be the grandest possible one.

"Let's go," Callie whispered.

Oscar sucked in his breath and stepped forward.

When he'd first seen the flags, Oscar had thought the strange birds pictured on them were perched upon oddly colorful nests, but as they got closer Oscar realized that that wasn't it at all.

"Why are the birds on fire?" he whispered to Callie, pointing up.

Callie glanced up. "They're phoenixes. They do that."

Two guards stood perfectly erect at either end of the iron gates, holding matching spears. They were dressed like birds themselves, in bright red uniforms lined with gold roping (a specialty of the Barrow's own Master Joseph) and adorned with glinting gold buttons. On top of their heads sat enormous fuzzy hatlike objects, shaped like upside-down haystacks about half an Oscar high, lined with red, yellow, and gold feathers. The hats seemed to suggest flames, if flames were made of feathers and looked ridiculous.

Oscar glanced up at Callie. She was not laughing.

So he would not, either.

Callie approached the guards and bowed deeply. "I'm the healer's apprentice, and this is the magician's hand," she said, flashing her pin and motioning to Oscar. She bobbed her head at him slightly, and he understood he was supposed to bow, too, so he jerked himself stiffly forward. "We were invited." She handed one of them a thick piece of paper. The guard squinted at it, then turned it around and examined it from different angles. Then he held it up to the sunlight and squinted some more.

Callie's eyes slid over to Oscar and then rolled ever

so slightly back. He understood now: This was what she did when people were ridiculous.

"Everything seems in order," the guard finally said. "I trust you'll be leaving before nightfall."

Oscar glanced at Callie. He trusted that, too.

"Certainly," Callie said.

And so the guards opened the big gates, walking in perfect synchronization, legs kicking up strangely as they took their giant steps. It seemed like a lot of work to open a door. Oscar tried to roll his eyes back, ever so slightly. But Callie wasn't looking.

They entered into a large courtyard made of a dizzying pattern of yellow and white stone bricks. Each brick was a square, each four bricks formed another, and then sixteen another—you could spend your whole life counting how many squares were in the courtyard. Or at least you could if you were Oscar. He looked up quickly.

A four-tiered fountain stood proudly in the middle of the courtyard, with streams of water spilling exuberantly down, because in the City apparently even water was a decoration.

A three-story, horseshoe-shaped building framed the courtyard. Oscar hadn't known buildings could bend like that. The white stone of the building was the same as they had in the Barrow, but it looked so much cleaner and brighter up here against the bright blue sky—and much more sparkly, due to the gold trim that edged everything. Each story was lined with huge person-sized windows, and every one had a window box bursting with bright, rich pops of enormous flowers, more beautiful than Oscar had ever seen.

"That's where the duke lives," Callie whispered.

"In which part?"

"All of it."

The City people milled around them, wearing their bright lavish clothes made from Barrow magic. In their swooshing layers and extraordinary colors, they popped and swirled and glittered against the white stone around them—which made them look just as bountiful, brilliant, and unearthly as the flowers above. There were many thousands of them walking within the walls, and they all looked like this.

The sky touched everything; Oscar had never been this close to it before, and the sun poked at his eyes. With the wind came a thick salty smell—*the sea*, Oscar's mind whispered to him. His stomach shifted.

It was all wrong. Too many colors, too many people; strange bricks underneath his feet; foreign and possibly poisonous air in his lungs; the lack of magic pulling at his skin. And even with so much around, it was so terribly empty. Everything in Oscar clenched. He felt like a farm animal who had wandered into the Barrow by mistake. He tightened his fist around Block.

"Come on," Callie whispered, tugging at his arm. "This way."

They moved through the courtyard, the City people oblivious to the children passing by. Oscar and Callie were made of grays and browns and bones and skin and had no place up here. They were like mice skittering through a congregation of peacocks.

They skittered under one of the archways beneath the building and found themselves on a small street lined with thin, rectangular houses packed side to side like mismatched books on a shelf. Here, the houses shone with color—pink, yellow, blue, purple, green. More flowers burst out of window boxes and pots by the doorways, and they were all perfect—nothing wilted, nothing thirsty, nothing straining for sun or shadow.

That was the thing with the City, Oscar realized as they walked. It wasn't made of gold or encrusted with diamonds. No enchantment made the place truly shine. It was just that everything was unstained by anything like wear or want, so carefree as to sport exuberant embellishments—swirling patterns in the wrought-iron balconies, gold door knockers with faces of animals, sculpted frames around the doorways, ornate ridging on the roofs, little statues on the staircases, flowerpots with flowers painted redundantly on them, even a fountain with a sculpture of a baby with big fluffy wings. And the people were the same way: gilded with plenty, unsullied by suffering. Someone who thinks of possessing a fountain made of a winged baby with water shooting out of its mouth must not have too many troubles.

Callie motioned to the statue. "I know. It's ridiculous. People in the east pay them so much rent the villages barely get by, and they're buying vomiting baby fountains."

They turned a corner and walked toward a man dressed in pleats and puffs and one carefully placed feather who was accompanied by a little girl, no more than five, with swinging skirts and a great velvet bow in her hair. She carried a little rag doll in her hands. The girl stopped when she saw them, and then reached up as if to touch Callie's thick curls.

"Julia!" said the lord.

Even Oscar knew you weren't supposed to do that.

"Your hair is pretty," the girl said.

"No, it's all right." Callie bent down and let the girl stroke her hair. "Thank you. Your hair is pretty, too, Julia."

"It is," said her father, shining like a star. "She's perfect."

"That's how they're supposed to look," Callie muttered as they walked on. "Glowing. All my time with Madame Mariel, I've seen only one City child be sick, really sick. And that was three years ago. They're all so *healthy*. Or at least they used to be. Here we are."

Callie motioned to a pink house that looked as if it had been built yesterday. "These are the people who sent for me today."

Oscar beheld the house. No stone baby burbled here, but there were two matching statues of men wearing wreaths on their heads—and nothing else. Oscar's eyes darted away as Callie brushed off her cloak, fixed her hair, and poised herself to knock.

"Wait!" he said.

"What?"

"Wh-what do I do?" His eyes felt like they were as wide as his face. "What do I say?"

Callie turned to him and put her hands on his shoulders. "It will be fine, Oscar. It's just like the shop. Just pretend. That's what I'm doing."

Caleb's not here; is there something I can help you with?

"Callie—"

"What?"

"I don't know how to pretend."

Callie's hands tightened on his shoulders and she looked him in the eye. "Well, pretend you do."

A woman in a simple black dress let them in and led them immediately down a hallway into a parlor. The house interior was like nothing Oscar had ever seen—a chaos of colors and patterns and objects and textures. The walls were covered in thick, intricately patterned paper; the furniture was all swirls, plush, and gilt; and *things* were scattered everywhere—tiny statues and figurines and vases and little tables perched on delicate bird legs that seemed they couldn't hold more than the lace that covered them. Nothing made any sound, but it was still the noisiest place Oscar had ever been.

Callie was greeting a lord and lady while Oscar focused on a small blue speck in the rug under his feet and tried to keep the noise from drowning him. "I am Madame Mariel's apprentice," she was saying, voice like a bell. "She is out on urgent business—"

"Everyone's gone!" the lady said, throwing up her hands. "Caleb, the healer . . . What business could they possibly have that's more urgent than this?"

"It's all right," Callie said, as sure and mighty as a tree. "She is deeply concerned, and so she wanted me to come right away to see you and gather information. I'll tell her everything and then come back." She held her hand out toward Oscar. He started. He had forgotten he was there. "This is Oscar, Master Caleb's hand. He'll be assisting me."

Oscar started to bow. Callie shook her head slightly. No. No bowing.

The parents didn't even blink, just led the two of

them up the stairs and into a bedroom, the mother whispering things to Callie as they walked. A little girl with black ringlets and plump cheeks was sitting on a big yellow chair in the front of the room, looking just as perfect as the rest of them, though her shoulders were hunched and her eyes were too wide, as if she'd been startled once and had never gone back to normal. She was biting her lip and yanking on a ringlet. She kicked her feet in the air slowly, rhythmically, revealing shiny red shoes. Oscar looked at Callie.

"No," said the lady to his unasked question. "In the bed."

The lady motioned toward the other end of the room, where there was a wide bed and a pile of lush blankets on top. Except it wasn't a pile—a boy was underneath it all, a little younger than Oscar. He was as limp as a doll, like the one the little girl on the street had been carrying. His whole body seemed sunken into the bed, like the bed had come with the boy already in it. The boy's head turned at his mother's voice, revealing a face that was entirely the wrong color—some whitish-greenish-grayish hue, lips and all.

Oscar took a step back. Callie inhaled, brushed off her apron, and went over to the boy. "Hugo," she whispered, "my name is Callie. I'm here to help you. How are you feeling?"

The boy whispered back, but whatever he'd said, it was only for Callie. She held her head close, murmured something, and then took his other hand and frowned.

She put two fingers on the boy's wrist and held them there, murmuring quietly to him. Oscar felt a familiar pressure on his skin. He glanced over. The girl in the chair had fixed her eyes on him. She was still swinging her legs slowly, and her face was set in a strange expression, just like the one on the face of the boy they'd met in front of the shop who didn't recognize his mother.

Oscar clutched Block in his hand. The air was thick with the noises of the boy breathing, the parents fidgeting, the rustle-swish of the girl's skirts, and the steady banging of her feet against the chair. There were so many sounds; he had no attention left for anything else.

Callie was saying things to the parents—something about warm compresses and hot tea and massaging his limbs. Oscar stepped to the left to make way for her, and his eyes accidentally caught the girl's and her legs stopped swinging. Her eyes did not let his go. Oscar flinched.

Then he realized: he had seen her before. Sophie, the girl in the shop with her father that first day. The lord was Lord Cooper, who had been so curious about Oscar and had asked such strange questions: *Might I ask, how long do you remember being here?*

She had watched him then, too; her gaze refused to let him go until it took in every bit of him. Now her eyes were asking him something, telling him something, and Oscar felt himself getting sucked into the great gap between her need and his comprehension.

He looked at Callie helplessly, but she was busy with Hugo, so he glanced back at the girl—though it meant meeting her eyes. Those eyes looked like Pebble's whenever the kitten was crouched in a corner hiding from Wolf. Oscar reached over with his non-Block-clutching hand and petted her on the head. It always worked on Pebble.

Sophie tilted her head and now looked curiously at Oscar. And it was only when her expression changed that he realized what the one before had been telling him—the girl was frightened.

Oscar sucked in a breath. His chest hurt. He opened his mouth but could find nothing to say to her. He shook his head helplessly. He was not made for this.

"I'll consult with Madame Mariel as soon as she returns," Callie was telling the parents. She sounded so truthful when she was lying. "And then I will come back up. Please send word if anything changes."

Callie motioned to Oscar. Time to go—though the boy was still flat and gray. Sophie's face shifted back again, and she was holding Oscar with those frightened eyes as if trying to keep him there.

He could do nothing. He looked away.

When they left the house, Oscar, for the first time ever, was glad to see the blue sky. Next to him, Callie's perfect posture had collapsed.

"Callie," he whispered, "can you help him?"

"I don't know," she said quietly. She pressed her hands on her cheeks. "I don't know."

"You looked like you knew what you were doing in there!" The words came out too loudly.

She sighed. "I know many things, Oscar. I've assisted on hundreds of healings, and I've read a lot. But—"

"So, what's *wrong* with him?"

"Well," Callie said quietly, "his pulse is faint. His hands and feet are swollen and cold. And he's just . . . weak, everywhere."

It wasn't what he'd meant. Oscar didn't want to know the boy's symptoms; he wanted to know what was *wrong* with him so someone could *fix* it and no one ever had to look like that again.

"I don't understand," he said. "I thought the City was protected. That's the whole point, magic serves the City, and so everyone is blessed—"

Callie's face darkened. "Well, not anymore."

CHAPTER TEN

Last Words

They visited three more houses, and at each it was the same—a young child flat in a bed, parents with the shine gone out of them. A girl could not eat. A stiff-looking boy said he hurt all over, and as he talked his lungs seemed to be trying to yank the words back. And another had gone to sleep at night healthy but when he'd woken up he could not see or hear.

It was all wrong, everywhere, and so was Oscar. At each house, Oscar lingered in the shadows. He had nothing to say to the parents, to the children, to anyone. His body was there, but the real Oscar was tucked away somewhere else, somewhere dark with four walls and a ceiling and at least two cats.

He stayed in that place until, at the last house, the boy's father—a tall, older man with eyebrows like cat tails—grabbed his shoulder. Oscar jumped as if he'd been pulled from a dream.

"You're the magician's hand? Caleb's?" the lord said, voice just like his grip.

Oscar stiffened and nodded slightly. *Is there something I can help you with?*

"You tell him he needs to come to the City. You tell him something's very wrong up here."

"He'll come," Oscar said. "I know he will."

The man leaned into Oscar and held him with his eyes. "Do I have your word on that?"

"I—"

"Oscar," said Callie quickly, standing up. "Why don't you go wait outside? I want to talk to Lord Baker."

A few moments later, Oscar was sitting on the front step in between two potted plants that looked like cypress trees in miniature. He eyed one. It was like there was a whole universe somewhere of inch-high people who lived in their own tiny little forest, and the City people were taking their trees for their own. The noise in his head buzzed steadily, and he pressed his arms as close into his chest as he could. It did not stop hurting.

Callie had been right to dismiss him. He did not belong here. And now Callie knew it, if she hadn't before.

She could have just told him what was wrong with the children and he could have made something for them—he could look at a list of ailments and know what to do (*comfrey, calendula, juniper berry*). Name a problem and his mind would sift through pictures of book pages, browse the pantry shelves, pluck from his memory bits of things Caleb had said, until the answer took shape in his mind. But when these problems took flesh and became people, people with wrong-colored faces and cold skin and grasping breath and unseeing eyes and faint words, the books and shelves and bits of things went away, and all that was left were scared little sisters and angry fathers and no answers, and Oscar had nothing for them.

When Callie came out, Oscar sprang up, nearly overturning one of the tiny-people trees.

"Callie," he said, eyes stinging, "why am I here? Why did you bring me up here?"

"Oscar—" She blinked at him and then glanced at the house she'd just left. She took Oscar's arm and led him down the stairs and into the street. "Don't worry about Lord Baker," she said. "Sometimes when people are upset about something, they take it out on the nearest person, especially if that person can't get angry back. Do you understand?"

Not really.

"But you can't make promises for Master Caleb,

especially to City people. You can't. All right? They'll expect you to keep those promises."

He nodded, pretending.

She put her hands on his shoulders. "Oscar, I brought you here because I thought you could help me figure out what's causing all of this."

"But I don't belong here! You could have just *told* me—"

Callie shook her head. "No. There's something underneath. More than we can see. And we can't just look at all the different pieces. We need to put them together."

That was the problem. He couldn't look at anything but the different pieces.

"Oscar, listen to me. I wanted you to come because you might see something I don't. I wanted your point of view."

"On herbs?"

"On everything. Master Caleb's not here and Madame Mariel's not here and these children need us. The healer's apprentice and the magician's hand. We're the best they have right now."

"But—"

She held up her hand. "Yes, when Caleb comes back. But"—she leaned in—"he's not here and we are and they are sick right now and I want to help them and I don't know how. They need me and I can't help them." She put her hand on his arm. "Please help me."

He could not say no.

Callie exhaled and started walking. "It can't be a coincidence," she said. "Something's making these kids sick. The Baker boy can't move his legs. The Collier boy's muscles are stiff and he can't seem to get enough air. The Miller girl can't eat. Hugo—his heart isn't working right. It's like . . . like there's something *broken* in each of them. But not the same thing. They're sick, and . . . Oscar"—she turned to look at him—"*I don't understand.*"

Her eyes were so big as she looked at him, and shining a little. He thought of Hugo's little sister and her eyes and her red shoes and his utter lack of anything to give her.

"I—" Oscar said. As he stood there, wordless, his mind made a map of the streets they'd traveled, and the houses of the sick children rose up from them. He saw no pattern, but something must be there—a current running between the children, some invisible force traveling from one to another. Something dark was in that current, moving from child to child, altering itself as it moved so it couldn't be named, let alone traced. All they had in common was that they were young children, and—

His head snapped up. "Callie, what if it's the plague again?"

Callie's eyes widened. "But," she said, her voice a

thick hush, "that was ages ago."

"Before. But what if it . . . changed somehow? What if it can get around the magic?" It sounded so strange to say, but it was possible. One year you spread garlic all around the berry bushes and it keeps the monkey beetles away. The next year the monkey beetles decide to eat the garlic. Things have a way of getting around barriers when they want to.

"I don't know," Callie said. "Nobody ever talks about the plague. I don't know anything about it; do you?"

"Not very much. But"—he looked at her cautiously— "I know where we can find out."

It was the first time Oscar had ever brought anyone below stairs—it was the first time he knew of anyone going down there at all besides the magician, the apprentice, and the hand, and when he opened the door to the cellar, he half expected some force to push them back.

"It's very dark in here," Oscar said, taking a step down. "Be careful."

In fact, the cellar had never looked so dark before. It was like the City had blinded him. He looked back to Callie to make sure she was all right. His heart fluttered like he was handing her a secret with each step—what if Caleb came back and found them? What if Wolf had never died at all and was just lurking in wait to catch

Oscar doing something wrong? Or what if he *had* died and was still lurking in wait?

When they stepped into the cellar, something hurled itself at Callie—though it was not Wolf, unless Wolf had become small and fuzzy and orange after his death.

"Pebble!" Oscar said as the cat crashed into her legs. The kitten flopped on her back and rolled around in front of Callie as if Callie were catnip.

Callie's face broke out into a smile as bright as all the lanterns up and down the hallway. She squatted down and rubbed Pebble's belly. "Good kitty," she whispered.

The cats multiplied around Callie—now Crow, and Bear, and even Cat. Callie's smile broadened as they presented themselves to her, one belly at a time. Oscar had never seen them all like this; one person made them all come out of the shadows.

"Did you name them all?" Callie asked.

"Well, in a way," he said. The cats had really named themselves.

He glanced over at his pantry. Someday, he would like to show it to her. But instead he motioned her forward into the hallway, shooting a look at Cat. *Master Caleb's not back, is he?*

Cat blinked back, unperturbed.

"This is incredible," Callie said, as they walked down the long hallway. "There's a whole world down here!"

When they got to the library Callie just stood in the doorway, mouth open. It was not Oscar's. He had not conceived of it or built it; he was not even supposed to be in it. But still, Callie was marveling at it, and pride tickled his chest.

"I've never seen anything like this," she breathed. "It's like a library in a book!"

A book in a library. A library in a book. Oscar let out a little laugh, and then coughed to cover it up.

Map yowled from his position on the chair, and Callie hurried over and gave him his due. The rest of them would come slowly, one at a time, and casually settle into different places in the library as if they had planned on being there anyway—except for Pebble, who didn't do anything casually.

Oscar went over to the shelves. He was no good for Callie up there in the sunshine, blinking at some senseless jumble of bits. But down in the cellar, he could help.

He went to the Aletheian history section and pulled down the plague book. The little green book next to it fell over, so Oscar pulled it down, too.

"Here," Oscar said, calling to Callie. "This is about the plague." He indicated the thick book in his hand. "This one might be, too."

Callie took the books and sat down in one of the big chairs. Map immediately jumped on her lap and flattened himself against her.

"I'm going to look at some of the plant-magic books," Oscar said. *At the bits.* He could at least try to help the kids feel better. That would make Callie happy. But even the bits were jumbled in his mind now with baby fountains and horseshoe buildings and naked statues and minia-ture trees. He tried to take the muddle of the day and pick the important pieces out. *Weak heartbeat, swollen hands, cold limbs. Vomiting. Pain and breathlessness. Blind and deaf.*

"That's right," Callie said. Oscar flushed—he hadn't realized he had been thinking out loud. She leaned back in the chair, shaking her head. "I wish they had more in common. Then we'd know where to start. There's noth-ing except they were all weak, and they all seemed . . ."

"What?"

She cocked her head. "I don't know. They all seemed like something was . . . missing. Did you feel that?"

Oscar shook his head.

Callie shrugged. "Illness takes things away from people sometimes," she said. She exhaled and started looking through the big book.

They worked quietly for a while, Oscar going through books hoping one of them would tell him what he was looking for. Every once in a while Callie would stop and tell him what she'd read. But none of it sounded like the country he knew—it was like hearing some tale of a far-off land. One Oscar did not particularly want to visit.

"The plague came from the continent—it came in on ships," she told him. "Once the plague swept through the coastal countries, most of the islands stopped all trade and forbade any boats from coming in, to keep themselves safe. But the duke thought the magic would keep Aletheia safe."

Oscar bit his lip. Wasn't that the whole point of the magic?

"So," Callie continued, "it started in the coastal villages in the west, children getting sick first." She looked up at Oscar meaningfully. "Um . . ." She scanned down the page. "Fevers and rashes and weakness and vomiting. And then it just swept through the villages south of the river."

Oscar sucked in his lips. There were no villages there now.

The map of Aletheia appeared in Oscar's head. He saw it—the great expanse of the eastern country, and the river snaking up across the south and to the west, slicing off the Barrow and surrounding areas from the rest of Aletheia, and he saw the shadow moving in from the southwest.

"Everything starting dying all up and down the river," she continued. "The whole western side of the island. Everyone was getting sick but the wizards. Even in Asteri."

"But," Oscar interjected, "I thought the plague didn't last that long. Especially not in the City."

Callie blew out air and motioned to the book. "It seems to have lasted."

Callie read on quietly for a while more. The book Oscar had been studying lay open in his lap—he could read so much more on Callie's face than in the pages in front of him.

"It spread over the whole island," Callie said after a time. "Whole villages were dying. It wouldn't stop until—" Her eyes grew wide and her mouth hung open. But her eyes kept traveling the pages. Oscar mashed his lips together and waited, counting silently to himself.

She looked up, finally. "Well, then the duke decided to institute a quarantine," she said, her voice heavy. "As soon as someone showed signs of being sick, they were arrested and taken into Asteri and kept there."

"Because it's magic," Oscar said. "To heal them."

"No. No. The duke lived in the east then; the capital was there, all the people with money lived there. Asteri—it sounds like it was run-down. Filthy. So they sent people there. Not just people with the plague, but their families, too, in case they'd been exposed . . . and then . . . they locked them in. Oscar"—she inhaled and leaned closer—"the City walls weren't built to keep people out. They were there to keep people *in*."

Oscar stared at Callie. "What if . . . what if someone got better? Would they let them out?"

Callie pursed her lips and shook her head.

Oscar sat back. The Shining City, infused with magic, blessed by providence, where the residents wanted for nothing—that was where people had been sent to their deaths. The duke had kept the plague from killing the entire island by condemning the sick and exposed to the City.

"Oscar!" Callie said, drawing him back to the library. She had the little green book open now. "Look at this one. It's all handwritten, different entries. It's like a diary—"

"Can I see it?" Oscar breathed.

Callie handed him the little green book, and he opened it carefully and flipped through the pages. Yes, it was a wizard diary, started after *Secrets of the Wizards* left off, after the plague hit. Only no one had copied this book and put it into type and produced it for library shelves. It was an actual handwritten account kept by a wizard, and somehow Caleb had it.

"I'm just going to look at this awhile," Oscar said, plopping himself down on the floor, not taking his eyes away from the book.

The journal belonged to Galen—the wizard who

had appeared at the end of the chronicle. It began:

> *This is a true account of the wizards and the plague of Aleth-*
> *eia. The duke has ordered us not to write about the plague in*
> *our chronicle anymore. He believes he can erase his sins—but*
> *the land remembers, always. I will record our efforts for the*
> *wizards who follow us, should such a thing curse our land*
> *again. We will leave empty pages in the official chronicle before*
> *the wizard's entries recommence. These will be the unwritten*
> *words on those pages.*
>
> *History condemns secrets to their death.*

With his breath stuck in the upper part of his lungs, Oscar flipped the page and plunged into the book.

When the plague began to sweep the continent, the wizards told the duke to stop all trade and sea traffic to Aletheia, as so many other island nations had. But the duke said the magic would protect Aletheia; there was no need to close the ports. And Aletheia was growing so wealthy from sending magical goods and its unusual array of natural resources out into the world, and that was good for the island, too. The wizards could not change his mind.

The plague began in the southwest, where the ships came in. The wizards told the duke to quarantine the area, but he refused; because the magic was all gone from the east now—if people could not go into the west, however would they get magic? Magic was the Aletheians' birthright.

With no official quarantine, the wizards asked the people of the east to forgo magic until the plague left. But they did not listen, and when an easterner crossed into the west for magic he crossed back carrying something far more powerful—and four days later half his village was gone. The duke ordered the wizards to find a cure, but they could not. Then he told them to build an impenetrable wall around Asteri to protect the vulnerable, and after they did he took the sick and locked them all in. And then their families.

And still the plague spread.

Galen's entries—formerly pages long—grew shorter and shorter. Like:

The plague has killed everything along the western banks of the river and the shores around the sea. Now, that earth is not just barren but a vacuum. One cannot plant a seed or light a match in this land, and one cannot carry magic across and expect it to survive the journey. Perhaps this will stop the spread. If it isn't already too late.

No. The magic had not kept Aletheia safe. It killed everywhere it went. It wiped out whole swaths of villages, took so much out of the land that it killed not just life but the potential for life.

Galen wrote:

The duke has given up on Asteri, left the people locked in there to die. He asks us to put all our efforts into protecting the east. He says it is for the good of all of Aletheia. But you cannot save a body and kill its heart. We feed him illusions and lies while giving the sick in Asteri everything we have.

Later, simply:

The plague does not affect us. Our magic does not affect the plague.

And then, the next page:

There is something in the magic we have that is greater than the magic we can do.

And then:

It is beyond us. We do everything we know, everything we can conceive of, we do things we don't know, and it is beyond us. People will keep dying until nothing remains in Aletheia but us and our monstrous failure.

Everything is sick. The plague is in the land now, and if it does not kill all the people first, the land will.

The plague sucks everything dry. It takes and takes. It is sucking away the magic we do. All we have left is the magic we have.

And finally:

We, the wizards of Aletheia, are the sworn protectors of this land and its people.

We are the guardians of a dying people, a dying land. All we have to give truly is ourselves.

We will be the last of the wizards. Our bodies and spirits will die. Only our essence will live. We tended to the magic, and now we preside over its death. Perhaps the world will be safer for it.

The spell has been cast. We will go take our places. May the magic that has kept us safe heal the city and the whole land, from the disease and from all it has left behind. May our lives do what our powers could not.

We are all agreed.

And then, signatures. Each one made by a different hand—some scrawled quickly, some elegant and embellished. One after another, filling the page, and pages after that. There were so many—several dozens at least. There might even have been—

A hundred.

Oscar frowned. It didn't make sense. How could there be a hundred wizards living at one time, when there were only a hundred wizard trees?

Oscar stared at the entry again. His heart thudded. Suddenly, he sprung up and pulled another Aletheian history book off the shelves, quickly flipping through until he found what he wanted.

A map. Before the plague.

And there it was, a country so like his—but different. All along the southern border there were villages right up to the river. When the river bent northward, the villages followed. And at the very southwestern end there was a hill, and upon it Asteri. And around the hill—

"Callie!" he exclaimed. Her head shot upward and he brought the book to her. His face felt so hot, like something inside him was burning. "This map. Of Aletheia. Before the plague. What do you see?"

"Um, the Eastern Villages," she said. "A capital in the east. More villages by the river where the plague-lands are now. And Asteri."

"What's missing?" He was not testing her. He needed to see if she saw what he did.

She inhaled. "The Barrow. There are some trees around the hill, but—"

"But there's no Barrow."

Galen's diagram in the wizard chronicle popped in his head—the two trees, one with arrows going up from the roots, another with arrows going down. Oscar had been wrong; Galen's sketch of the trees feeding the roots was not a diagram of how the wizard trees worked, but a theory of how they might work. It was not an analysis, but a plan.

"Callie," Oscar breathed, "wizards haven't been coming down to the Barrow and becoming trees since the beginning of time." His voice sounded strangely even, like the words it spoke were nothing at all. "They died, just like everyone else. Or they used to. All the wizards during the plague, *they made the Barrow.* They turned themselves into trees, to infuse the ground with the magic. To try to kill the plague from the soil up."

The air in the library held on to Oscar's words, refused to let them go. They hovered in the room like phantoms, and Oscar and Callie could only gape at them, faces as wordless as the empty pages of the official chronicle.

The trees were not Aletheia's gift to the wizards for their service, not living monuments to great men and women. They were monuments of a desperate act, necessitated because of foolishness and greed. The trees were not the wizards' respite. They were their sacrifice.

CHAPTER ELEVEN

Deciduous Ghosts

Oscar and Callie sat in the library a while longer, Callie scanning the books for more information, Oscar just sitting inside his mind. There were no answers about the children, but they did not even know what the questions were anymore. The world had ruptured once again. Even history could disappear under your feet.

The island of Aletheia teemed with magic—magic so powerful that when a plague ravaged the continent, Aletheia still thrived. For centuries great wizards had worked the magic to keep the island prosperous and marvelous, until slowly the magic faded, and eventually the wizards, too. But their power, their core, lived on in the trees they became, ensuring that the Barrow would thrive for all eternity. Even as the sorcerers replaced the wizards, then the magicians after that, and now the magic smiths, their essence lived on in the Barrow, feeding the soil magic so the blessed people of Aletheia's Shining City could flourish, as was their due.

This was what they had always been told. This was the legend of Aletheia.

But no. It was just a story. Just pretend. The plague came, the Duke of Aletheia put all his faith in magic, and three-quarters of the island died. The plague ate away at the island's lifeblood—the people, the land, the magic itself—and it would have consumed the whole place had the wizards not performed their last, greatest spell.

The wizards gave themselves, and a cursed, blighted City was birthed anew. And somehow the magic in the Barrow lived on, and soon there were sorcerers, and then magicians, and magic smiths after that—the purveyors of petty little charms for a gluttonous populace.

Once, people were walled into a City of decay and death. Once, there were villages on land that was now barren and toxic. Once, wizards fought with everything they had, and then despaired. Once, they encircled a hill and waited to take root.

Callie put the rest of the pieces together from what she'd read in the history book. The spell worked—more than the wizards knew. It did not only rid Asteri of disease; it turned it into a jewel, one that shone so brightly the plague survivors flocked to it. Even the duke made the new Asteri his home. And, soon after, he offered a tremendous bounty for the first person who could draw magic from the earth again.

The official Aletheian history book did not tell the story quite this way. It made no mention of the wizard's sacrifice—simply, the magic had eventually saved its chosen people from the plague, just as everyone had known it would. The wizards themselves simply disappeared from the history of the plague. They lived only in the white spaces between the lines.

Even the past was a lie.

Callie and Oscar walked upstairs together in silence, and Callie slipped out the door into the night. When she was gone, Oscar could only crawl into his room and clutch Block in his hands.

In the morning, Oscar woke up, got dressed, laid out food for the cats, and got water. He swept the shop and dusted the shelves, in case any dirt had accumulated overnight, and then surveyed the store and set to work restocking whatever needed restocking.

When Oscar opened the back door, the smell of fresh bread greeted him like an embrace. A basket was waiting for him. Oscar took it in, and the cats began to circle pointedly. He divided up a loaf for them and set the pieces on the floor. And then he saw the piece of paper at the bottom of the basket:

> *Oscar,*
> *I expect you can read this note.*
> *Please come see me, as soon as you can.*
> *Your baker,*
> *Malcolm*

Oscar rubbed his chest. Malcolm had tried to warn him, tried to tell him not everything was as it seemed. *Magic is big and beautiful and terrible. The wizards understood, but no one understands anymore.* Oscar could have asked more questions, could have paid more attention. Malcolm had told him, but Oscar hadn't heard.

A familiar feeling burned deep in his stomach, like a pestle grinding into his gut. Maybe he would have heard Malcolm if only he knew how to listen.

Oscar perched the little cat on a shelf below the counter and then opened the shop, peeking his head up the path to check for Callie's dark head bobbing toward him. It did not, but two villagers came in a few minutes later, and soon Oscar could think of nothing but customers.

In the first two hours the shop was open, Oscar sold six different protective items. It wasn't until he sold the seventh—a thick leather chain Caleb had made that you tied on your doorknob to protect the house from hexes, robbers, and bear attacks—that he noticed the pattern.

"Something else has happened."

The buyer was Master Christopher, who owned the marketplace tavern. He raised his eyebrows. "And a good morning to you. To address your comment, no, something has not happened. Several things have happened. You should watch yourself."

"What?" Oscar breathed. "Tell me!" He knew enough now to realize he was not supposed to talk like this to customers. But in this particular moment he didn't feel like figuring out how to say anything other than what he meant.

"You should watch your tongue, too! Someone's been prowling the marketplace at night, little hand, attacking our wares. Madame Aphra hung twenty yards of cloth to dry outside last night, and do you know what she woke up to?"

"Bits?"

Christopher narrowed his eyes. "Hmmm. Yes. A small pile of bits. Same thing with Madame Alexandra's leather, the pieces she had just enchanted. And"—he looked around, though he and Oscar were the only ones in the shop—"Madame Catherine says the Most Spectacular Goat is missing."

Oscar stepped back. No.

"Better protect the shop while you can, little hand. Someone is sabotaging the marketplace."

Pictures arranged themselves in Oscar's mind—the sack of Wolf, then the gardens and the glass house, then the cloth and leather in bits. "What if it's not sabotage?" Oscar asked.

"What else could it be? A very enormous bear?"

"The pieces don't fit," Oscar said.

"What an odd thing to say," Master Christopher said.

In the early afternoon, a gentleman and a Wolf-age young man from the City came in. They seemed to be father and son, and neither of them looked troubled in the least. Oscar surreptitiously looked over the young lord. He did not seem to be suffering from any illness, unless there was a disease that made someone's left nostril flare in a perpetual slight sneer.

Following closely behind them was Master Thomas, the blacksmith, who bobbed his head at Oscar and headed toward the wards. A farmer was in the shop, too, looking at animal repellants. The father and son went over to the gaming shelves and began browsing

through decks of cards. *Strictly for entertainment,* Caleb
had labeled them. Magic was illegal in Asteri's game
houses—Caleb had invented a detection system for the
house proprietors and then a way to mask the magic on
his own goods.

Soon, a man and a woman from the village came
into the shop, heading directly for the counter. "Is Caleb
back?" the woman asked.

"No," Oscar said flatly, and then crossed his arms.

The man grunted.

"Do you know when he intends to return?" the
woman said.

"He didn't tell me," Oscar said. And then added,
for Callie's sake, "Is there something I can help you
with?"

The man crossed his arms and straightened up. He
was very tall. "Yes," he said, staring down as if Oscar
were something he was contemplating squashing.
"When he gets back, you can tell him that someone's
attacking us, and he needs to care more about the village
and less about his wealth and fame."

"Giles," the woman muttered, "he's just a boy." She
turned to Oscar. "I'm Mistress Eliza. My husband and I
make jam." She looked over at Master Thomas, who had
stepped closer to the group. "We were in the northwest
strip of the woods looking for berries this morning, and

the oddest thing happened. We were in front of one of the wizard trees, and suddenly the whole thing . . . faded. Except for the stump."

Oscar went cold.

"What?" the farmer said.

"We looked around at the other wizard trees," Eliza continued. "And at first they looked fine, but when you looked directly at them, the same thing happened. And then one disappeared entirely right before our eyes. Again, just the stump was left."

"Just the stump," Mister Giles repeated. "And not a fresh one, either."

"This is an assault!" Master Thomas said.

"The tree had been chopped down," Mistress Eliza said, eyes wide, voice breathless. "Some time ago. And four other trees seem to be the same. Ghosts."

"There's another magician," the farmer proclaimed. "That's who's attacking us."

Master Thomas folded his arms and considered. "That does seem a likely theory," he said, speaking carefully.

The older City gentleman called out, "Does that mean his magic is better?"

Giles turned, glaring. He took a step toward the man and opened his mouth, but just then the gentleman's son pointed at the counter. At Oscar.

"Look," he exclaimed. "The little boy's crying. Over trees!" He laughed.

Now Mistress Eliza was glaring at the father and son. Everyone in the room was still as a cat before pouncing.

"Well, I think it's time to go," the gentleman said, putting his hand on his son's shoulder. "We'll be taking our business elsewhere."

The pair left the shop, slamming the door behind them. Oscar put his hand to his wet cheek.

"I don't understand who would do this," the farmer said. "They must be trying to harm us. Drain the Barrow."

And then the villagers were rumbling again, so loudly it seemed the shelves might shake. Oscar just stood there shivering, slowly turning to ice.

"Do you think it hurt?" Oscar asked, his voice cutting through the noise. "The trees?"

Everyone turned to look at him.

So it was not a normal thing to say, it was not a normal thing to think, but Oscar thought it anyway, and he needed someone to answer.

Giles eyed the farmer and Master Thomas. He gestured to the door, and they all moved toward it. Eliza went back to the counter. "No," she told Oscar, cushions on her words. "I don't think they felt a thing."

"Just tell Caleb to come by as soon as he can," Giles

called, voice now gentle, "and we'll tell him everything we saw. . . . Remember, Giles and Eliza, all right?"

Mistress Eliza put her hand on Oscar's shoulder. "Don't worry," she said. "It will be all right."

"How?" Oscar asked.

"What?"

"How will it be all right?"

Mistress Eliza blinked. "It just will."

She gave Oscar a smile, and the trio walked out the door, leaving Oscar alone.

He stood in the store for one minute, not able to think, not able to move. Then suddenly he was at the front of the shop locking the door. He was not being loyal; he was not working hard. But it was very difficult to know how to function in the world when every truth turned out to be just an illusion.

So he slipped out the back door, walked down five buildings, and tucked around to the front of Madame Mariel's.

Callie opened the door, her hair tied up on her head, her gray apron on top of her dress. She seemed surprised to see Oscar—to be fair, Oscar was surprised to see himself there.

"I'm glad you're here," she said, voice low. "There's another one." She motioned him inside.

At first he thought she meant another tree, but when

Callie led him through the front parlor into the back room of Madame Mariel's, he saw a City boy lying in the small cot. The boy's face was covered in some kind of scaly rash. Oscar stiffened.

A lady in a cream-colored dress with a purple-and-gold bird printed on the skirt stood in the corner. The bird was not on fire.

"This is Oscar," Callie explained to the lady and the boy. "He can help." She turned to Oscar. "This is Jasper, and his mother, Lady Foster. Jasper fell ill overnight."

Oscar leaned in close to Callie. "I have something to tell you about the wizard trees," he said.

Callie started slightly. "All right," she whispered. "We'll talk more about that later." She went over to the stool by Jasper's bed, motioning him to follow. "Could you come look at Jasper's rash, please? I'm hoping we can make him more comfortable. I've been using some agrimony and yellow dock," she added, motioning to the mixture at her side.

Oscar looked over at Jasper. The boy blinked back at him. He looked like he didn't understand anything, either. And the rash—

"It's really scaly!" Oscar said.

Callie coughed. The boy glanced at her. The rash *was* really scaly—almost like bark falling off a tree.

Callie turned her attention back to the boy and

began to rub the salve into his right arm. "This is just a couple of herbs," she said to him, voice like aloe. "It will help your skin. And then we'll figure out what's going on. We'll help you feel better."

"But"—Oscar looked at Callie—"we don't even know if it's the plague yet! How can—"

"Oscar!" Callie sprang up and knocked the stool over.

"The plague?" exclaimed the lady.

"Don't worry!" said Oscar.

Callie's head snapped toward the lady. "He's speaking figuratively."

Oscar frowned. He was being quite literal.

The lady took a step backward, shaking her head. "The plague is back?" she breathed. Her face was a mask of fear.

"We don't know," said Oscar. "It only *might* be back."

"*Oscar!*" said Callie. Her voice was like a falling guillotine.

Oscar blinked at Callie and took a few steps back. Callie shook her head at him, very slightly. It hit him like a kick.

Callie turned her attention back to the boy, righted the stool, and sat down. The boy seemed to have grown even paler and was looking at Oscar like Oscar himself had brought the plague.

"Now," Callie murmured, "can you tell me how you feel?" Jasper's eyes grew wide and he shook his head.

Callie studied him for a moment, then leaned in. "Do you think you can say something?" she asked. "Can you tell me anything?"

The boy opened his mouth, but nothing came out except a low, inhuman groan. His eyes popped.

Callie was so totally absorbed in the boy, for her there was nothing else in the room, in the marketplace, in the universe besides him. There wasn't even an Oscar who had so much whirling around in his head that he could barely stand still and all he wanted to do was tell her about the trees.

A flash: a reflection in his head, a whisper from the past. A picture of a smaller Callie and her brother, a little-boy version of Callie herself, all eyes and hair, but in some sickly wrong color. Maybe he had a rash, too; maybe he looked like something was missing, too. *Illness takes things from you,* Callie had said.

Oscar inhaled. "You need to heal him because you couldn't heal your brother!"

Everyone stopped to gape at the words as they hung in the air. Callie suddenly looked as sickly as the boy in Oscar's imagination. She was blinking rapidly, and her mouth hung open.

The boy's mother exploded from the corner. "Who

is this boy? Where is Madame Mariel? Where is Master Caleb?"

Callie's face went blank. She stood up carefully. "Oscar," she said, brushing off her apron. "You can go now."

Oscar turned and fled. As he left the shop, he heard Callie's voice carrying from the back room.

"I'm sorry," she was saying. "Don't listen to him. He doesn't know what he's saying."

Oscar ran back to the stop, chased by the invasion of darkness. He headed into the back room and then lost the will to go any farther.

History told lies; someone was murdering wizards and prowling along the outskirts of the marketplace; Oscar's whole world was in bits. Sickness was haunting the City, though the wizards had given their lives to ensure otherwise. The magic was failing, and so was Oscar. Everything he said, everything he did, everything he thought and felt, it was all wrong, and he never should have left his pantry.

If he hadn't, no one would ever have looked at him the way Callie just did.

Then, in the darkness, a wisp of light tickled at Oscar. He was in the kitchen of the most powerful magician in a generation. If another magician was doing this, it couldn't be a coincidence that he or she was only attacking when Caleb was gone.

Another magician could not be more powerful than Caleb. Whoever it was, Caleb could find him and stop him. Caleb would do it. If he only knew what was happening.

Maybe Oscar could do nothing else against the ineffable dangers of the world, maybe he was useless and broken and all wrong, but at least he could try to figure out exactly where Caleb was and how to get a message to him. He was Caleb's hand; he could do that much. And then everything would be better. Caleb could even help the City children—all the parents were asking for him anyway—and then Callie would be glad.

Caleb would want to know, anyway. He would want to know all these things. He was the magician, the closest thing to a wizard they had.

So Oscar got up, went down the cellar stairs, then strode right through the main room into the hallway and to Caleb's workroom.

This was very much against the rules. This was so against the rules that Caleb had never even had to tell him the rule in the first place. But the world was changing under Oscar's feet, all the rules were changing—why not this one as well?

He would want to know. He'll be glad I told him.

He entered the room and walked around slowly, turning on every lantern he could. Cat stood in the doorway, thumping his tail. *Do not go astray, little mouse.*

The room was several times larger than Oscar's bedroom and was filled with shelves and cabinets, a worktable and tools, a desk with all kinds of books and notebooks on it. And everywhere, vials and tubes and jars and tools and strange machines and contraptions. It all hit Oscar at once, and he had to take a step back.

No. There had to be something, some letter or diary that indicated where Caleb might be and how to get in contact with him. Oscar took a deep breath and stepped forward, trying to focus on one thing at time. There were more bookshelves in here, lined with thick, old-looking books with black covers and strange gilt titles in a language Oscar didn't recognize. Even looking at them made him feel like ten spiders were running up and down his skin.

Cat thumped his tail again. *If you were a kitten, I would drag you out by the scruff.*

Hanging on the wall above the worktable were all kinds of tools. Oscar recognized a few woodworking and engraving ones, but the rest were completely outside his experience. On the table a few more tools were scattered among a pile of wood scraps.

Underneath the table were two large clay jugs—one

labeled *Plaguelands Dirt*, the other, simply, *The Sea*. There was a cabinet next to the table, and Oscar opened it up to find a large assortment of weapons. He closed the cabinet. The next one was filled with animal traps. The next with odd-colored potions.

On one table sat test tubes, vials, and some device made of a mounted cylinder and, beneath it, a glass lens. Above the table were jars of strange fluids, plant clippings, bugs, spiders, hair and fur, and some bits of small rodents. There was even one rat cut into perfect halves. Oscar's eyes fell on a dead sparrow, and he looked away.

Oscar should not be in here. He should leave.

But still he stayed.

On the wall above the writing table was a series of drawings. Figures of people, made of ovals and rectangles and joints, and next to them some small drawings of children's faces, perfect like dolls.

He opened up a notebook. Dated entries, Caleb's handwriting, but not any language Oscar knew. Some sketches and scribbling. Oscar flipped through the entire book and then the next. It was all the same: chaos.

A small book on Caleb's desk had a series of diagrams of the human body in it: first a drawing of a naked person, then on the next page it was like the skin had been stripped off and the body was all muscles, then on the next, bones, then organs and a great network of veins.

Underneath that was a ledger with a few pages of entries. Names, dates, and a number of coins Oscar could not even fathom.

Some spell work, perhaps. Or all those mysterious imports. The names were familiar somehow—perhaps Caleb had told Oscar something about the ledger, but Oscar was too stupid to remember what.

The desk drawer was filled with letters—some in Caleb's hand, but most not. And these were all written in another language, too.

Nothing was here, no place names, no plan, no carefully thought-out note left for Oscar about where to reach him in case of emergency.

Oscar looked around the room, feeling panic tugging at him. This had been his last hope of helping. Now all he could do was stand around and let the world fall apart.

Thump. *If you were a kitten, little mouse . . .*

Oscar's eyes fell on a small shelf in the back of the room, lined with jars. He stepped closer. The jars were filled with some thick liquid and all labeled with names of different animals—*goat, pig, horse, deer, bear, ape,* along with some Oscar had never heard of. And the last— Oscar picked up the jar and held it to his lantern to look more closely—*human.* He dropped the jar. It did not break. And that was good, for if it had, he would have been covered in blood.

Oscar took three steps back. But the room was not done with him yet; the blood had called to him, and now something else was calling.

Oscar stepped three paces away, to a dark corner of the room. And then he looked at the rug beneath his feet, bent down, and pulled it up.

A square door was cut into the floor, about as long as Oscar himself. It was so well masked by the floor that most people would have missed it, but it was the sort of thing Oscar noticed. And the door wanted to be opened. So Oscar opened it.

Under the door was a compartment in the floor, and inside that compartment was a strange figure. Oscar held up the lantern.

It was a doll. Or like a doll. Made of wood. About a foot smaller than Oscar, the size of a small child. Its limbs were jointed at the elbows and knees. You could tie strings to the doll's body and make it walk..

Oscar reached down and picked up the doll's arms. They bent, just as human arms should. Slowly, carefully, he picked up the doll and cradled it in his arms.

Its head was nothing, just a head-shaped block of wood. Its limbs flopped and its waist rotated slightly as he picked the doll up. The wood felt warm and hummed just the way Block did. It called to him, like something familiar and lost.

He looked into the doll's faceless face. He bent the head around. It moved, but the neck was stiff. *Wooden.*

Yes, the wood gave Oscar the same combination of peace and yearning that the wizard trees gave him when he put his hands on them.

But how had Caleb—

The truth slapped Oscar on the cheek. It was not some new magician cutting down the wizard trees. It was Caleb. Caleb was cutting them down and using the wood for magic.

The spells from *Magic and the Mind* popped up in Oscar's head: a spell to implant memories. Living Enchantments. The Breath of Life.

And flashes: the boy from today laughing and pointing. The villagers and their faces when he'd asked about the trees. The sickrooms and Oscar in the shadows. The shop: *Orphan, simple, odd, not right.* Caleb's voice: *You are an odd little boy.* Wolf: *Do you know what a freak you are? You don't even know where you came from, do you?* And the shadows of the past: *Look me in the eye, boy.* And the feeling, always, of living in a different pocket of air from everyone else, not knowing how to break through it. And this, the aloneness, pressing down on his chest, the most constant company of his life.

And the look on Callie's face today.

And then he understood:

I am made of wood.

I am made of wood.

CHAPTER TWELVE

The Magicians

There is a way the truth hits you, both hard and gentle at the same time. It punches you in the stomach as it puts its loving arm around your shoulder. *Yes, I am terrible to behold,* the truth says. *But you suspected it all along, didn't you? And isn't it better, now that you know? Now, at least, it all makes sense.*

So Oscar cradled his brother for a while, and then put him back in the compartment and closed the door.

Caleb had made him, enchanted him, given him life. Maybe Caleb had made him just to have a hand. *Loyal, works hard.*

Lord Cooper, Sophie's father, in the shop last week: *Might I ask, how long do you remember being here?*

Maybe none of Oscar's past was real. Maybe he'd never been in the Home at all. No, he couldn't have been. That's why the memories were so hard to grasp. They had all been planted, like a lily in a vegetable garden. Oscar could have been made five years ago, or even more recently still. Who knew what in his past was real? He was a blank page.

Maybe Oscar had been the first, the experiment. Maybe Caleb had learned from his mistakes and his next one would work better. Maybe that one would not be odd.

Maybe, maybe, maybe.

Nothing was real; nothing was sure. His memories were phantoms, his past a lie. He took the cat from his pocket and gazed at it. The cat hummed and buzzed. They were kin. No wonder he felt more comfortable with the trees than with people.

How strange to leave the boy—for Oscar was sure the doll was destined to be a boy, like he was—under the floor like that. Still, he was just a wooden doll—whatever Caleb would do to give him life had not happened yet.

Wolf: *He can do things no one's ever done before.*

Mister Malcolm: *There is danger in small enchantments. Small enchantments make us dream of big ones.*

Oscar's mind went blank; his head began to roar. His skin felt like it had thinned into tissue paper. Even the air against it hurt, threatened to break through. Really, it was amazing his body and all its systems worked as well as it did; Caleb was a most marvelous magician indeed.

Oscar stayed huddled up as tightly as possible for hours. Cat stopped thumping his tail and came in to sit by him, but even his purrs felt like an assault. Oscar couldn't help it. There was nothing at all to him besides his heart and that roaring and this frail, tissue-like skin.

Gradually, as morning began to dawn, his body regained its memory of how to be a working boy again. *Yes, your mind works. Yes, your skin can survive this air. Yes, your heart will stay in your body. Yes, your muscles work, and so do your joints, while we're at it. Yes, you are a creature that thinks and moves and walks and even talks, though you don't enjoy it very much. You may be a doll, but you can do these things.*

Oscar picked himself up, walked out of Caleb's studio on his working legs, and shut the door with his perfectly articulated hand.

It was all quiet now—his whole body, his mind. Everything felt very still; it was unlike anything he'd experienced. He felt like a lantern with no light. All he had to do was walk up the stairs, feed the cats, go get water, do his chores. He swept the shop and dusted the shelves, in case any dirt had accumulated overnight. He surveyed the store and set to work restocking whatever needed restocking.

His routines had always felt right. And now he knew why. He had been made to do them.

And then, noise in all the silence. A knock on the kitchen window.

Callie.

He opened the back door but stood in the doorway.

Callie's face looked wrong. He did not understand it. Her eyes were red, and she looked like she was half ghost. He had learned some of her expressions, but he did not know this one. He had to learn what other people simply understood—and now he knew why. This understanding was a human ability, and Oscar did not have it.

"May I come in?" she asked, voice low.

Oscar could not come up with a way to say no, so Callie moved past him and then stood in the kitchen. She did not say anything. Neither did Oscar.

"Is there anything you want to tell me, Oscar?" she said, after a while.

I am made of wood.

"No?" She folded her arms. "Oscar," she said, speaking in almost a whisper, "I know you haven't had a lot of experience with . . . people. But you have to think before you talk. When people are sick, your job is to make them better, not insult and scare them. You . . . you have to think about how the things you say might make other people feel."

A human ability. Oscar did not have it.

Callie was looking away now, holding herself close. "And you have to be careful," she said, voice wavering. "What you said to me, it was . . . not right. When you say the wrong thing, when you hurt someone, you tell them you are sorry. That's what you do. You could have come by later, and you didn't. Now I'm standing here in front of you, and you haven't even said you're sorry."

"I am sorry," Oscar said.

"We're going to have to talk more about how you need to be with sick people. It's delicate, and—"

"No," Oscar said.

"No what?"

"No. I am not going to visit another sick patient. I must tend to the shop." He motioned to the things on the counter. Stiffly.

She narrowed her eyes, "Oscar, are you angry? Because—"

"No," he said.

"I need to talk to you about something," she said.

"I have to work," he said.

She took a step back. "What's going on?"

"I don't need help anymore, Callie," he said. "Or rather, I can't be helped. It's not going to work. Ever."

"What about the children?" Callie said. "They're sick."

"They don't need my help," he said. "It's not what I'm for."

Callie put her hands on her hips. Her mouth dropped. She shook her head so slowly.

And then she blinked. Twice. And her eyes were shining again.

"Callie," Oscar said quickly. "There is just something wrong with me, that's all. And it can't be helped. I . . . I wasn't made right."

"So," she said, her words clenched like a fist, "you don't want me to come anymore?"

What was he supposed to say? He did want her to come. But nothing he wanted was real.

"I see," Callie said, after he did not answer. Then she shook her head slowly and strode to the door. When she got there, she turned around, eyes flashing. "I got a letter last night. From my village healer. That's what I came to tell you. He said Madame Mariel never came to call again. He said my parents moved away two years ago. After my brother died. My brother died. He never got better at all."

Oscar stared. Callie put her hand up to her eye and wiped a tear away. His wooden heart broke. "You were my only friend, you know," she said.

And then she left.

Oscar looked at the floor.

It would have been nicer, if Caleb had made him so he didn't feel things.

He looked at the herbs on the counter, then at the awaiting shop. It was almost time to open. He could feel the bustle and noise and assault of the day to come.

He should open the shop. Right now.

But instead, he went out the back door.

The bakery was a few buildings down from Caleb's—the only shop in the main marketplace that wasn't run by a magic smith. Sometimes the smells from it traveled all the way down to Oscar's pantry like a beckoning finger. He could not smell anything today.

Oscar knocked on the bakery door. Dimly, he noticed that the window, which was usually filled with bread and rolls and cakes, was empty, and the shop was closed.

Malcolm opened the door and read Oscar's face. "My boy, are you all right? Did something happen?"

Malcolm ushered Oscar in and pulled out a chair for him, and then presented him with a roll and a glass of water. Then Malcolm pulled out a chair and sat down.

"Tell me what's wrong," he said.

Oscar blinked. Words came out of his mouth. "Caleb's gardens were destroyed. His glass house came down. Someone must have attacked the gardens."

"I see," Malcolm said, leaning in. "That is very upsetting."

Oscar began to pick at the roll, peeling little bits of crust off. "Someone destroyed Madame Aphra's cloth. And Madame Alexandra's leather."

Malcolm clasped his hands together, and his gaze did not waver from Oscar. "Yes. I know. What else?"

"The Most Spectacular Goat is missing," Oscar said.

"I know," Malcolm said gently. "It is very sad. She is a spectacular goat. What else?"

"They think it's another magician. One we don't know about. Trying to sabotage the Barrow." Oscar had bits of bread in his hands, and he rolled them around with his fingers. They were cool and soft on his skin.

"Yes. It seems a possibility. Though a troubling one."

"There are sick children in the City," Oscar added quickly. "Sicker than City children are supposed to get."

A pause. "Did Miss Callie tell you that?"

Oscar nodded. There was more to the story, but he did not feel like telling it. He picked off another bit.

"I see. Is there more?"

Oscar pursed his lips together. "Someone chopped the wizard trees down. Five of them. In the northwest strip of the forest."

Malcolm straightened. His eyes darkened. "How do you know this?" he asked, voice suddenly careful.

"A Mistress Eliza and Mister Giles. They were up there. There was an illusion spell, and it failed, and . . . they saw the stumps." Oscar's eyes flicked up at Malcolm. "The wizards sacrificed themselves!"

He'd thrown the words out in the air, thrown them at the baker, because he could not hold them in anymore. But Malcolm caught the words without even flinching. "I am glad you know," Malcolm said solemnly. "It is important to understand what the island is really made of."

Oscar looked down at his hands. "Why doesn't anyone remember?"

"The truth is there for anyone who looks closely enough," Malcolm said. "But I don't think anyone wishes to look."

"But shouldn't they know?"

"They should. But that would mean looking at what drove the wizards to it. The fable is so much . . . cleaner."

Oscar set his gaze on a crumb on the floor, slowly gathering words to him before sending them off into the air. "What could someone do with that wood?" he said finally. "From a wizard tree? If . . . they were going to use it?"

"Use it?" Malcolm's brow furrowed, and he moved his gaze to the wall. Oscar watched his face, looking for something to hold on to. But so many things were passing over it, like leaves in the wind. "Well," he began slowly, "the wood would be very powerful. The magic in it . . . I imagine you could do whatever magic you wished with it . . . if you were so inclined. If someone is using the wood . . ." He shook his head. "No, I cannot imagine anything more powerful."

Oscar's eye twitched He stared at the plate in front of him.

"My boy," Malcolm said after a time, "is there something else?"

Oscar shifted. He tore the roll into two pieces. And then each of those into two pieces. "I did something wrong yesterday," he said. "I said the wrong thing. To Callie. She had a little brother and I said . . . the wrong thing. And now . . ."

"That is difficult," said Malcolm. "It is a terrible feeling to hurt someone who you care about. What you must do is make amends. There are few among us who say the right things at all times."

"But I always do this," Oscar said, looking as close to Malcolm's eyes as he could. "Everyone tells me. There are ways to do things, ways to act with people, and I do not understand them. I cannot understand what people mean when they talk. I do not do things right. I do not feel things right. I do not see things right. I am not . . . I'm not made of the same thing as everyone else."

The baker took in a deep breath. "I think if you'll look around, my boy," he said gently, "you'll find that no one is quite right. But we all do the best we can."

Oscar looked down. He was not like everyone else. And the more that people did not see him for what he was, the more alone he was.

"What about everything else?" Oscar asked, eyes now stinging. "What about the gardens, the goat, the trees? If there's someone doing this, they have to be stopped! You are a magician. You can help. Can't you help?" Someone had to stop it, before the whole world came crashing down.

Malcolm leaned back in his chair and sighed. "I *was* a magician, Oscar. A very long time ago. But I cannot help."

"Why not? We need you. Caleb's not here. We need a magician!" Oscar could feel his heart racing.

"Magic won't solve everything, Oscar," Malcolm said. "It often has the peculiar ability to make things worse. And there are some things beyond a magician's power to fix."

"Well, you could try."

Malcolm gave him an odd look. "I am sorry. I know this is hard. Magic is not ours to use, my boy. We think it serves us, but that is only magic playing tricks. Magic only makes us hungry for more magic. We need it more, we rely on it more, and thus it has more control over us. Do you understand?"

Oscar looked at the floor. *No.*

"Oscar," Malcolm said, taking a deep breath, "I was going to come talk to you today. I am leaving."

"Leaving? Where?"

"To the Eastern Villages. This is not my home anymore. I have been planning this for a long time. And if magicians are attacking their own, it is time to go. Your news today only confirms what I had planned."

"When are you going?"

"Today."

"Oh."

Malcolm leaned forward and took Oscar's hands. The touch was like fire on his skin. His eyes looked into Oscar's, and Oscar could not look away, though he felt himself burning. "I think you should come with me."

"What?"

"You can be the baker's apprentice."

Something rose in Oscar's chest, like a flower blossoming all at once. It grew until it filled him and threatened to spill over everywhere. The words Malcolm spoke touched a longing so deep Oscar hadn't even known it was there.

His eyes fell on his plate. There was only a carcass of the roll left; the rest was in bits. He grasped the flower, clutched it close, so close he would never forget the feel of it.

And then he let it go.

It was a life for someone, but not for him.

"I can't leave."

Malcolm sat back, releasing Oscar's hands. "I intend to bring my cats. And there will be room for more. There is no magic to dislike them there. And," he added, "we could bring Miss Callie. Villages always need healers, and she is quite naturally gifted."

"She says she isn't."

"A good healer is gifted in ways other than magic, Oscar."

"I can't leave," Oscar said.

"Why not?"

"Because." Because this was everything he knew. Because he lived in the cellar, in the pantry, in his small bedroom. Because there was the library, the hallways. Because his feet knew how to walk on these paths, his lungs how to breathe this air. Because he knew all the trees. Because he was loyal and hardworking. Because this was what he was made for. And what would happen to a boy made of wood if the magic that bound him failed? What would happen to him out of the arms of the forest, away from magic, with nothing around him but emptiness?

No wonder he was so bound to the forest. No wonder being away from it pulled on his skin.

"I have to stay."

"Well," Malcolm said, "I hope you will change your mind."

Oscar did not speak. His eyes filled, spilled over.

Malcolm put his hand on Oscar's shoulder. "I will leave you instructions for how to contact me, and anytime you want to come, anytime you need me, you just send word, and I will come get you. This is my word to you. Do you understand?"

And he took Oscar by the hands and looked him in the eye. And Oscar took a deep breath, and then met his gaze. There was a whole sky in there. But this one Oscar wanted to fall into.

It was a life for someone, but not for him.

When he got back to the shop, all the lights were on and the front door was open. Oscar's heart skipped and his head filled with possibilities—Callie, some robber, some angry City lord, some magician determined to ruin the Barrow.

But when he walked in, he found it was worse than all of that.

"Master Caleb," he said.

The magician was standing at the shop counter,

filling the whole room with his presence. He was bent over studying a letter he had clutched in his hand, and the air around him was crackling. At the sound of Oscar's voice he popped up, and his eyes flared.

Caleb strode in front of the counter and threw his arms to the side. "Why was the shop closed?" he asked, voice bigger than the room could hold. "It's Thursday, one of our busiest days. What if the duke found out? What could the emergency possibly have been? It must have been *dire*."

Oscar shrunk. "I—I'm sorry."

"What?" Caleb spat, taking another step. He was as big as a giant. "Do you think the money to run this place makes itself? Do you think the duke will lessen his fees just because you didn't feel like working the shop? Do you think that just because I'm a magician, the rules don't apply?" He grabbed the money box from the counter and held it up. "Is this really all the money for the *week*?"

Oscar had heard Caleb yell before, had seen him angry before, but all that anger had always seemed to be spinning tightly around the magician, always held by his gravity. Now it was flying through the air, completely uncontrolled.

"What is wrong with you? What is wrong with everyone? Can't anyone solve a problem for himself? Do I have to do everything?"

Oscar stepped backward. "I—I'm sorry, I—"

He what? Tuesday he'd gone to the City to discover the plague had probably returned. Tuesday night he'd been busy learning that the whole mythology of the Barrow was a lie. Wednesday he'd spent fielding angry questions about Caleb's location. Wednesday night he'd discovered he was a creation of wood scraps and dark magic. And today he had gone to visit the only magician the Barrow had left because he was so desperate for someone to help him make sense of everything—except that that magician had given it all up for bread.

Callie had taught him to apologize. But no, he was not sorry.

He straightened as tall as he could. Which was not very tall, but it still felt right.

"Master Caleb?"

Caleb had moved back behind the counter and was pointedly counting out money from the money box. He glanced up.

"You cut down the wizard trees."

Caleb's gaze did not waver, but the room shuddered. He lowered the money box slowly onto the counter, straightened, and folded his arms. "Did I, now?" he said. His words sounded oddly like a caress.

Oscar felt his lip twitching. "You did," he said. "You cut down the wizard trees. At least five. And you"—he couldn't bring himself to say it—"left the stumps. Your illusion spell faltered—"

Caleb slammed his hand on the counter. "What did you do?"

"I didn't do anything. You did! They're wizards and you killed them."

"There is no such thing as wizards," Caleb said. "Not anymore."

"They're the trees!"

"They left us," Caleb said.

"They sacrificed themselves! To save the City!"

"And then what?" he said, throwing his arms out. "They left us with all this magic and no one left who knew how to use it. If the first sorcerer had not found a way, it all would have dwindled and died. And then where would we be?"

"I—" Oscar started. He had no idea how to answer. How could you answer a question about something that had never happened?

"The wizards left us," Caleb said, articulating each word like some terrible spell. "They left the magic to die. And then there would be no protection for anyone— against disease, misfortune, hunger, want, vulnerability." He banged the side of his hand against the counter with each word. "How is that protecting Aletheia? How?"

Oscar's face went hot. "That doesn't mean you can cut them down."

Caleb was in front of the counter now, walking slowly toward him. "Who says I have, Oscar? *You?* My dull little hand? Have you told anyone your theory? Do you think people will believe you?"

"No," Oscar said.

Master Caleb was in front of him now, staring him down. "It is up to me to shepherd the magic, serve the City, make the Barrow thrive. Me! The wizards left us; I have to work with what we have." Caleb's chest heaved. "I should turn you out for your disrespect, little hand. But instead—"

He lifted his hand high and—*crack*—slapped Oscar on the cheek. Oscar's palm flew up to his face like a startled bird. His cheek roared, and it felt like a bottle had shattered inside his head.

Caleb drew up. "I will find a new apprentice to replace Wolf," he said, voice steady. "You will go back to the cellar where you belong; I see being upstairs gives you grand delusions. And if you ever speak of this, to anyone, I will turn you out and leave you in the plaguelands. All you have to give is your loyalty, do you understand? That is your only worth."

Oscar held his cheek and tried to blink his brain back into place. Caleb was right: his loyalty was all he had to give. He began to make his way to the basement, below ground where he belonged. But when he got to

the doorway he stopped and turned. "Master Caleb?"

"What?" Caleb snapped.

"I want to know why," he said. "Not about cutting down the trees, but . . ."

That was it. He couldn't say it. It was his one chance, and he could not commit the truth to words.

But Caleb did not ask him what he was talking about. He folded his arms and appraised Oscar. "There was a need," he said. "That is all."

Oscar nodded slowly. At least it was the truth. He walked into the back room, and down the stairs into the dark cellar. His pantry awaited him.

This was what he'd wanted. Even though his cheek stung and he could still feel Caleb's fury lashing at him, he should have felt relieved. He had his four walls and ceiling back, his small little days, his mortar and pestle and his beginnings, middles, and ends. There would be no more shop, no more customers, no more journeys to the City, no more world shifting under his feet. He had it all back, everything in its place. He should feel relieved, happy.

He should. He should.

Oscar sat in the pantry for hours. He should work, but he did not. There was so much in his head, so many places to get lost. Oscar wandered and wandered and could not find his way out. Some cat or another sat next to him; another slept noisily in a corner. He put his hand on the cat and got lost some more.

Nighttime. Caleb came down the stairs and walked by the pantry without stopping. Oscar was not working, but Caleb did not check. Somehow, this was even worse.

He wondered, dimly, if Caleb might notice anything amiss in his workroom. But what would Caleb do, slap him?

After a long time, Oscar went upstairs to do his nightly chores. This was what he'd been made for.

After feeding the cats, he found himself wandering into the shop. It was very dark. He straightened the shelves where the protective spells were, trying to make them look less picked over. In his head he ran through what he would need to make—just as he would every night for the rest of his life. But the gardens had been torn up, the glass house destroyed. Eventually, Oscar was going to run out of things in his pantry. And Caleb would have to tell the customers, *I am sorry; I have no more; would you like some bits?*

And Oscar laughed a little to himself.

And that was when the front wall crashed in.

CHAPTER THIRTEEN

Dirt

I t was like the entire front of the shop exploded—like someone had loaded a giant cannon with stone and wood and glass and shot it into the room. Bits of door and wall and window flew toward Oscar like they themselves were attacking. He crouched down, covering his head by instinct. His whole body took over, never giving his mind time to consider that there might be something worse coming.

There was. Oscar sensed it before he saw it, something dark and hulking and altogether wrong. Dull thuds, like a stone mallet hitting the ground, and some suffocated groaning. And chaos all around, like Oscar was inside a jar of water that someone was shaking violently.

His eyes popped open.

In the rubble and dust that had once been the front of the shop, a creature hulked and crashed about. Not a creature, a monster. Not made of sky but of earth. A giant, as tall as the shop, and person-shaped, with thick arms and legs and a sphere for a head, but mostly it was an enormous lumbering *thing* made of dense, wet black soil, with bits of moss and patches of grass and fungi and sticks and decomposing plants mixed in. Every time the creature moved, its surface rippled, as if the soil of its body was shifting and churning. Wet black clumps dripped off its arms as it swung them around.

It swiped across a shelf of charms, pushing as many as it could into the center of its face. And then it did the same with a shelf of tinctures: the creature ate them, glass and all. The floor filled with the remnants—broken bits of charms, shattered glass, oils spilling everywhere.

It brought down everything on the east wall of the shop, devouring everything it could—jewels and potions and salves and herb packets and spell kits and decoctions and teas and so many small enchantments. And then it froze, arm raised in mid-swing, and turned its blob of a head slowly toward Oscar.

It had no face, but Oscar could tell it was studying him all the same. It tilted its head back and forth and then let out a strange muffled roar. A maw opened in the front of its head, gaping and endless, like if you fell into it you would drown in the earth. If you made it that far, that is—the thing had teeth made of sharp rocks, with little patches of moss caught between them.

Then another beast appeared in the doorway to the back room, a hissing thing with a demon face, spikes of fur standing straight up along its spine, and a tail like a puffy club.

Cat.

The monster took a lumbering step back.

Then Crow appeared next to Cat, growling like an earthquake. And Cat sprang at the creature.

"No!" Oscar exclaimed, bursting to his feet.

The creature groaned and swatted the cat away. Cat landed in the corner with a thump but sprang up again. Now Bear was next to Crow, and the two cats prowled slowly forward.

Oscar jumped up and put his hand on whatever was on the shelf behind him—a smooth glass vial with some red liquid in it. He was by the love potions; they would have to do. He hurled one at the creature, and glass exploded on its chest. The monster slammed its hand into the spot where the potion had hit and then stuck its hand in its mouth and sucked the liquid off.

Cat sprang again, leaping, claws first, onto the monster's back. It swiped, and chunks of soil fell to the floor.

Crow went for its leg with her mouth, batting soil away with her paws. The monster wriggled and writhed at the cats' touch. Bear made for the other leg. The monster kicked at Bear, but she sprang out of the way. Oscar hurled another potion at the creature, and another. He screamed as he threw the glass jars, he screamed terrible things, and the whole shop was glass and fur and soil and hissing and shrieking and lurching and little bits of magic scattered everywhere.

The monster kicked Crow away and swept Cat off it again and took a step toward Oscar, and Oscar was running out of love potions. And then—

"HEY!"

A voice exploded above the chaos. Oscar's head whipped toward it. Caleb was in the doorway, filling it as he'd never filled it before, his whole face like fire. Map and Pebble hissed at his side.

"GET OUT OF HERE, BEAST!"

Caleb shouted again and took a step forward, raising his arm out over his shoulder and swinging a glowing battle flail on a chain. Oscar could not move, could barely see or hear. The creature roared, and the roar was deathly, urgent, tragic—and even though the thing could kill him very very badly, somehow that roar still shattered Oscar's heart. The creature took a big lumbering step toward Caleb, then another one.

"Oscar," Caleb bellowed. "Go!"

Oscar looked from Caleb to the front door of the shop, which was now clear.

"Oscar, run! NOW! Now, my boy!"

But he could not. He could not run. He could not move, though the monster was stepping toward his master, though his master kept yelling at him to go. The monster lurched. The flail circled. The cats mustered their forces. The air was tar-thick with dirt and noise and motion and sweat and spilled herbs and rot, so thick Oscar was trapped in it.

But Caleb was here now. Caleb was here and the battle flail was swinging and the cats were remounting their attack and Oscar was in the corner and the monster was in front of Caleb now, reaching for him. With a flick of his arm Caleb swung the flail at the creature's torso. Soil sprayed the air, and the thing howled again.

The monster grabbed at the glowing ball. Caleb flicked it away and then struck again. Another burst of dirt, another terrible hollow howl, and the monster took another swipe at the chain, hitting it with its paw. Now the ball swung around the creature's paw, chain right behind it. Immediately, the monster clutched the ball to its chest, pulling Caleb forward. Caleb yelled, then yanked the flail back. A clump of dirt fell to the floor.

The monster roared and lunged toward the flail

again. It grabbed at the weapon with its pawless arm, and with a mighty swing of its other arm swatted at the thing holding the weapon. Caleb.

The arm hit Caleb directly on the side of his head and kept going, like it had hit nothing at all. Caleb's head snapped backward, far, too far; some unearthly sound cracked in the air, and the magician crumpled to the floor.

Quiet. Stillness. Absolute.

Then, a flash of gray hurtling through the air. The screech of one cat, the howl of another. And another sound—something high and desperate coming from Oscar.

Caleb lay on the floor, and then the monster was over him so Oscar could see only its hulking black form. Crow was on the thing's back, soil flew everywhere, and the creature started up and began grabbing for the cat.

Caleb still lay there.

"Master?" Oscar screamed. And then suddenly he could move, he could do nothing but move, he was running forward—toward the monster, toward the flail, toward his magician and master. The monster was over Caleb again, clutching for the battle flail. Crow went sailing through the air. Without a thought, Oscar threw himself at the beast, as if he were a cat, as if he had any power at all against such a thing. He beat his fists against the thing's back. *Get up, Caleb. Get up.*

A roar shattered the earth. Suddenly Oscar was in the air; his eyes and face and lungs were full of dirt; the earth was crushing him, taking his breath and body. Another roar, and suddenly Oscar was flying backward.

BAM. His whole body slammed against the path outside the shop. His head hit the stone, everything in him thwacked, and sickly shocks traveled up his back. Oscar screamed. For a moment he heard nothing and saw nothing but some soundless explosion in front of his eyes, like the sun was bursting open.

The monster had thrown him out of the shop. Swatted him away like a gnat. Caleb was still in there, maybe still on the floor; maybe he hadn't even gotten up yet; maybe he was hurt and needed help.

Help. He could get help. Though aftershocks of pain rumbled through his body, though his head roared and his stomach turned, Oscar pushed himself up and made for the nearest shop.

It was nighttime in the marketplace, and anyone who had a home would have gone there already. But Oscar screamed and banged on the doors, his need spilling over everywhere, and by some force of luck or magic people answered. In moments a small group stood in front of Master Thomas's place: the blacksmith himself; Madame Aphra, the weaver; Madame Olivia, the bookmaker; and Madame Catherine—once the proud owner of a Most Spectacular Goat.

The blacksmith disappeared into his shop and came back with two swords and two axes and distributed them among the adults, then gave Oscar a small knife. "For protection," he said. "You go hide in my shop now, all right?"

The magic smiths went off into the night and Oscar waited three beats and crept after them. He was so scared he could die from the fear, if the pain in his body did not kill him first, but still he followed them—knife out in front of him. As if that knife would do any good against the monstrous thing.

Just pretend, Callie would say.

His ears were roaring and his body trembling and everything inside him aching and reverberating; still, he expected to hear something echoing from the shop into the night—yelling and crashing—he expected to see some battle spilling out past the wreckage. But everything was silent and still. Though he wanted more than anything to go hide under a counter at the blacksmith's, Oscar crept forward.

And then he was outside the shop, peering in. And there was no chaos at all, no swinging swords, no swiping hands, no shattering stock, no glowing iron star. There were just four magic smiths, standing together with their backs to him, weapons at their side, still.

Oscar burst in and slipped around the edge of the group.

The shop was completely ravaged. It looked like an angry giant had taken a hammer to it. What had once been carefully stocked shelves were now fragments on the floor. Even the counter was smashed. There was nothing on the walls but broken pieces of things, and the floor was a chaos of wood and glass and stone and powder and liquid and soil—clumps of soil, large and small, everywhere.

And in the middle of it all lay Caleb, eyes open, body broken—just the way Oscar had left him.

Hands falling on Oscar's shoulders. Pulling him back. The other adults moving in front of Caleb's body like a wall. Madame Catherine, voice firm: "Come outside with me."

"No," Oscar said, shaking himself loose. "I want to see."

And he stood there taking in the body of Master Caleb, once the greatest magician in the Barrow. He took a slow step forward and got down on his knees in front of the body of his master, his creator.

This was not Caleb. It was a thing, with all the Caleb-ness gone from it. Death takes the person and leaves his shell behind, like a hollowed-out tree.

Oscar owed this man everything, even his birth.
And tonight he owed him his life. Master Caleb was his
father, or the closest to it Oscar would ever have, and
now he was gone. Oscar did not know what he was supposed to be feeling right now, what all the adults behind
him would be expecting him to feel. He did not even
know what he was, in fact, feeling. Except, whatever it
was, it was a lot. Too much. More than bodies could
hold.

"Oscar," said Madame Catherine, who was suddenly
next to him, "do you want to come back with me?"

Oscar shook his head. "Do you have somewhere to
go?" Madame Aphra asked.

Oscar nodded.

"We'll come back tomorrow and clean up. Would
that be all right?"

Nod.

"And maybe you can tell us what happened. Would
that be all right?"

Nod.

"Would you like us to take Master Caleb now?"

Nod.

And soon the adults had wrapped up the shell of
Master Caleb and taken him away, and then there was
no more Caleb in Caleb's shop.

A mewing: a filthy, bedraggled Bear stumbled in

from the back room. Her formerly white puffy fur was caked in dirt, and clumps of soil hung off her stomach and sides. Her front legs and her muzzle were entirely black.

"Oh!" Oscar exclaimed, standing up. "Bear! Are you hurt? Where is everyone?"

He looked around. Three sets of paw prints led out the front room of the store. But there should have been five. Bear was standing next to the pile of rubble where the counter had been, squawking. Oscar darted over and started moving the rubble aside to reveal Cat pinned at the bottom, as dirty as Bear.

The animal looked up at Oscar in a daze. Two of his legs were bent in very bad ways. Broken.

Oscar choked out a noise. "Oh, Cat, I'll—"

But Cat yowled and looked pointedly at the back corner of the room. Crow was lying there, curled in a ball on her side, her flank covered in glass and splinters of wood and bits of blood. She was shivering. As Oscar went to her, she blinked up at him and whimpered.

"I'm going to make you feel better," he whispered, trying to cover the breaking in his voice. "Wait here. I'll be back." He darted downstairs and grabbed a few things from the pantry, and soon he presented the cat with a mixture of milk and valerian root in a bowl. "This is for the pain," he said, dipping his finger in and letting her lick it off. He did the same for Cat. Then Oscar crouched next to Crow and picked the glass and splinters out of her, one by one. "You're very brave," he told her. "You are a remarkable cat." He washed the soil and blood off her, moving in firm, sure strokes across her flank, and then wrapped her in bandages laced with witch hazel and chamomile.

Though the shop lay in rubble around him, though Caleb was now just a shell, though the earth had come to life and gone on a rampage—there was a task; there were Oscar's hands; there were herbs and bandages, and shards to pick out and wounds to treat, and this trembling, trusting cat who needed Oscar not to be afraid.

"You're going to be all right," Oscar said. It was not a lie. Oscar would make her all right.

He rubbed a salve of oat straw and nettle into bandages and gently set Cat's legs, then carried first Crow, and then Cat—who did not much like it—down the stairs and placed them both on his bed. It didn't take too long to find Pebble, who was hiding under Oscar's bed, or Map, who was behind the chair in the library. Both were filthy, but they were all right. They were all right. With the cats on his bed—Bear had settled there, too, and was beginning to bathe herself, a process that was going to take rather a long time—Oscar took his blanket and pillow and laid them on the floor. He put

Block on the table to watch over them all, then lay down on the blanket. After a few moments Pebble had tucked herself into him.

Oscar put his arms around the kitten. And after a while he started telling her things, though he spoke loudly enough for the rest of them to hear. "Master Caleb was killed tonight," he said. "He was killed trying to save us. The monster broke his neck, and that broke him forever. Master Caleb—" He paused. "He's gone now. He did something terrible, but . . . he did good things, too. And he kept us well. And it's all right if you are sad."

Oscar rested his hand on Pebble's back. "I know it is very scary right now. We don't know what's going to happen. But I will take care of you. Maybe I can sell herbs on a cart or . . . or something. I'll figure it out. But I will make sure you are taken care of, all right? You don't have to be scared." He curled up closer to the cat. "You don't have to be scared."

CHAPTER FOURTEEN

Shells

I n the morning Oscar got up, got dressed, laid out food for the cats (though in the cellar—a change), and got water from the well. Then it was time to sweep the shop and dust the shelves, in case any dirt had accumulated overnight, and survey the store to see what needed restocking. This was going to be much more complicated than usual.

Every time his mind flashed a scene from the night before, he closed his eyes and squeezed it away. Every time his mind began to whisper worries at him, he did the same. Sometimes it was helpful to be made of wood.

Oscar's head hurt, his body ached, and everything inside him felt very heavy, but still he worked, putting rubble in the wheelbarrow, wiping up liquid, sweeping up pieces of glass. He reached for a clump of soil, and then his hand recoiled.

After a while, Master Thomas and Madame Catherine came by. They spoke to him in voices that were supposed to be kind but made everything flash and whisper again. They led him into the kitchen and sat him down, and the two adults crouched in front of him just so they would be at the perfect level to stare him in the eyes. Or try to, anyway. They told him they would see if the carpenter could come and build something where the wall used to be, as soon as possible. They did not mention Oscar's future, probably because they didn't know what would happen to him, either.

It would be funny, Oscar thought, if they tried to send him back to the Home, where he'd never been in the first place.

"Now, Oscar," Master Thomas said, putting his hand on the back of Oscar's chair, "can you tell us what happened?"

Oscar shook his head.

Master Thomas tried to look deeper into Oscar's eyes, and it was like he was gouging them out. "I know it must have been awful," he said, his voice low. "I can understand why you don't want to relive it. But you're the only person who has seen this creature, and it's attacking us, and it killed Caleb, and so we need your help."

Oscar squeezed his eyes shut and unfurled the truth before them—*a monster made of earth, not fast but big, not smart but strong, smashing down the wall, eating the contents of the shelves.* He told them the whole story, and now other people knew it, too, and he could not imagine it was not real. They asked him questions, and he answered as best he could.

"We're going to put every magic smith on this," Thomas said. "We will hurl all the magic of the Barrow at this thing. We will find it and destroy it, and whoever is controlling it, too. Don't worry."

Oscar grabbed on to the words and held them. At least they were paying attention now. Someone was doing something, finally.

The adults left, and Oscar went back to his tasks of putting Caleb's shop back together again. Caleb had always said how important it was that a magician's shop look impeccable, because if he could not keep his own shop looking good, what good could his magic be?

"Oscar!"

He looked up. Callie was standing in the ex-doorway, gaping at the shop. "Are you all right?" She breathed, stepping inside, taking in every last broken bit. "Oh, Oscar . . ."

Lips mashed together, she took in the whole disaster;

she took it in for a very long time and then straightened, picked up the broom, and started to sweep.

"Where did all the dirt come from?" she asked, after a time.

"Aren't you angry at me?" Oscar asked in reply.

"What?"

"You were very angry yesterday morning."

Callie's eyes popped. She inhaled, as if about to say something, and then shook her head. "Well," she said, "I'm not anymore."

"That's good," said Oscar.

Every once in a while someone would stop by to gawk at the shop, and each time it made him feel like his skin was rippling. But the fourth person left very quickly, as did everyone after that. Oscar finally figured out that that was because Callie kept glaring at them.

They worked all day, and finally the shop didn't look rampaged upon anymore; it just looked abandoned and barren. Half the shelves were either broken or gone altogether, the rest were completely empty. Two of the windows were broken; the counter was gone. The shop was a ghost. A shell. Oscar looked around and tried to make it all work in his head, in his body. But there was no sense to be had.

"Come on," Callie said, touching his arm. "We need to eat."

Callie led him to the kitchen, got Oscar some water, and then searched the cupboards. She pulled out some potatoes, onions, and carrots and started chopping them.

"I don't eat that," Oscar said.

"What?"

"I eat bread. And sometimes cheese. I don't eat that."

She stared at him.

"It has chunks," he added.

She narrowed her eyes, and then kept chopping. "We're going to need to restock your pantry soon, Oscar," she said. "There's not much in here. I can go get you more food." She tilted her head and asked carefully, "Do you think Caleb left any gold?"

Oscar hadn't thought about it. But yes. There was the cash box, and a big Oscar-sized safe filled with coins.

Actually, there were three Oscar-sized safes. Caleb had probably left a lot of gold.

Callie finished chopping, and then threw everything into a pot, poured a jar of stock inside, and set the chunky brew on the stove. Then she wiped her hands and sat down next to Oscar. "You need a place to go," she said, looking at him like he was a bird that might flee if startled. "You can come stay at the healer's shop if you want. I don't . . . I don't know when Madame Mariel is coming back. I don't know what I'm going to do when she does. But now those children need help, and . . . I'm not leaving them. I could use an assistant. You could stay at the healer's and be the apprentice's apprentice."

"No."

"Why not?"

A flutter in Oscar's chest. "This is my home. I can't leave."

"Oscar, there's a wall missing."

"That's all right."

"But—"

"Caleb has a lot of money. That will keep us for a while."

"Us?"

"The cats and me." He could feel his voice growing louder.

"But still. Eventually—"

"This is where I live."

Callie's face scrunched up, but she didn't say anything else. Oscar looked through the doorway into the shop.

It was Caleb's shop, but now there was no Caleb. A magician's shop without any magician. Oscar could prepare herbs as he always had, but no one would buy anything that they knew was made by an eleven-year-old boy, even though they'd been buying the same things all along.

But the shop and the cellar were his whole world. You couldn't leave the world. Oscar would stay, and tomorrow he would get dressed, feed the cats, get water, sweep and dust the shelves, and see what needed restocking.

Anyway, Oscar was not a boy like other boys. Without the magician who made him, what would become of him? It wasn't like he could go to the healer if he got sick. Maybe he wasn't even supposed to last. Oscar was a puppet with no master now, and he could almost feel the strings dragging behind him.

Callie sipped her tea and kept glancing over at Oscar, in the manner of someone who has something to say but doesn't want to say it.

"Oscar," she finally asked, "can you tell me what happened?"

Oscar pressed his lips together. "There was a monster," he said after a while. There, that was true.

Silence. Then: "Can you tell me anything about the monster?"

Oscar looked at the floor. The fluttering in his chest had turned into churning. "Master Thomas said the magic smiths are going to go after it."

"About time," Callie said darkly.

"So we don't have to worry anymore," Oscar said.

Callie looked at him sideways. He understood. His words sounded as false as when people said them to him.

She waited. Oscar looked at the floor again.

"Can you tell me anything else?"

"They think someone is controlling it. Another magician. They'll go after him, too. They'll go after everything."

"And," Callie said, words tiptoeing up to him, "what do you think?"

Oscar kept his eyes on the floor. "I'm not sure."

Callie sipped her tea again. She exhaled and pulled out a pin from her hair. It all came tumbling down, everywhere. Oscar could only barely see her—he did not know if he could ever move his eyes from the floor again.

"All right," Callie said. She got up and went to the stove and began to stir the pot. The smell of the food spread through the air, and soon Bear and Pebble appeared from the cellar. Callie kept her back to Oscar and kept stirring. It made it easier to ask what he wanted to ask.

"Callie?" Oscar began. "When your master dies, how are you supposed to feel?"

Callie stopped stirring, and looked at Oscar over her shoulder. "I suppose, you might feel a lot of things." She spoke slowly, picking her words like she would pick flowers. "You might feel sad. You might feel a little scared, too."

Oscar frowned. "But . . . what if they'd done something really bad? How do you feel when someone's done something really bad?"

Callie turned around fully, and he could feel her eyes prying at him. "Like if they were cruel to you?"

"No. No. Something else." His eyes flickered up to Callie. "Something really wrong."

Callie took a step forward. "Oscar, what did Caleb do?"

He hesitated. This wasn't how the conversation was supposed to go.

"Oscar," she said firmly, "tell me."

Oscar paused. It seemed funny to tell her, now that Master Caleb was dead.

Callie took the pot off the stove, pulled out the chair, and turned it so it faced him. "Listen to me," she said, eyes focused on his face. "There are strange things happening, there are sick children and a monster is attacking the marketplace, and if the magician has done something terrible, I would like you to tell me."

"He cut down the wizard trees."

"*What?*"

"Not all of them," he said quickly. "But at least five."

Callie gaped. "I don't understand. Why would he do that?" She was staring at him as if he himself had cut down the trees.

"Well, maybe it's only five," Oscar mumbled.

"Oscar!" Callie sat up, pushing the chair back. "It doesn't matter how many! How—how could he do that? Why would he do that?"

Oscar swallowed. Caleb in his head: appearing in the doorway, swinging the battle flail, telling Oscar to run. Then: Caleb gone, the broken shell left behind.

"Well, the wizard-tree wood is so powerful, and—"

"And *what*?" She hit the *t* so hard it felt like a slap.

A lump rose in his throat. This was not going right. "Well, um, here." He reached out into his pocket and took out Block. "Hold her in your hand."

Callie's eyes flared, but she took the wooden cat from Oscar. "It's warm," she said. "It feels like it's almost— humming." She gasped and popped out of her chair, dropping the cat like a burning thing. "That's *wizard-tree* wood?"

"Yes." That had not gone right, either.

She looked at him in horror. "Caleb chopped down trees to make little *cat figurines*? What does it do, tell the future? Grant eternal life? Turn you into a cat god?"

"No, uh"—he snatched Block off the floor and gripped her tightly—"no. I made this one. It doesn't do anything. It's just nice."

"I see," Callie said. She crossed her arms. "So, what did he use it for?"

"I'll show you!" Oscar said. "I'll show you what he was doing."

Callie stared at him, eyes narrowed. "Well?" she said. And then: "Oscar?"

So he got up and led her down the stairs.

When he opened the door to Caleb's workroom, Callie gasped. She stepped inside and then stood still, her eyes wide, looking slowly around the room like she was memorizing it.

As he followed her in, he could feel the magic in the room tugging at him, trying to get him to do its bidding.

Callie took a few steps forward, eyes never stopping their survey. She beheld the books, the potions, the strange contraptions, the vials and tubes and jars, the desk and all the notebooks on it, the animal bits, the blood.

"It's under here," Oscar found himself saying.

Breath caught, he lifted the rug. Callie was watching him now, mouth open, eyes intent, as still as a cat in the shadows. When he lifted the trapdoor, the wooden doll was there, just as he had left it. So Oscar gathered the doll carefully in his arms and held it up.

Callie inhaled sharply and fixed her eyes on the doll. Oscar could not read her face, could not tell whether she thought it was an abomination or found it beautiful, in a way.

Why couldn't he read her face?

"May I see?" Callie whispered. She held out her arms, and Oscar passed the wooden thing to her as if it were a baby. Callie took it in her arms and then took it in with her eyes. Its limbs flopped and its head rolled to the side, and in a second Callie readjusted, as if to make the doll more comfortable.

"This is what Caleb was doing," Oscar said.

"I don't understand," Callie breathed. "What is this for? What was he going to do with it?" She did not take her eyes away from the doll.

Oscar squeezed his eyes shut. He did not want to say the words. But if he did, then she would have a piece of the secret. It would be nice not to carry it all alone.

"He was going to transform it," Oscar said, voice quieter than the air.

Callie's head snapped up. "Transform it into *what*?"

"A boy."

Callie froze. Her eyes locked on to Oscar's in that way they had of trying to pull out all his secrets.

"A real boy," Oscar said. "Almost. You would have barely been able to tell the difference. He was going to be a boy. But not anymore. Caleb died, so he won't get to be a boy now. He'll never get to know what it's like, to be real." Oscar could hear his voice shaking. "Almost real.

And he wouldn't have been alone. I could have helped him and taught him things and—"

"Oscar, *tell me what you're talking about.*"

Oscar glanced up at her. She was holding the doll so carefully, keeping its head propped up, keeping its limbs folded into her arms. She was cradling it as if it was the most delicate, precious thing in the world.

"Caleb made me. I was like that."

Callie's head popped up. She looked at Oscar.

One moment.

Two.

Three.

"What?" she said finally. "Why do you think that? Oscar, why?"

He looked down. "I just know. You know something when it's the truth. It explains everything. Why I am this way."

Callie looked down at the boy thing in her arms. The tears were rolling down her cheeks now. Nothing in the room moved except for the tears on her face. Then she looked back at Oscar.

"I don't care," she whispered.

"What?"

Her head snapped up. "I don't care if you're made of wood," she said, suddenly loud. "I don't care what you were once, do you understand?" Fire flickered behind

her eyes. "Even if this is true, I don't care. Now you're Oscar."

She exhaled. Her face closed. And then she crouched down and gently set the doll back in its home. After giving it one more look, she closed the trapdoor and pulled the rug back over the hidden compartment. "Come on," she said. "Oscar, come on; let's get out of here. Oscar?"

He looked down at the rug. It had the strangest patterns on it, like some great tangle of birds. Like the birds had all been flying in different directions and their paths got entangled and now they were twisted around one another, and the birds pulled and pulled but could not get away.

He swallowed. He pressed his hands together, and then moved his eyes to Callie. "I am sorry about your brother," he said.

CHAPTER FIFTEEN

Bait

When Oscar went out of the shop in the morning to collect some supplies from the forest, a barren marketplace greeted him. Four shops were closed for the day, and two had broken windows. No vendors were setting up stalls. Only two people were out, standing in front of the jeweler's across the way, speaking intently to each other. Oscar stood as still as an empty stall, gaping. Maybe if he looked long enough, everything would go back to the way it was.

It didn't.

Swallowing, Oscar headed into the forest. For now he would collect what he could in the mornings, and then spend the afternoons preparing herbs for the shop—back before any of this had happened many of his days looked this way. It was almost ordinary. It would be a while before he had enough stock to open the shop again.

A thought, caught: *Maybe Caleb will be back by then.*

Caught, then dropped, like something burning.

Yes, it was almost ordinary. Except his master had died, except City kids were getting sick, except the earth was a monster. Oscar did not stray too far from the shop. It was his to mind now, for Caleb. He was loyal and hardworking. He picked flowers and took cuttings from plants and scraped off samples of bark and collected some mushrooms.

When Oscar got back to the shop, he parked the cart by the back door and began carrying his harvest inside. He'd just brought in the last of it when he heard someone clearing his throat

Oscar peeked out of the back room. There was a City gentleman standing in the front of the shop, looking like he couldn't remember whether he'd put on his pantaloons that morning.

"Your front door is missing," the gentleman announced when he saw Oscar.

"Your hat has a big feather on it," Oscar said in reply.

The gentleman told Oscar he was looking for a necklace. The jeweler had carried necklaces made of diamonds that would cause any lady who received them to forgive the sins of the person who gave them to her. But the jeweler's shop was closed, and he would not open it up, no matter how hard the gentleman banged on the door.

"We don't have anything like that," Oscar said.

"What about a ring?" the gentleman asked, adjusting his feather. "With the same magic. Nothing too engagement-y, if you know what I mean, but—"

"We don't have anything like that, either." Oscar blinked. He'd interrupted. "You could try apologizing," he added.

The gentleman peered at Oscar, then shook his head. "I'll try the perfumer."

That morning, Oscar tried to work in the back room, where he could keep an eye on the shop, but people kept coming in. It turned out it was hard to close a shop with no door. So Oscar gave up on the kitchen and spread out the plants in the middle of the shop.

The villagers talked to him now like he was a person. They asked him how he was, if he needed anything; some even brought him food and explained it was for him to eat.

One by one they told him what had happened in the marketplace overnight. There had been more attacks. In the shoemaker's shop, everything on the City-wares side had been torn apart. The jeweler had arrived to find every one of his enchanted jewels gone, and most of the shelves down as well. And in the back room of the tavern, where once there had been a great stack of barrels of Master Christopher's special brew, only small wet wooden bits and a sticky floor remained.

"What about the healer's? Madame Mariel's?" Oscar asked.

No, the healer's shop was fine.

Yesterday, while Oscar and Callie had been cleaning the shop, the magic smiths were out in the forest, searching for some sign of the creature, and though they had gone to every corner, even past the forest and the meadows up to the desolate wilds of the plaguelands, they had found nothing.

But they had set a trap. A large pile of meat, with smell-amplification charms spread out for half a mile around it, and a cage above that just waiting for something to fall upon. They were using all the magic at their disposal, they'd assured everyone.

"Do you think that's enough?" a woman asked Oscar. "All the magic at their disposal?"

"Don't you?" he asked. Everyone always had thought it was enough before.

Meanwhile, the City people seemed to have no idea what had passed, as if the walls that kept out intruders also kept out any news not directly concerned with their lives. As the villagers watched, a gentleman with a purple cloak and a perfectly trimmed beard swept in, took in the shop, and then waved his hands to indicate the marketplace outside.

"What's happened down here?" he said, hands everywhere.

"Monster," Oscar said.

The gentleman straightened. "What kind of a monster closes a haberdashery on a Saturday?"

Oscar squinted.

"No matter," the gentleman said. "I need a luck charm. Your best one."

Oscar cleared his throat. "I'm sorry," he said. "They were all eaten."

The gentleman raised his eyebrows. "I don't know what it is you're saying, little boy, but I need a luck charm. Now. I have some very important business tonight."

"That is too bad," Oscar said, "because they have all been eaten."

The gentleman's face paled. "What am I supposed to do?"

"I don't know," Oscar said.

The man stiffened. "The marketplace better get itself back in order," he said. "The duke will hear about this."

"Like he'll care," muttered a villager.

"Must be nice to have those walls," said another.

Finally the carpenter, Madame Sabine, came, and everyone left the shop. After a while the front was closed up with something resembling a wall. "This is my special wood, Oscar," Sabine told him. "Even Master Thomas couldn't make anything as strong as this. I can't put in a door yet; after Master Thomas and the others get back from checking the trap, we're going to put something up around the marketplace, Perhaps I can come back tomorrow—"

"Or even later," Oscar said.

As soon as she left, Oscar sat in the middle of his very closed shop and exhaled. It was so quiet all of a sudden, a quiet you could wrap yourself up in. He cleaned the floor and moved things into the kitchen, then went downstairs to give Crow and Cat their remedies. They were still in Oscar's room, and one of the other cats was always with them, though Oscar had not quite figured out the rotation. Cat, who could not move around yet, spent his time sitting on Oscar's bed in a half fume, half sulk, and so Oscar made a point of filling him in on everything that had happened, the best he could. Oscar understood: Cat was in charge—that was what he was made for.

As he told Cat all about the trap the magic smiths had set, a picture appeared in his mind: A pile of meat, a cage hanging above. A trigger somewhere that would cause the cage to fall. And the smell enhancers radiating outward into the forest.

It should have been so simple: The smell lures the creature; the creature eats the bait; the bait triggers the cage; the cage falls on the creature; the creature is trapped. A perfect chain of events, a perfect system.

Still, Oscar couldn't quite make it all fit. He held the monster in one side of his mind, and the picture of the meat and the cage in the other, and could not quite put them together for some reason.

And it wasn't just because the monster had no nose.

He went back upstairs, trying to hold the whole plan in his head, trying to mash the pieces together. Eventually, Callie appeared at the back door.

"I have a patient soon, but I wanted to check on you," she said as he opened the door. As she stepped inside, she looked around at the suddenly stocked counters. "Where did this food come from?"

"Some villagers," Oscar said. "A few of them. They kept bringing me food. I'm not sure why."

"Oh, Oscar," Callie said, sad moon eyes shining a little. "Because they wanted to be kind. I know it might be hard to believe, but sometimes, people are kind."

A week ago Oscar had not known that. And then Callie had crumpled the City lady's card in her hand.

"Now, have you heard anything about the magic smiths?" she asked, taking off her cloak and setting it on the counter.

"They didn't find anything," he said. "They're setting a trap, though." He glanced up at Callie. "They say they are using all the magic at their disposal."

Callie's eyebrows went up. "I suppose that means Master Charles will attack it with perfume."

A grin tickled at Oscar's cheeks. "Or," he said, "Master Julian could give it a really ugly haircut."

Callie glanced at him. Her mouth twitched. "Oscar, you made a joke!"

Oscar felt his cheeks redden. He made jokes. He just didn't usually say them out loud.

"Really, for all the magic smiths we have," Callie said, "it doesn't seem like any of them actually do anything."

Oscar thought. There were magical ales, enchanted jewels, wear-proof boots. There were things for luck, things to sprinkle on money to make it grow, things to win disputes, slow aging, increase strength, enhance beauty. There were dresses that would never fray made of fabric of extraordinary colors, and hats that were simply extraordinary. There was Madame Lara, the soothsayer—though it seemed to Oscar that not predicting the monster attack was a large oversight on her part. There were so many pretty things—little statues of birds that sang when you asked them to, tapestries whose pictures shifted, flowers that never went out of bloom, delicate little eggs painted like shining worlds. There was silver that never got tarnished, and glass that never broke, and extrastrong wood, and, apparently, necklaces that made the recipient forgive the giver.

Small enchantments, all.

Callie exhaled and leaned back. "Do you remember the duchess's son, who we met on the path? Ronald, who can't remember anything?"

Oscar nodded. That was Ronald's name in his head now: Ronald-who-can't-remember.

"The duchess sent word. He's worse. It's like . . . his brain isn't taking anything in. She said he's talking very strangely, too, like he's a clock that's running slow." Sighing heavily, Callie perched her elbow on the table and dropped her forehead into her hand. "I don't understand," she said, gritting her teeth. "With the plague, people had the same symptoms, but now . . . I don't know how to help them. It just can't be random, Oscar; there's got to be a common thread. I'm reading every thing I can, but—"

"You should make a map," Oscar said.

"A what?"

Oscar frowned and thought. He was making perfect sense to himself. "Um," he said, searching his head for the right words, "it's like . . . each child is a country, and you place them somewhere in your mind, like your mind is the world, and—"

Callie was staring at him like he'd turned into a bubble mushroom.

"Um, I'll show you." He opened one of the drawers and got paper and a pen. "A map." He drew some blob children on a piece of paper. "How many are there?"

"Five. No, six. That we know about."

"All right. So now, you do that in your head, but with each child and what's wrong with them, and then look at the map and see if you notice anything."

"The map in my head?"

"Yes."

"Of each child and their disease, all at the same time, and I . . . look at it?"

"Yes."

"Oscar, I can't do that. I'm not even sure what you mean. Can you do that?"

Oscar scrunched his brow. "Yes."

"Well," Callie said, "what if I actually drew a . . . map?"

"I guess that could work," Oscar said.

So Callie took the piece of paper and wrote the names of the children underneath the blobs. Oscar had pictured the children in different places, but he did not correct her. And then she wrote down their ailments, blob by blob.

Callie sat back, looking at the sheet in front of her, face set in concentration, while Oscar watched carefully.

After a while, she let out a long exhale and patted the map. "I have to go. I have a patient," she said. "Let me know if you hear anything about the trap. And I'll do the same." She stood up and picked up the paper. "Thank you for this," she said. And she left, taking her map with her.

And here was that lightness inside Oscar again. He put his hand to his chest, to keep it there.

The next knock on the back door was definitely not Callie—it came from someone much larger, much more insistent. It did not say, *Oscar, can you hear me?* It said, *Oscar, wherever you are, open this door right now.*

The knock belonged to Master Thomas, who thudded his way into the room as soon as Oscar opened the door. Too loud, Master Thomas was too loud.

The blacksmith was accompanied by a rush of unsettled air, and his face looked like it was cast in iron. He looked Oscar in the eye, and oh, how Oscar wished he would not do that.

"Oscar," Master Thomas said, "I need to know if you were telling me the truth." His voice sounded careful and sharp at the same time, like a butcher slicing off a thin cut of meat. And still too loud. Oscar's stomach hurt.

"Um"—Oscar could not think, not with all the thudding, but still he tried to run through everything he'd ever said to Master Thomas—"I'm sure I was."

The blacksmith's eyes narrowed. His voice became less careful. "This is not a joke, boy. Were you telling the truth about what attacked the shop?"

"I—yes!"

"We caught something in the trap last night," Thomas said. "But it wasn't some earth monster. It was an enormous bear."

Master Thomas stared Oscar down, as if these words should have great significance, as if Oscar should understand and be very, very sorry. But he did not understand. It made perfect sense that the trap would catch a bear. Bears liked meat.

"I don't understand," Oscar said.

Master Thomas took a deep breath. "It's very important that you tell me the truth," he said. "Did a bear attack the shop?"

"No!" Oscar exclaimed. "It wasn't a bear! Didn't you see all the dirt around the shop?"

"This was no ordinary bear. It was very enormous. Most of the smell-enhancing charms were gone; there must have been forty of them. Unless someone stole them, the bear ate them before the meat."

"It wasn't a bear!" Oscar said.

"Young man, I know a bear when I see one." He locked eyes with Oscar again. "I want you to think very carefully. Very carefully. And if you come up with anything else you want to tell me about that night, anything at all, you let me know, you understand?"

He narrowed his eyes, and then turned and left, closing the door particularly firmly behind him. Oscar just stood. His eyes stung. His face was hot. His lungs sucked in breath.

But for once, Oscar did not feel like there was a pestle grinding in his gut, like he should tuck himself into a ball somewhere so he would never do or say the wrong thing again. There was no pestle, and if he'd had one he would have liked to grind it into Master Thomas's eyes.

No, he understood the words behind Master Thomas's words. Master Thomas did not want him to think very carefully. He did not expect him to come up with anything new to tell him. Master Thomas thought he was lying.

So this was what it felt like to be angry.

What do you do when your head is hot and your insides are boiling and your skin can barely contain all the dangerous things bursting forth underneath? The pantry pulled at Oscar—he could climb in there and shut the door and never come out.

But instead, he slipped outside and ran to the healer's.

When Callie opened the front door, Oscar opened his mouth, and the words started to erupt. She glanced behind her. "Come in," she said softly. "I have a patient." She gave him a meaningful look.

A moment. Then, pressing his mouth shut, Oscar grasped the erupting things with all his might, and held on to them until they settled.

Something was wrong. Something that was not about Oscar. Though Callie wore her usual professional aura just as surely as she wore an apron, there was something not right about it. It looked put on, uneasy, like a mask that didn't quite match her body.

She led Oscar to the back room. A gentleman in a long green cloak was standing in front of the door.

Flashes: a noisy house, an airless room, Callie's murmuring, a rustle-swish of skirts, and a face colored all wrong. The shop, an amulet, the questions, and the girl who did not stop looking at him.

Lord Cooper. Father of Hugo. The boy with the cold limbs. Oscar looked over to the cot, expecting to see a greenish-whitish-sickish face. But it wasn't Hugo there at all. It was his sister, Sophie.

Oscar stepped back. In his mind he saw ringlets, plump cheeks, shining red shoes kicking in the air, eyes searching Oscar for something he had no idea how to give. Now the girl looked like a little ghost in a bright red dress. All shell and no girl.

He closed his mouth; he dared not say a word. He just backed into the shadows and listened to Callie's murmurings. Her father sat perched in a chair in the corner. Callie started rubbing something on the girl's arms now. "How does that feel?" she whispered.

However the girl answered, it was too soft for Oscar to hear. She didn't even seem to move.

Callie slowly rubbed the ointment along her torso and arms, face and neck, telling her at every moment what she was doing, loud enough for Lord Cooper to hear. Though she spoke of limbs and skin and heat, it almost sounded like she was casting a spell.

Callie said something to the father about bringing their carriage up to the shop door, and sometime after that he was holding his daughter in his outstretched arms, carrying her like a limp doll.

Oscar watched, willing the girl to look back, to stare at him again. She did not.

After Callie shut the door, the healer mask broke off and fell to the floor. Inhaling loudly, she plopped down at the table and looked at nothing.

Oscar plopped next to her. "What's wrong with her?" he breathed.

A moment. Then Callie looked up at him, her eyebrows doing their Callie-thinking thing, and her jaw set. She held up her hand and then pulled over a piece of paper that was lying on the table. The map. She drew another blob.

Sophie, Callie wrote. And then she tapped the pen on the table.

"What is it?" Oscar asked. "What was wrong with her?"

"Hold on," she said, staring at the paper. "I'm thinking."

"About what?"

She glanced at him. "About how I need quiet to think."

Oscar opened his mouth and then shut it. Words seemed to want to burst out anyway, so he swallowed them back and stared at the table and started counting. Meanwhile, Callie was examining the map of the children, eyes prying at all its secrets.

Oscar kept counting, while Callie stared. Her face looked like a slowly tightening knot. When he got to 76, she opened her mouth and he stopped, but then she closed it again. So he kept going. When he got to 134 the same thing happened.

And then, when Oscar got to 245, Callie leaned back in her chair, blew air out of her mouth, and shook her head slowly. He watched her, trying to decide if he should keep counting. But then she looked at him, and her eyes were blazing, and her Callie-ness was back.

"Oscar," she said, "these aren't diseases. Think about it." She pointed at the map. "Ronald who can't remember. Jasper who can't talk . . ."

Oscar frowned. "Well," he said slowly, "there are diseases of the mind. I have a whole book under my bed that Wolf left me—"

Callie set her jaw. "Oscar, Sophie had no heartbeat. None. She's still alive. I don't know of any disease that lets you be alive with no heart."

Oscar stopped.

"All these kids," she breathed, "they're not sick. They're failing."

"I don't understand."

She started pointing at the blobs at the paper. "This girl can't eat, physically can't take in food. This one's mind isn't working. This boy can't see or hear all of a sudden. This one's skin is cracking open. And this one, I think he's *hardening*. Don't you see? These aren't diseases. The kids are breaking down."

Oscar shook his head slightly. It was so much easier when the map was in your mind.

Callie turned to him. "Oscar," she said, grabbing his hands. "Listen to me. You aren't made of wood. The City children are."

CHAPTER SIXTEEN

Decoctions

O scar could not speak. His throat was all lump. He could only duck his head down and lose himself in the floor.

Callie grabbed Oscar's knee. "It's true, Oscar. The children are made of wizard-tree wood and spells. But the spells are breaking apart now. The children are breaking down."

"But I'm—"

"No," she said firmly. "You remember how I said the children all had something missing?"

Oscar could not answer, could not look up.

"Well, they do. And I felt it from that little girl we ran into on the City street, the one who touched my hair. She was perfectly healthy. I felt it but I didn't pay attention then. There's just something"—Callie pursed her lips and thought—"*lacking* in them. And that boy, I couldn't place it at the time, but his arms were hard. Like wood. Like skin on top of wood."

"But," he said, squeezing the words out, "even if they are made of wood, it doesn't mean I'm not."

"I don't think so," Callie said firmly. "It's not like that with you."

"But . . . but there was only one doll. There are so many kids."

"That you *found*, Oscar. There's one doll you found. There are five wizard trees down—at least. Can you imagine how much wood that is? Oscar, this is Caleb. If he had the power to turn wood into a *child*, do you think he wouldn't try to make as much money from it as he possibly could?"

"But those City kids are so . . . perfect."

Callie sat back in her chair and exhaled. "Well, you know what the City people are like. Maybe that's the whole point."

Somehow the evening had snuck up on them while they were busy with other things, and the light in the healer's shop was fading quickly. Callie lit the lantern on the table and then slid the map over to Oscar.

"Look at this, Oscar," she said, pointing, "Just look at it."

She got up and started lighting lanterns around Mariel's front room, while Oscar studied the map. The blobs looked back at him, each wearing its wounds as words. He could see them now in his head, see the whole of them. Their bodies were failing them—or if not their bodies, their minds. Oscar could feel his lungs take in air, his heart beat, his blood course, his mind record everything around him. Breathing, digestion, circulation, talking, seeing, hearing, remembering. They were systems, and in the children they were failing.

He kept his eyes focused on nowhere. "If this is true," he said softly, "then what about me? Why am I like this?"

Callie turned to him, eyebrows raised. Oscar could hear the words in the air before she said them:

Why are you like what?

No one is quite right.

But she did not. She crossed her arms around her chest. Her eyebrows tightened. The corner of her lip twitched, just a little.

"You're Oscar," she said finally. "That's all that matters."

He did not understand. But this was Callie, and so he had to believe her.

Callie huffed, then adjusted her apron and sat back down as if that was the end of it. "Now," she said, sliding the map back over, "let's say I'm right. Let's pretend. Let's say these are all spells failing . . . somehow. Maybe they weren't put together right, or maybe Caleb was supposed to be doing maintenance, or maybe it's something to do with the missing wizard trees."

Oscar opened his mouth to ask her what she meant, but then the pieces began to fit together in his mind. A grove of five trees, gone. That area of the Barrow earth no longer fed by the wizards. Empty. A hole in their protection.

"A hole in the magic," he said.

No wonder Caleb's illusion spells had faltered. They were right on top of the hole.

Callie tilted her head. "Yes, that's what I think. But it doesn't matter, really, what caused it. Just—saying I'm right, saying these are failing spells—is there something we can do? I mean you and me? The apprentice and the hand?"

Oscar's eyes went to the flickering lantern light. A simple question, cutting through the noise. A spell is failing. The magic is fraying at the seams. Can you put it back together again?

"Yes," he said. "I think so. I think we can make something. At least—"

He was going to say *at least temporarily*, but he could not finish the sentence, because at that moment the door burst open, and Oscar jumped out of his chair, knocking it over. It was no soil monster who appeared from the dark of the night—but rather Lord Cooper and his great swooping green cloak, followed by the carriage driver, who was clutching his left shoulder. And Lord Cooper was bearing a gasping, sobbing Sophie in his outstretched arms.

Callie popped up from the table. "What happened?"

"Our carriage was attacked," Lord Cooper breathed. "By some beast."

Callie sucked in a breath and Oscar stiffened. They glanced at each other, and somehow in that glance a book's worth of words passed back and forth.

"She's hurt," Lord Cooper said, holding the girl out like an offering. "It swiped at her, and—it hit her pretty hard. In the chest, I think."

It was like a lantern flared on inside Callie. She straightened, her face transformed from worried to purposeful, and she seemed to grow three years in the space of a second. "Come to the back room," she said, herding everyone through the doorway. Lord Cooper was carrying his daughter like she was made of feathers. Callie motioned to the cot. "Put her there. Slide her on as gently as you can—that's right." She pointed to the carriage driver. "What is your name, and what happened to your arm?"

"Pierre, miss. I crashed into the seat," the driver said in a half-choked voice, "but it can wait. Take care of the little miss."

With a swift nod Callie pulled the stool up next to the cot and started talking to Sophie, while Oscar stood in the doorway, neither in the back room nor out of it. Sophie's pale face was red and chapped with tears, and all her features were clenched up. She clutched at her abdomen, and even from where he was standing Oscar could see she was trembling. His mind flashed to Crow in the corner, bleeding and shaking, flank full of glass.

Callie was standing over the girl now, murmuring questions, placing her hand gently on Sophie's side. The girl let out a whimper.

In a blink Callie was up, getting a pair of scissors from the shelf behind her. She looked over her shoulder and told the lord, "I have to cut her dress off." She was not asking permission.

Lord Cooper did not object. He didn't even seem to be there, really—he sat on the stool, chest rising and falling, half watching Callie work, half somewhere else entirely. Lost. "It swiped at the carriage and took off the side," he told the room. "And then it tried to take her.

The horses got spooked and ran. If they hadn't . . . I don't know how we would have gotten away." He closed his eyes. "It was enormous. And so dirty. Was it a bear? It must have been a bear."

Callie had the red dress off now, and she carefully lifted up the girl's white shift. Her back tensed. She did not move for one moment, two, and then she slowly angled her face toward Oscar.

"Oscar? What we were talking about earlier? Can you make something like that?"

Her voice grabbed hold of him and pulled him forward. She looked at him, and he looked straight into her eyes for one full heartbeat. And he read them perfectly.

"Yes." And then he ran back to Caleb's shop.

His head was full of ice and noise, and it was everything he could do to sort through it all. His hand went to his other arm and squeezed, tight.

The question had been simple: *Saying these are failing spells . . . is there something we can do?*

Yes. You can strengthen the spell.

At least, he was pretty sure.

He had never made anything like this before, never heard of something like this being made. You usually used these kinds of herbs to help with a decoction—sometimes there was something inherently unstable about the mixture you were making and you needed something there to mend any ruptures, convince the herbs to work together. Sometimes you wanted the herbs to be a little louder than they were on their own: you needed something to coax them out. And sometimes you needed something to fuse them together so tightly they would never remember being separate in the first place.

Repair, amplify, bind.

Dandelion, vetiver, goldenseal.

They were all hidden ingredients, helper herbs that no one really noticed, because they just made everything work as it was supposed to. They were pieces from other puzzles, but perhaps they could be put together to make something new.

Oscar would have liked to think about it more, but there was no more to be had now, so he set a pot to boil and then ran down to the pantry and filled his arms with jars and ran back up. He put two handfuls of each herb in another pot, mixed in a bag of cornmeal, and when the water was ready he poured it on top of the mixture and stirred until it was thick. Then he took the steaming pot by both handles and darted back to the healer's.

When he got there, he found Callie holding Sophie's hand. A steaming cup sat on the little table next to the bed, and the room filled with the smell of licorice root—*for pain*—and valerian—*for sleep*. They were basic herbs, the sort any ordinary healer would use. But they were the right ones.

The driver was holding a towel to his shoulder, and Lord Cooper could be seen through the doorway pacing the front room.

"A poultice," he said to Callie, indicating his pot. In a flash she was collecting bandages from the cabinet. When Callie moved away, Oscar's eyes fell on the girl's torso. Her entire left side blossomed with a deep, terrible purple.

His eyes darted away, landing on Sophie's face. She was staring at him again, eyes wide as the world. Tears ran down her cheeks, but she was silent now, and mostly still. Her eyes called to Oscar, though nightmares flickered behind them. Oscar smashed his lips together and took one step into her gaze, and another. He was next to the bed now, and still she gazed at him.

And then Sophie opened her mouth, and Oscar leaned forward, because he knew that's what he was supposed to do. She whispered one word in his ear, the first word she had ever said to him:

"Monster."

He drew back and stared into her eyes. And he knew, finally, what the girl was asking of him.

• • •

Oscar paced around the cellar that night, trying to hold all the pieces in his head. No magicians were coming, no magic smiths with glowing swords. They did not believe in monsters. And Oscar no longer believed in magic smiths.

So Oscar paced. Bear watched him, and Pebble darted around the room. Oscar had put all the images of the night the monster attacked in a box and buried it deeply in his brain. Now he unburied it and dumped out all the contents to make a map.

And he saw this:

The monster, swiping the contents of a shelf into its mouth.

And this:

The love potions Oscar threw at it smashing against its chest. The monster stopping to wipe itself off and then suck the potions off its hands.

And this:

The glowing iron flail smacking into the monster's chest. The monster clutching for it.

And from the attacks on the marketplace:

The boots for the City people. Master Christopher's special brew. Madame Aphra's dress cloth. The Most Spectacular Goat.

And:

Master Thomas and the very enormous bear in the

cage—all the smell-enhancing charms around the trap missing.

Oscar stopped. "It's all magic," he told Bear. "It's eating magical things."

Bear flicked her tail. Oscar started pacing again, as Pebble darted through his legs. The sketch from Galen's book flashed in his mind—the regular tree and the soil feeding it. The wizard tree, feeding the soil.

A grove of wizard trees, now stumps. A hole in the magic. The system shut down. The wizard trees had been cut down, and the earth around them was starved for magic.

"No," Oscar whispered to himself. The monster was not made of earth—it *was* the earth, birthing a monster to serve its monstrous need.

There was no rival magician, no one pulling the strings. The monster was alone, with no master. Just like Oscar.

"It's *hungry*," he said.

Yes, Sophie was made of spells, and that's why the monster had attacked. She was full of more magic than anything in Aletheia.

She and the other children, that is.

Oscar stopped cold. He looked at Bear. The cat gazed up at him. The lantern inside Oscar flared.

And then he headed for his pantry.

His first job was to make a remedy that Callie could give to the other children tomorrow. He'd made Sophie's quickly, because she'd needed it quickly, but now he had more time. He stood in the pantry and scanned the shelves. Oscar had no idea what Caleb had done to the dolls to make them children—the magic was a thousand times beyond his understanding. Even if he knew what the spells were, he couldn't fix them. He was no magician.

This was all he could do:

Repair. Amplify. Bind.

Dandelion, vetiver, goldenseal.

A tea, to work from the inside out, and a salve, to work from the outside in. Sometimes in remedies it was better for the herbs to be infused; sometimes it was better for them to be absorbed. But this wasn't a remedy, really, and the children's bodies were illusions covering a churning tangle of spells. The herbs needed to work their way to each spell, weave themselves so gently into it that nothing else frayed in the process, then join all the bits together so the tangle could become a working whole. A tea and a salve, to meet in the middle, double in power, and find their way to every little spell.

Making a tea is easy—you just combine the herbs, watching the mixture carefully to see the moment when they become more a whole rather than parts. But a salve is a system built on these moments. First you boil the herbs long enough to coax out their gifts—you will feel it when this happens. Then you strain out the water, pour oil into the herbs, and keep simmering until the oil now has these gifts. You will be able to tell. Then, beeswax, just enough to give the mixture thickness, not enough to take over. When you have just the right amount, you stop adding. And then you stir and keep stirring, and you stir some more, until the oil and wax come together. At each step there is a small moment of transformation that cannot be overlooked or rushed. And these moments should not be, because they are beautiful.

So Oscar worked in the kitchen, curtains pulled and lanterns flaring. Block sat on the counter, watching him. The healthy cats crept up from the staircase one by one to keep their eyes on him. Bear and Map sat and watched, but Pebble chirped at him and could not seem to settle herself down.

"This is for the City children," he told them. "It will help, I think. At least for now."

That was the problem. Nothing living lasts forever. The herbs' power was natural and would fade after a time. Caleb had probably assumed that if something went wrong he would be around to fix it.

As soon as the salve was done, Oscar poured it into jars and set them aside. The night that had worked its way in around the curtains was still deep and thick—a good thing, as Oscar had plenty left to do before sunrise.

At the first touch of morning Oscar was ready. He put the remedies in a bag, poured water in a canteen, and tucked Block in his pocket. Then he found some paper and a pencil and sat down.

He studied the paper, as if words might manifest upon it if he only concentrated hard enough. He was not very good at writing. He had a thousand things to say to Callie and a hundred words to say them with. Not to mention all the things that he did not want to say.

This was the result:

Dear Callie,
 Had to go collect plants. Gone all day. These are for the children. Give each child both.
          —Oscar

He looked at the note. Writing it had taken an eternity, and by all rights the words should have transformed into poetry somehow. There was so much else in his head—what the herbs were, how they were all helper herbs and now they were all going to help one another. He wanted to explain about the tea and the salve meeting in the middle, doubling in power, going at the spells from all sides. But this would have to do.

He exhaled and looked around the room. Now that the night's work was done, a tendril of fear was beginning to creep up his back. He clenched his fist and closed his eyes and tried to breathe it away. Then his eyes popped open. He had one more thing to say to Callie. She would understand, if it came to that.

PS. Take care of the cats. Two in my room.

He folded the note and dropped it in the bag of remedies. If he left it in front of Callie's door, she would find it first thing and could go treat the children.

That done, Oscar went downstairs and put out food and water for Crow and Cat, who were both sleeping.

"Wish me luck," he whispered to them.

And then it was time.

The sack was loaded. He was ready. There was a hole in the magic in the northwestern strip of the forest. That's where Oscar would go.

CHAPTER SEVENTEEN

The Hole

The marketplace was still fast asleep when Oscar left the shop, untroubled by the encroaching dawn. The giant bag he'd prepared was tucked behind the back entrance, still covered in the dull wool blanket Oscar had left on it to keep the whole thing looking as uninteresting as possible.

But really it was a very interesting bag, filled with everything he could find in Caleb's office that had liquid or powder in it, as well as an enchanted leather sack with some of Caleb's magical blankets stuffed inside, and an animal trap from Caleb's special collection.

The soil was hungry. It wanted magic. Oscar would give it magic. Then it would not be hungry anymore.

To get to the northwest strip, Oscar had to walk behind the marketplace and past the village and keep going through the forest all the way around the City. This was a daunting prospect, more so when you had a giant bag strapped to your back. Though Oscar was used to going back and forth to the gardens, and this was not that much farther a distance.

Not *that* much.

Most of the forest lay to the east of the hill, except the narrow bands that wrapped around it on the north and south side like embracing arms. There was not much to distinguish the northwestern strip; it was the home of some scattered hazel trees, an overgrowth of shepherd's purse, and the forest's second-best patch of stinging nettle—though that was not a plant Oscar collected often. Nothing lay beyond it but the northern swath of barren plaguelands that separated the Barrow from the great sea.

Oscar walked on, farther north than he had been for several months, and in that time the wizard trees seemed to have aged hundreds of years. Maybe the trees around the marketplace had done the same; maybe Oscar was so used to seeing them he hadn't taken the time to really look. But their majesty seemed not just old but worn somehow, like a throne in a castle ruin. Their bark was dark and peeling; their branches were sagging; some had wounds in the darkening trunks. As Oscar took in the trees, a sharp, gnawing, measureless feeling swelled inside him. A tree put a comforting branch around Oscar's shoulder and gently named the feeling for him—sadness.

The walking was hard work, and his muscles began to mutter protests. That meant he had walked a long time, it meant he was growing closer, it meant that fear had gone from tracing a finger gently on his neck to wrapping around it with a cold bony hand. He could still escape—the fear was in front of him, and all he had to do was wrench free and run in the other direction. But he kept walking forward, straight into its embrace.

Finally, ahead of him—a hole in the forest. A swath of gaping sky where there should have been none. Like someone had taken a sword and put a great slash in the world.

There was no illusion here.

Oscar stood frozen as the emptiness crushed him from all sides. It felt like someone had reached his hand into Oscar's chest and plucked out everything warm it could find.

Willing himself forward, he approached the first stump warily, stepping like the forest floor might disappear under his feet if he put any pressure on it. And why not—everything else that was essential had already disappeared.

The stump came up to Oscar's knees. The top was jagged and splintery, a mismatch of edges and lines and points. It had darkened, and moss covered it like a blanket, like a shroud. The trees had always seemed so enormous, but without the tree part the stump looked the size of an ordinary table. And it was just a shell.

Looking away quickly, Oscar walked on to the other stumps, keeping his eyes on the ground ahead of him, trying to swallow back the things rising in his throat. Even though he was not looking at the missing canopy above him, he could still feel its lack crushing against him. And the quiet—the usual chirping, cawing, skittering, rustling, creeping sound of the forest was gone.

The sun seized its opportunity, boldly presenting itself to undergrowth that had no idea what to do with it, as if it was the sun that had been in charge the entire time. The other trees stretched their branches weakly, like children in a village after all the adults have suddenly disappeared.

It wasn't just a hole in the magic. It was a hole in the world.

Oscar took a deep breath. Everything hurt; his body had done all the work it had in it for the day. But he could not rest—the ground was hungry.

The first thing to do was set the trap.

The trap was just a precaution, just in case all the

magical items caused the monster to come out. Though Oscar was dearly hoping the daylight would keep the monster away—and then once Oscar had completed his task, it would never emerge from the soil again. If the earth wasn't hungry anymore, it would not need the monster.

Really, the bear trap he had picked looked like a monster itself, made mostly of a jaw with terrible pointed teeth and a long chain dragging behind it as a tail. It should have been as heavy as an iron brick, but Caleb's trap was as light as a cat, the long chain like velvet roping. Oscar wrapped the chain around the thickest oak tree he could find, then he placed the trap a few feet away and set it, as easily as pulling on a handle. *Click.* He covered the trap with leaves, and then he took the leather sack with the enchanted blankets in it and hung it on a tree branch right above the trap. If the monster did come, it should go for the most concentrated area of magic first, and then Oscar could do his work. The magic smiths had put out a sack of meat and gotten a bear. He would put out a sack of magic to get a monster.

Bait. Lure. Trap.

He reached into his pocket to give Block a squeeze and then picked a jar from Caleb's workroom out of his bag: this one held arrowroot, rue, and some strange golden powder. He shook the jar—for no good reason at all—and then slowly scattered the contents carefully around the soil near the closest stump.

"Here," he breathed. "Take it. Eat up."

More.

Oscar jumped and looked around. It wasn't a voice, or even a sound. The word was suddenly just there, pulling on him like an insatiable urge.

More.

Oscar's breath caught. He looked around again, and then quickly opened a jar of some pink viscous fluid and drizzled it on the ground.

More.

Another, quickly. And another.

He scattered everything he could. He threw small glass tubes so they smashed, their contents drizzling into the soil. He spread powder everywhere, dumped potions at his feet. It was the entire mission of Oscar's body to give the ground as much magic as it could as quickly as possible. It was messy business, and soon he was covered in the powders and potions. He could at once win love, succeed at business, expose treachery, and confuse a foe.

More.

He kept on, feeding the soil with potions and decoctions and globs of ointments and small little vials of mystery goo. He fed it everything he had, his heart thrumming, his head roaring, his chest heaving.

And then the bag was empty. It was all gone.

More.

There was no more to be had. This was his plan; this was supposed to work, supposed to sate the earth. Oscar sucked in a breath as the thing kept tugging at him, harder than ever before, so hard it might pull him apart. All he had left was the bag with the blankets, but that was for the—

Monster.

He felt it before he saw it—a dampening dark presence, a rotting smell infiltrating the air. Oscar whirled around. And gasped. On the other side of the wizard stump, a dark form was rising up from the earth. It was undefined at first, just a mass of soil, but as it rose, the form began to take shape. The monster was growing out of the soil like a tree out of the earth—there was no separation between the two. It picked up one leg, then the other, separating itself from its home, and then shambled toward the leather sack hanging from the tree.

Oscar's whole body contorted. Every single muscle seized up; his bones locked together. Oscar was not going to move, not ever again. His eyes darted to the pile of branches on the ground where the trap was.

Please work please work please work please work please work please work.

The thing lurched for the bait. Its front leg slammed

down directly on the pile of branches. The trap sprang, and the creature fell forward, landing on the ground with a muffled *bam*.

Oscar could not breathe.

The creature pushed itself up with its arms, and its head swiveled around frantically. It tried to tug on its trapped leg. And then an anguished suffocated noise emanated from it, one that shook Oscar's bones.

Oscar backed away. His skin burst with sweat. He should leave; this would be the precise time to leave; he should turn and run. But he could not.

Run, Oscar.

The thing moaned and tried to crawl on the ground with its arms. Oscar squeezed his eyes shut and told himself to run now. But, still, he could not, and when his eyes popped open, the creature was crawling forward— one arm's length, two. Groaning, it picked its way off the ground and stood up.

It had only one and a half legs now—where the bottom half of its right leg should have been, only a view of the forest remained. The creature spread its arms out, and its head pivoted slowly from left to right.

Then it reached into the earth, scooping up more soil into its arms. Which it used to start to form itself a new leg.

And then Oscar ran.

He did not think where he was going. His brain ceded complete control to his body, which had one task—*get away. Far. Now.* And in the most opposite direction from the monster possible.

He tore through the forest as fast as he could, skipping over rocks and stuttering across the fallen branches of hazel trees, skittering over clumps of shepherd's purse, scraping himself on stinging nettle. It didn't matter. *Get away. Far. Now.*

But the thing was following him. He did not look, but there were four loud sounds in the air: Oscar's frantic footsteps, Oscar's heavy breathing, Oscar's pounding heart, and a soft rhythmic muffled thudding. Earth against earth. *Boom-BOOM, Boom-BOOM.* The forest around him cowered at the thing's approach, bushes bristled, branches snapped. Oscar willed his body forward, *faster, now, faster, you can do it.* He ducked around trees and skipped over bushes—but the creature followed him still. He should have been quicker, more agile than this great shambling stumbling stupid thing, but no matter what he did, the thuds stayed behind him.

He did not look.

A flash of something straight ahead—a change in the light. Oscar kept running, and it wasn't until he was darting through the wall of trees into the empty air that he realized he'd reached the end of the forest. And, in front of him, the plaguelands.

The plaguelands looked just like they sounded, an endless desolate sea of dry dead earth and scattered rocks and a few pieces of rotting wood, of bright-beating sun and boundless blue sky. It was the world, after its end.

But—*boom-BOOM*—there was no choice, so Oscar plummeted. He yelped, the vacant air assaulted him, but he kept going. His feet kicked up dust as he ran, and he kept inhaling it, and soon his mouth and lungs felt as harsh and desiccated as the world around him.

About fifty steps in, Oscar stopped. Something was missing. He couldn't feel the monster near him any-more, couldn't feel much, really. No, there was no magic here, but it was even emptier than that. Nothing else lived in the land—nothing growing or breathing or even moving—and though the wind rushed around him, the air seemed as dead as the ground, like it had given up long ago.

Breath caught, body poised to spring, Oscar turned his head slowly back. The monster was standing a few steps in front of the forest, arms up, back hunched, legs stooped, faceless face angled toward the ground, as if trying to understand it. A cloud of dust stirred around its feet, and a halo of darkness hung around its body—it looked like the creature was slowly infecting the air.

Oscar stood there, heart slamming, sucking in

poison dust. It was not like he had anywhere to hide. He was the only actual thing in the entire landscape in front of the monster.

And, he realized with a shudder, he was doused in magic.

He sucked in breath as the plaguelands dust stung at his magic-drenched clothes and skin, like hundreds of very tiny mosquitoes were sucking his blood.

The monster muffle-roared again, and it swiveled its head from one direction to the next, looking back toward the forest and then toward Oscar. Back toward safety and home, forward to feed its hunger.

Go back go back go back go back.

And then what would happen? If it went back?

Sophie's eyes, the red shoes, a rustle-swish of skirts. Caleb on the floor, broken. Crow in the corner, bleeding and trembling. The shop in ruins. The gardens. Wolf. Oscar's whole world.

Oscar inhaled. He felt a spark in his chest, a spark of something that had been there for so long he'd never bothered to notice it. It flickered and then flared.

He turned. He picked up a rock. He hurled it at the monster.

"Come get me!" he yelled.

And then he hurled one more.

Run, Oscar.

And so he ran.

Silence.

For a moment.

And then:

Boom-BOOM. Boom-BOOM.

Oscar ran ahead, away from everything he knew, deeper into everything he feared. His mind was back in charge, tugging his body along with it. He wanted to be back in the forest, his home, under the protection of trees and shadow and night and magic—but so did the monster. He was hungry, and lonely, and did not fit quite anywhere. And neither did the monster. And so he would keep running.

The dust was beginning to burn against his skin now—or else that was the sun. Oscar's muscles were burning, too, and it felt like there was a knife in his side. Maybe the wind was stabbing him.

He chanced a look over his shoulder. The monster was about twenty paces behind him—the wind taking bits of soil for itself, blurring the outlines of the creature against the sky.

Boom-BOOM.

The forest receded in the background, and as Oscar ran he felt something tugging at him and then letting him go—like the thread that connected him to the Barrow had snapped.

Oscar coughed and ran and stumbled and ran more. He checked over his shoulder, and behind him the monster stumbled, too. Maybe its thread had broken as well. He could hope.

The creature seemed fuzzier—less defined. And less sure in its steps. The plaguelands were nibbling away at the magic thing, bit by bit.

But not quickly enough.

Yes, the creature was diminishing. It could not run like this forever. But neither could Oscar. He would collapse in a heap, and then the thing would have its prize.

But maybe, maybe, they were far enough away that it couldn't find its way back.

Or maybe that was a little farther away yet.

And so Oscar kept running, hurtling his body into the void.

He barely noticed when the view in front of him changed from the great cracked barren land. Or when another presence started to hang in the air. So it was some time before he saw the unmistakable truth in front of him.

Just ahead, the world ended. At least all the world Oscar knew.

He'd mistaken its sound for that of the wind, mistaken its scent for that of the plaguelands dust, mistaken that strange strip on the horizon for some alteration in the landscape. And the landscape did alter. There was a stretch of sand, and then the fathomless sea.

Oscar had never seen the sea before. He hadn't known that it stretched on until it joined with the sky and that after that the world was just some infinite blue. He hadn't known that the waves looked like hungry beasts themselves, growing in might until they crashed against the shore, grasping at the land and taking whatever they pleased. He had not known that they were like animate thunder. He had thought the worst thing you could drown in was the sky.

There was a dark brown blotch in the water that matched one on the shore—an old rotting dock with its entire middle missing. There had been civilization here once, but the plague had consumed it.

He dared a glance back at the creature, and—though it was stumbling and fuzzy and the wind kept taunting it with pieces of itself—it was moving faster. The monster was deep in an alien world, maybe so deep it could never go home, and the only hope it had left was this magic-soaked boy with a little piece of wizard-tree wood in his pocket.

For it was only now that he was covered with potions that the monster chased him. The monster had not been interested in him at all in the shop; it had thrown him aside like garbage. Because unlike the City children,

Oscar was not made of wizard-tree wood and spells, but of flesh and bone and heart and brain and blood. He was a boy—born, not crafted. There were no strings dragging behind him.

He was just a boy. Just Oscar. That was all.

And it was Oscar and the monster at the edge of the world.

If he were magic, maybe he could last a little longer. But his muscles were real and they were gone now—he was empty limbs and bones that would surely collapse into a pile. He did not want to be eaten. And maybe the magic on him would give the monster strength and it would find its way back to the forest, back to the Barrow, to Sophie and Callie. Maybe it would eat everything.

If he had any muscles left, he could start darting around the shore, seeing if he could outlast the monster. But he didn't. And he couldn't. He was human.

And so he made his choice.

Oscar closed his eyes and ran forward, and the waves beckoned to him, and still he ran, and then the ground underneath his feet turned soft, and still he ran, and then his feet squelched, and still he ran, and then water sprayed in his face and lapped at his feet, enticing him inside.

And he stopped. And looked.

The monster shambled forward.

Oscar could not breathe, could barely move, but he only had a few things left for his body to do, and then it would be over.

He kicked off his boots, and immediately the water began to ooze around them to investigate. As the water started to gently pull at his feet, he looked back and took the best breath he could muster.

"COME. GET. ME."

And then he hurled himself into the waves.

Water pushed against his face and splashed in his mouth, tickling his lungs. It pressed against him everywhere, grabbing him and pulling at his clothes. The sea was not empty at all, but monstrously alive.

It felt so dark in there.

He flailed and bobbed, trying to find his feet, trying to find the sky, trying to find anything. Tendrils of slimy plants grabbed at his leg, and Oscar's foot slammed against the sea floor.

He gulped in air. He was up to his shoulders in the water. He looked frantically around for the oncoming creature. The water could not take him yet.

The thing was coming for him.

Oscar pushed himself toward the remains of the rotting dock. His hands flailed out in front of him and his feet pushed against the uncertain floor. One last push—and his arms wrapped around the dock post.

It was mostly rotted, but still solid and there, and Oscar held on with everything he had.

It wasn't much.

The monster was at the shoreline now, just a few yards away, batting at the water that hit its face. Oscar's clothes hung thickly against him—the sea might already have robbed them of their magic, his bait, so he focused all his energy on the little block of cat-shaped wizard-tree wood in his pocket. *You are magic,* Oscar told it. *You are magic. Not made of spells, but magic all the same.*

Bait. Lure. Trap.

The thing groaned and pawed in his direction, then took an uncertain step into the water. The waves touched it gently, an exploration, an invitation.

The monster took another step, until half its legs were submerged. Blackness spread out in the water around it.

Oscar hung on to the dock desperately as the water pressed in around him. He wanted to shout, *Come get me,* but he had no breath left for words.

The sea was calling to the creature just as it had called to him. Each wave lapped at it, each one a taunt. And an enticement.

The monster yowled and lunged forward. *Crash,*

responded the sea. The monster flinched and looked around. *Boom,* responded the sea.

A chunk from the monster's shoulder was missing. But its arm still reached for him.

I'm here, Oscar thought. *I'm here. Come and get me.*

It was only a few feet away now, and even though much of the monster seemed to be gone, the head and the torso and the arms and the horrid rocky mouth were still there, and that was probably enough. Oscar let out some choked plea and then grabbed for the other pole.

The monster roared and hurtled itself toward Oscar, its body falling into the water entirely. A terrible muffled yowl as the waves lapped and goaded and hungered and consumed, and the monster was gone. A dark thickness lingered on the water, and then that too washed away.

Oscar clutched at the pole, keeping his eyes fixed on the spot where the monster had been. The creature could rise again, could be in the water now, moving toward him, ready to pull on his leg and take Oscar down down down. And Oscar would not be able to hold on to the pole, he barely could now, and the sea was grasping at him.

But the thing did not emerge. Still, Oscar could hear the echoes of its anguished roar—it was a monstrous, miraculous creature, and none of this was its fault. It was just hungry.

Oscar closed his eyes. Block was in his pocket, shining

and warm. He wanted to put the cat in his hands, but he had no movement left. Still, he knew the cat was there, and that was something.

Water splashed over his head. The wind seemed to beckon to him, or maybe it was echoes in his head. Maybe it was the wooden boy in the floor calling to him. If only Caleb had told him, if only Caleb had transformed the doll in time—Oscar could have taught him things, things about being a real boy. But the water was holding Oscar close and telling him beautiful lies, and since it was the end, he chose to believe them.

Chapter Eighteen

The Land Remembers

It was a man's arm that pulled Oscar out of the water—strong and sure. That he remembered.

There was a great green cloak: it wrapped around Oscar like the sea, like a smile. That was true, too.

There was something pounding on his back. There was water. The water was certainly true.

There was a flash of red shoes, and a rustle-swish of skirts.

That was probably wrong.

And there was a horse, and he was on it, and there was an arm holding on to him, and that seemed like it couldn't be true, but probably was.

It turned out Callie had not believed his note. It

turned out it had, in fact, worried her. It turned out she'd remembered where in the forest the chopped-down wizard trees were. And it turned out she'd known that he would go there.

The night before, Callie had not allowed the men to move Sophie, so the little girl had slept on Callie's cot while her father and the driver stayed at the tavern. And when the men arrived at Callie's the next morning, they found Sophie had gotten much better overnight. It was miraculous, really.

How can I ever repay you? Lord Cooper asked.

And Callie pointed to the map of the Barrow.

So Lord Cooper and his driver rode up to the north-western strip of the forest and found the grove of stumps, a bear trap, and a great mess of vials, tubes, and jars. And some boy-sized boot prints leading away. The prints stopped as soon as the forest did. The men rode around the plaguelands but saw no trace of anything at all until they got to the shore, where two boy-sized boots lay at the water's edge, without the boy.

Oscar learned this part of the story later, much later. First there was a cot, a blanket, some tea, and then a long dreamless sleep. And, somewhere, a small warm purring body curled up against his chest.

Then: Oscar waking up to find himself in the back room of the healer's, Pebble at his side, Oscar's hand on her, making sure she was real.

She was. She was the softest creature. Oscar kept his hand on her back, feeling the purrs rumble through her body, teaching their steady contented rhythm to his mind and heart and breath, and slowly the pieces of him began to move back together, one purr at a time.

Oscar raised his head. He was alone in the room, excepting Pebble. His old clothes were hanging by the fire—he seemed to be wearing a nightshirt made for a boy several Oscars bigger than he.

And: next to the fire, his boots and the little wooden cat.

And flashes: traps, monsters, maws, the beating sun, the endless sea, pumping limbs, pounding feet and heart, pounding waves, sucking breaths, dust in his mouth, water in his mouth, trying to keep running, trying to keep breathing, trying to keep his head above water, trying to hold on to the dock—and, everywhere, the unrelenting footsteps of the monster.

He closed his eyes and curled up around the cat. Behind his eyes, the monster shambled into the sea while the waves ate away at it, and still it pressed forward. Its hunger was more all-consuming than its need to survive. The hunger mattered more than the monster.

Oscar shuddered. Pebble chirped and began to press her head against him.

They were not done yet. There was still a hole in the magic. The earth was still hungry. The monsters would keep coming.

He squeezed the cat, and then got dressed and put his boots on and tucked Block back into his pocket where she belonged—solid and warm.

"You're up!"

He turned. Callie was in the back doorway—hair tied back, apron on, arms on her hips. Her eyes danced around his face.

Oscar bit his lip. He could not read her expression. He had worked so hard to learn her—what if the sea had taken that away from him?

"Are you feeling better?" Callie asked, stepping closer to him.

Oscar nodded hesitantly. That, at least, was true.

"Good." She stared at him. Oscar stared back. Her eyes shimmered. And then narrowed.

And then she stomped on his foot.

"Ow!"

Callie's eyes flared. "Why did you do that?" she yelled. "You could have been killed!"

"I didn't think—"

Her expression cut him off. "No, you didn't."

"But . . . I didn't want—"

"I don't care!"

He sucked in his lips. Her arms were wrapped around her body, and her eyes had in them an entire litany of scolding.

"I'm sorry?"

"You should be. Don't ever do anything that stupid again without taking me with you." She squinted at him pointedly. "Now, I am going to give you some tea and some stew with lots of chunks in it and you are going to eat it all and tell me what happened."

"But I only eat—"

Callie narrowed her eyes.

"I mean, yes."

Oscar did his best to tell her the story—he choked out bits as he choked down lumps of stringy meat and slimy, soft vegetables. He tried to tell it like a story he had heard once about a boy somewhere, instead of something that had happened to him. Callie listened, eyes big, and when he was done she gazed at him like she'd watched the entire thing happen. She did not speak, and Oscar swallowed and let his eyes drop.

"Oscar," she said finally, "you are very brave."

He could not say anything after that.

Callie got up and served him a second bowl of stew and filled him in on the events of the morning.

"Lord Cooper will drop by—he wants to tell you how grateful he is. He would have done it before, except you'd nearly gotten yourself drowned." Callie raised her eyebrows at him meaningfully, and then went on. "But Oscar . . . Sophie is doing so much better. I think she'll be fine. It worked. Whatever you made *worked*."

Something tickled at his chest, and the lightness floated up. The corner of his mouth went up in a smile.

"I still need to go up to deliver the remedies to the other children."

Oscar frowned—she was supposed to do that when he was going after the monster. That had been his plan.

"I've been a little busy taking care of you," Callie snapped.

He quickly made his face as blank as he could. Apparently he was going to be hearing about this for some time.

"But, Oscar, these are just the children we know about. What if there are more? How do we find them? Remember the lady in the shop the day after Wolf was killed? The one who left Caleb her card?"

Something's wrong with her, the lady had said. Oscar had forgotten. He'd been so focused on the card; everything else had been crumpled away.

"I got a letter from Madame Mariel yesterday," Callie said, shifting. She leaned toward Oscar, eyes wide. "She's not coming back."

"What?"

"She *is* on the continent. She said she's going to stay there. She wants to set up a healer's shop there. She says it's because the Barrow is no longer safe. Of course it can't have anything to do with the fact that there's no duke to tax her there."

Oscar stopped. "But . . . she won't be able to work magic."

"I don't think she plans to tell the people on the continent that," Callie said. "She asked me to sell everything and mail her the proceeds."

"Are you going to do that?"

"No."

Oscar swallowed. "So . . . what are you going to do?"

Whatever answer Callie was going to give was interrupted by a sharp knock at the front door, immediately followed by Lord Cooper strolling in, his green cloak trailing behind him. Callie and Oscar stood up.

"Miss Callie," he said in greeting. "Mister Oscar."

"How are your children?" Callie asked, brushing off her apron.

"They are recovering well, thank you. Hugo seems much better after we gave him your remedies last night." He looked over at Oscar. "I wanted to come down myself to check on our boy. Are you feeling better?"

Oscar nodded.

Lord Cooper knelt down and put his hands on

Oscar's arms. "It was very brave of you to try to find the bear that attacked my Sophie," he said. "But next time let adults handle the bears."

"Oh, he will," said Callie quickly.

"That's my boy," said the lord. He ruffled Oscar's hair, and Oscar did everything he could not to flinch.

The lord got up to go.

And Oscar opened his mouth.

"Why did you do it?"

The lord froze. Callie's head turned to Oscar. But she did not stop him.

"Why did I do what, young man?" the lord asked slowly, turning to Oscar.

"Why did you get magic children?"

Lord Cooper appraised Oscar and Callie for a long moment.

"If we hadn't figured it out," Callie interjected softly, "we wouldn't have been able to help them. It would have been easier if you had told us."

The lord exhaled slowly. "Caleb promised children who would never get sick," he said, voice quiet. "Never suffer, never have any problems at all. A boy got sick and died a few years ago. It was horrible. That wasn't supposed to happen!" Even at the words, his face darkened. "And this way, we could have what we wanted. A boy and a girl, three years apart in age, and nothing could go wrong with

them." He looked at Oscar and Callie, as if for approval.
"We'd never have to see them suffer at all. You want your
children to have the best of everything—"

"But—" Oscar sputtered. "They did suffer."

"They were not supposed to!"

"Didn't you ever think they could fail?" Oscar asked.

"No!" the lord exclaimed, shaking his head. "They're
magic!"

"But," Callie interjected, voice soft, "they're made of
wood."

"Wizard-tree wood!" Lord Cooper interjected.

"What happens if everyone has wooden children?"
Callie went on. "What if they never become adults?
What happens if they can't have kids? What happens to
all the *people*?"

The lord's brow furrowed. "The City is blessed! It
will endure as it always has. Others will carry on. My
wife could not bear the thought of having children and
watching them suffer. Losing them." He looked straight
at Callie. "Could you?"

Callie flushed and looked at the floor. "It happens,"
she said quietly, after a moment. "That doesn't mean
they shouldn't have existed in the first place."

A twinge in Oscar's chest. He reached his hand over
to her. He could squeeze her arm; he could put his hand
on her back, on her shoulder; he could turn and put both

his hands on her shoulders and look her in the eyes. People had done all these things to him in the past week. He could do them. Almost. He reached his index finger out and placed it gently on her arm and then took it away.

The lord drew himself up. "Miss Callie," he said, "I am very grateful to you and Mister Oscar for saving my children. This has been unbearable. This was not supposed to happen. They're magic!"

Callie swallowed. She wiped one eye and straightened, all business again. "Lord Cooper, there are other children like yours."

"Yes, there are."

"Do you know how many others?" she asked. "We need to help them. If they haven't started having problems yet, they might soon."

"I would say . . . over fifty."

Callie let out a long burst of air. Oscar simply burst. Over fifty.

"You see," the lord explained, "everyone else has them. You wouldn't want your child to be the only one who had flaws. What would it be like for them?"

Oscar could not speak. Over fifty little Sophies, all with their systems failing. They were so small; he was grown-up compared to these children. He knew things now; he had done things. They should be allowed to do things, too.

The surnames of the children they had visited popped in his head and arranged themselves—*Baker, Collier, Cooper, Miller, Piper, Wright.* And suddenly he knew where he'd seen them before: the ledger, in Caleb's office. Over fifty names. And such big numbers attached to each one—so many coins. Caleb had exacted a high price to manufacture children.

"Lord Cooper," Callie was saying, "If you could write down the names of—"

Oscar leaned over and whispered, "Master Caleb has the names."

When Lord Cooper turned to go, his face looked odd, like that of a cat who had secretly taken more than her share of cheese. His eyes caught Oscar for a moment, and then lingered there. "When I first saw you in the shop," he said, voice low. "I thought you were . . . like my children. Caleb's first attempt, perhaps."

Oscar's face went hot. Callie stiffened.

"You do not approve," the lord continued, eyes still on Oscar. "But, young man, wouldn't it be a nice thing, to be made of magic?"

"Thank you, Lord Cooper," Callie said, voice like a knot. "You may go."

After the lord disappeared out the door, Callie sank slowly into her chair, and Oscar followed suit.

"I don't understand," Oscar breathed. "Fifty magic

kids? Because everyone wants children who can't get sick? That they don't have to worry about losing?"

"Lord and Lady Cooper did lose something," Callie said. "They lost the human children they could have had. They could have existed and do not."

Oscar wrapped his arms around himself and squeezed tightly. The magic children, would they ever realize what they were? Or would they just feel that something was missing, something at the core of what they were supposed to be? Would they find themselves oddly wistful for the real people they should have been, for the life they could have had?

It was like being an orphan, in a way. They would feel it, but they would never understand why. Oscar would never know why he didn't work quite in the same way as everyone else. All this time, the gray shadows of the Home had been obscuring some bigger void, one he hadn't even known existed until now. Wolf had said: *You don't even know where you came from.* Oscar had thought Wolf knew some terrible secret about his past. But no. Oscar was an orphan with no history attached to him, no story of the parents he had once had. Wolf had been taunting him because his past was unknowable.

Callie coughed a little, and Oscar looked up. She was staring at the table, twisting curls in her hand. "My brother was so much younger than me," she said in almost a whisper. "I saw him go from a baby to a child. He went from being this creature who ate and slept and cried to being . . . Nico. And suddenly . . ." She squeezed her eyes closed for a moment. When she opened them, they were wet. "Suddenly he liked playing in the fireplace and pretending it was a cave. And building things out of little scraps of wood. He made me little houses. And when I'd tell him stories . . . he loved that."

Callie hugged herself. "Suddenly he was a person." she said, voice as thick as the night. "It was amazing." Her lips pressed together, her eyes fell closed again for a moment, and volumes of history passed over her face After a time, she added, "The child Lord Cooper was talking about, the one who died, was the duke's son. Marcus was his name. Right after I first got here, the boy had a terrible fever. The duke screamed at Madame Mariel that she was supposed to be able to fix him. That this never should've happened in the first place."

Callie's voice slowly changed, and suddenly she sounded like she was talking to him, and not to some tiny patch of air. "And Mariel couldn't help him. She tried, but it was beyond her. The boy died a few days later. And soon after that, we were flooded with City parents looking for something to protect their children. Caleb was, too. They were all so afraid. Terrified. As if their own children were already sick. I'd never seen City people afraid, especially not like that."

No. City people were not supposed to be afraid of anything. Wasn't that the whole point?

"That's where I met the duchess. The mother of Ronald-who-can't-remember. While we were there, while the duke was screaming, she just sat in the corner, like a shadow. Like she'd died and was already a ghost. That was a long time ago. But Ronald . . . I wonder if he was the first one. A child who would never fall ill . . ."

"They'd never have to watch their kid suffer," Oscar said quietly. *There was a need,* Caleb had said. *That was all.* Not for a shop boy, as Oscar had thought. He had not understood that there were many different ways to need.

Callie slowly traced a finger along the tabletop. "I've been reading about the City during the plague," she said. "It was so awful in there. People would try to escape, but the walls kept them in. Everybody was dying, all around, hundreds a day, and their families were locked in, too, and they could only watch. . . . When you lose someone, it hurts so much your body can't contain it." She swallowed. "The wizards said the City was just a wound at the end. Maybe there are scars. Maybe the ground still carries all that grief. Maybe the whole land is still . . . traumatized, somehow, and the people who were born there have it in their blood, the way some people in the Barrow have magic in their blood."

"The land remembers," Oscar said. The wizards had told him so.

"Maybe that's why the City people are the way they are," Callie went on. "Acting so superior. Thinking they're chosen. If you're chosen, if magic exists for your benefit, nothing bad can ever happen to you, right? Then you don't have to be afraid." She glanced up at Oscar. "I'm not saying it's right. At all. It's horrible. It's so selfish, and now their children are suffering."

Oscar nodded slowly.

Callie dropped her hand on the table. "Well, it doesn't matter what we think," she said, straightening. "They're children now. This was never their choice. And they could all be breaking down. How many times did City people come in yelling for Caleb?"

Oscar bit his lip. "A lot." Over fifty children, all made of unstable spells, all threatening to fall apart at any moment. The decoction would keep them. But Oscar didn't know for how long. They could fall apart again, or something else could fail. Their spells could simply fade, and they would be nothing but wooden dolls again.

"Fifty children, Oscar! Do we give them all remedies? Even the ones who haven't broken yet? How do we know the remedies won't stop working, just like the original spells did? What do we do?" Eyes widening, she inhaled sharply. "What if Caleb was going to export them? What if he already did?"

There is danger in small enchantments, my boy. Small enchantments make us dream of big ones.

"There's something else I have to do," Oscar said. "It is very stupid." He looked up at Callie hesitantly. "Do you want to help me?"

CHAPTER NINETEEN

Endings

The monster was gone. Or at least it belonged to the sea now. But the monster was not the real problem. Even though it had very much acted like it.

Oscar explained to Callie about his original plan, about all the magic he'd dumped into the earth trying to feed it, about the unrelenting hunger that surrounded him, about how it was only after he gave the ground every last piece of magic that the monster had appeared, desperate and ravenous for more.

Everything and everyone was so hungry. The monster. The Barrow folk, buying everything up when danger lurked. The City people, clutching at pretty little enchanted things. Substituting magic for people. The shining people's ancestors, when the plague threatened, ignoring the warnings of the wizards, assuring themselves magic would keep them safe as they themselves brought death upon the entire island. They could have kept Aletheia safe, they could have kept the plague contained, but they had all cared for magic more than their own survival.

And, again, the City people, forgetting the lessons, believing the lies, letting the dark parts of their legacy be obscured by white space and blank pages.

Everyone was so hungry.

"So what are you saying?" Callie asked.

"The hole in the magic is still there," Oscar said. "The earth will keep bearing monsters as long as there's magic enough to let it."

"So what do we do? The apprentice and the hand?"

"I don't think . . ." He glanced up warily. "I don't think there should be magic anymore."

She drew herself up. "You think it should be destroyed?"

Oscar swallowed. "I think *we* should destroy it."

Callie's eyes widened; they took in the whole of him, the whole room, the whole Barrow, she took them all in, and then her eyes lit and her jaw set. "Great," she said. "How?"

• • •

That evening, Oscar and Callie sat in the library por-ing over the shelves, cats swarming around them. Books lay all around—Aletheian histories, atlases, the plague history, the official and unofficial wizards' chronicles. But while people had written volumes on finding magic, using magic, and making magic grow, and more volumes on magic's theories, ethics, practical applications, and even impractical ones—no one had ever written a word about making magic go away.

So they put away the books while the cats settled on their laps, and talked, and slowly they hatched a plan.

No one had ever tried to make magic disappear—but sometimes it disappeared anyway. Sometimes it got used up. And sometimes it was lost in a vacuum.

It was Callie who mentioned the plaguelands dirt, the way Oscar had described it sucking off the magic on his skin; and the sea, lapping away everything that had held the monster together.

It was Oscar who talked about the trees—Galen's diagram with the arrows going up from the soil in one tree and down to the soil in the other. And, underneath the ground, the roots spreading the magic through the soil. A network. A web.

Or a circulatory system, Callie said. With magic coursing through the roots like blood.

And so, Oscar said, if something else got into the system . . .

. . . it would course through the roots, Callie said. Like magic.

And they had their plan.

It was late when they were done—the cats were all balled up and sleeping. Oscar walked Callie upstairs. They were silent now; all the words had been said. But when Callie was about to leave, she turned to Oscar, raised her eyebrows, and blew air out of her cheeks.

He could think of nothing better to say.

Oscar kept an eye on her through the window as she walked back to the healer's, though he didn't know what he'd do if another monster appeared—except maybe send the cats after it. When she disappeared into the house, his eyes fell on the bakery. It was Sunday; bread day, once upon a time, when Oscar lived in the cellar.

Oscar rubbed his arm. With the bakery shuttered, the marketplace looked like it was missing its wizard tree. And so he sat down at the kitchen table and wrote a letter:

Dear Mister Malcolm,

There was a soil monster. It killed Caleb. It chased me into the sea and drowned. Now Callie and I are going to destroy magic.

*Then we have to stay in the Barrow to watch the City children.
They are made of wizard-tree wood. You should come back. You
can bake bread.*

—Oscar

That night, he dreamed of the plaguelands. But the dream was not like his sky nightmares. Everything was still empty and endless, and yet not monstrous. A boy was running through the land, moving toward the horizon— and at first it seemed like the boy was being chased. But the boy kept running, and nothing appeared behind him. When the boy finally disappeared into the horizon and nothing followed, it occurred to Oscar that maybe the boy might not have been running away, but maybe he'd been running toward something.

When he woke up, Oscar had the taste of the plaguelands around him. He rubbed his chest, but he was uneven, everywhere. He held the plan in his head, and his stomach shifted, just slightly. The earth that they were going to put into the forest had been so damaged that nothing could survive it—its nothingness was an even greater power than magic. Maybe a greater power than wizards. Once, Oscar had not believed such a thing could be possible.

When Callie arrived in the morning, Oscar was up in the kitchen reading Galen's journal again.

"Where's your cloak?" Oscar asked.

Callie shrugged. "Doesn't seem necessary anymore."

"Come look at this," he said, nodding to his book. "Near the end. Galen wrote about the plaguelands." He tried to sound casual, but he was rocking in his chair a bit. He grabbed onto the seat to stop himself.

It was one of the entries he'd read that night in the library—and at the time he hadn't thought anything of it. But now—now, he wanted to see if Callie saw what he saw.

She read:

The plague has killed everything along the western banks of the river and the shores around the sea. Now, that earth is not just barren, but a vacuum. One cannot plant a seed or light a match in this land, and one cannot carry magic across and expect it to survive the journey. Perhaps this will stop the spread. If it isn't already too late.

"I remember this one," Callie said. "What did you want me to see?"

Oscar's eyes widened. "Read it carefully," he said, motioning to the page. "He says the plague killed the land, and then talks about it being a vacuum. But what if that was . . . later? What if he's not describing what *happened* to the land, but rather what the wizards *did*?"

Callie squinted at the entry. Her eyes passed over the words, and then again. "I don't understand," she said.

"Here," Oscar said. His words were starting to pile on top of one another. "Look at the words. The plague killed the land, they say, made it barren. But what if the *wizards* did everything that came next? 'Now, the earth is a vacuum.' *Now.*" His face was flushed. "They couldn't get anyone to stop crossing to the west and back for magic. What if they *made* the plaguelands so people wouldn't have a reason to go to the west anymore?"

Callie forehead scrunched up, and she studied the words again, tugging on a curl. "I guess," she said, tilting her head, "it *could* be read that way."

"It could!" he said. "Yes!"

"But we don't know," she said softly. "It's not clear. It could have been the plague, too."

"It could," he whispered.

"Really," Callie said, "it doesn't matter, as long as it works. Whether the wizards did it or not, the plaguelands stopped the spread. And now they're going to stop the monsters from coming. It doesn't matter, as long as it works."

Oscar didn't say anything. But she was right: it didn't really matter, not in the end.

Still, it was a nice thing to believe.

Soon, they had plunged into the forest. Oscar had a

bag with the jug of plaguelands dirt from Caleb's work-room strapped to his back; Callie, one carrying the jug of seawater. This time they walked right into the center of the forest, the middle of the circulatory system, to the biggest wizard tree.

It was Oscar's favorite tree, the one with the honey mushrooms growing underneath, the one with the five massive branches rising up and out of the trunk like a flower.

Had it looked so old when Oscar had last been here? The bark was gray, fading. The leaves were thinning like an old man's hair. There was a long welt of missing bark in the middle of the trunk, and some kind of dark fungus was growing in the welt.

The tree looked so tired. They all did.

But maybe, without the hungry soil taking from them all the time, the wizard trees would not be so tired anymore. Maybe, now, the soil could feed them. Just like it was supposed to.

Oscar walked up and put his hand on the trunk. The gentle warmth pressed into his palm, a reassurance. Despite all the things churning inside him, the touch of the tree eased him a little, as surely as a cat's purr. As it always had.

"Is this the right thing to do?" Oscar whispered, running his hand along the trunk. "Is this what you want?"

No answer, just the same steady warmth. It was the same as it had always been, Oscar realized. Though this tree was drooping and thinning, though the magic had been used and abused, though its colleagues had fallen for no good purpose, though it was so tired, this feeling of some steady, generous vitality in all the wizard trees had never lessened. It was the essence of the tree, the truth at its core.

He'd always thought of this feeling as the presence of magic. But no other magic-laced thing had ever felt like the wizard-tree wood. It was the tactile translation of the ineffable warmth and peace Oscar felt in his chest when he was with the wizard trees, when the cats were with him, when Callie was there—and so he named the feeling love.

He nodded at Callie, and they both put their jugs down. Callie poured some seawater into the plaguelands dirt and began to mix it around with a stick. A poultice. Then Oscar scooped some of the mud up with his hands and began rubbing it into the exposed bark gently. Just a little, so it would work its way through the tree very slowly. He wanted to murmur things, but he could think of nothing to say.

Callie massaged the mud into the visible roots, and then poured the excess water around the tree. Whatever magic-destroying thing was in the plaguelands would be

in the tree soon. The soil would suck it up, and it would travel through the circulatory system, from root to root. And slowly the magic would dissipate, like a pile of dust in the wind.

It had all been such a beautiful lie. Such a warm blanket. The enchanted island. The storied history. The magic, always good, always acting in service of the people, always protecting them. The Aletheians, always so noble and worthy. The shining people, free of disease and want, so blessed they could have anything they desired—beauty, luck, health, wealth. Anything, even children made of wood.

It was a beautiful lie that they had all been telling themselves—that you could have magic without monsters.

"People are going to be very upset," Callie said.

Yes. They were going to be very upset.

They stood back and looked at the tree. The whole bottom of the trunk was covered in mud, but the tree had already begun to drink it in.

In a blink Oscar's throat swelled; his eyes filled with tears. Callie grabbed his hand and held it. They stood together, eyes fixed on the great tree, and together, they took notice. They carried the wizards' secrets, and they would remember.

After a while, Callie squeezed Oscar's hand. "Let's go home now," she said.

He gave the tree one more glance, and then turned and followed her. They walked in silence all the way home. But even as they approached the marketplace he could still feel the warm humming of the tree in his hands. Like he had taken it with him.

There were people in the marketplace again. Half the shops were closed, but villagers and merchants were milling around. Some were replacing the windows at the jeweler's. Madame Sabine and another villager were putting a wall back on the shoemaker's. Everywhere people were cleaning, rebuilding, putting the marketplace back together.

And some nonhuman noise from across the marketplace: a bleating. And a joyful chattering. In front of her shop Madame Catherine was bent over, rubbing the flanks of one very dirty, bedraggled Most Spectacular Goat.

Oscar swallowed. The tears came and did not stop. Callie wrapped her hand around his arm. He took in Madame Catherine and her goat, then closed his eyes and kept the image—something to hold on to.

The next morning, Oscar and Callie went up to the City to deliver remedies to the families they'd already visited, plus a few whose families had heard about what they were doing and had sent messages to Callie over the last few days about their own children.

Callie had been studying the ledger and was trying to figure out how to approach the families that hadn't sent her a message yet. Oscar would leave it to her. She was good at people.

"What about the duke?" Oscar asked as they walked up the hill. "And Ronald-who-can't-remember?"

Callie grimaced. "I know," she said. "It's funny with Ronald—with everyone else, we can fix what's broken, at least immediately. And we can probably fix the system that holds on to memories, so he can remember from now on, but whatever childhood Caleb implanted in his head might be just . . . gone." She stopped and regarded Oscar for a moment. "But, does it matter? It's not real. People don't remember much from when they're really young, but everything that happened is still a part of you. The facts of the memories don't matter, except what comes from the living of them."

Oscar nodded slowly, kicking up dirt as he walked. His only clear memory of the Home was riding away from it, but the shadows were part of him, all the same. The children didn't have any pasts, at least real ones. All they had that really belonged to them would be the lives they made now. If they were allowed to make them.

The guards with the absurd hats were waiting for them when they got to the City, and Callie showed them her stack of letters. As they passed through the gates, Oscar rolled his eyes. "What will they do with themselves without magic?" he muttered.

Callie let out a dark laugh. "I don't know," she said. "Work, maybe? Anyway, we got along just fine in the Eastern Villages without magic."

Oscar looked at the ground and took a deep breath. "Do . . . you think you'll go back there?"

Callie's lips tightened. "It's not my home anymore," she said. "It never really was."

"Are you going to . . . stay?"

"Oscar, my parents sold me. Madame Mariel abandoned my brother. And then she abandoned the Barrow. I am not going to abandon these children. They need us."

Us, Oscar repeated to himself. The apprentice and the hand.

"Who else will know how to help them?" Callie went on. "I . . . I can be a healer. We helped those kids; we figured it out. You just have to pay attention to the people."

Oscar nodded. He understood. People were Callie's plants.

"And," Callie said, "there are herbs that work without magic. I used them back home. Maybe not as potent, but people use them all around the world. Aren't some of the herb books in Caleb's library from the continent?"

"Yes," Oscar said. "A lot of them."

"And so," she went on, "I will need a garden."

She glanced at Oscar and then looked pointedly at him. And then stopped and stared.

"I will need a garden," she repeated.

"What? Me?"

"Yes. You know how to grow herbs. People will still need them even when . . ."

She didn't need to finish. *Even when the magic's gone.* "But what about Caleb's shop?"

"Oscar, it's not Caleb's shop anymore. It's your shop. The whole marketplace is going to change. But people always need medicine. You could grow herbs and sell remedies. In my town we had an apothecary."

Apothecary. It was a funny word, like a flightless bird. Oscar looked at the ground. "I'm not really made for people."

Callie exhaled. "You're not made at all, Oscar. Don't you see? After everything that's happened this week? You get to do the making."

He did understand. Sort of.

"And I can help you. And you help me. We have a deal."

"I don't know."

"You don't have to yet. We can just worry about today."

"Yes," Oscar said. "I'd just like to worry about today."

This was not entirely true. He wanted to think about tomorrow, and a tomorrow after that, too, one where every day was certain, where he could see the perfect structure to it, where he could count the steps one by one—not live with this white fuzzy emptiness that was in his head. He'd always had surety, so much so that it never would have occurred to him to want it. He hadn't known things could be any other way.

There were so many things it had never occurred to him that he could want. It was very human, to want things.

"We'll figure it out," Callie said. "Now, come on."

They went to the Coopers' house first to check on Hugo and Sophie.

It was Lady Cooper who met them in the parlor, full of happy words for Callie and Oscar. Lord Cooper hung back in the shadows, still looking at them like he wanted their approval.

Sophie, Lady Cooper said, had gotten up and walked around that morning, and Hugo had sat up in bed. It was a miracle, really.

"They'll stay healthy now," Lady Cooper added. "Right?"

She smiled, but something else flashed across her face. Oscar had seen it in enough people now to understand:

Lady Cooper was frightened.

Maybe Callie had been right. Maybe just as the Barrow had held on to the magic, the City had held on to the grief of the plague, and so grief coursed through all the City people's veins. Maybe they were really afraid of the fuzzy blankness, just like Oscar was.

Oscar glanced at Callie. She nodded slightly.

"We don't know," Oscar said, straightening. "They're made of wizard-tree wood and spells. We can't possibly know what's going to happen."

"Nothing like them has ever existed before," Callie said. "There are no books. We can only do the best we can."

The lady's face contorted. "But . . . what are we supposed to do?"

The words popped into Oscar's head: *You live with it.*

The children would have to.

They went to Sophie's room first. Oscar stood in the shadows while Callie sat next to the curly-haired girl on the bed. Sophie was more girl than ghost now. She was sitting up, and her big eyes widened when she saw Callie.

Callie smiled down at the girl. "May I touch your side?" she asked.

The girl nodded.

As Oscar watched, Callie put her hand gently on Sophie's rib cage. The girl did not flinch.

"May I see?" Callie asked.

The girl did not protest as Callie lifted up the white shift. Oscar saw a flash of olive skin and what looked like the memory of a bruise.

"It looks much better," Callie said. "Do you feel all right?"

Sophie nodded again.

Callie frowned. "Can you talk?" she asked.

Nod.

"She never did say much," said Lady Cooper from the back of the room. "It's just the way she is."

Oscar's mouth twitched. No wonder he liked her.

"I'm just going to put my fingers on your wrist," Callie was telling Sophie. "I can feel your heart there; did you know that?" As Callie leaned into the girl, Oscar could see the concentration in her shoulders. She stayed like that for a long time. "It sounds much stronger," she murmured to Sophie. "But I think we can get it even stronger still." Then she leaned back and looked at Lady Cooper. "I'd like to give her one more dose of tea. Is that all right?"

"Of course," Lady Cooper said. "Anything."

Callie stood up. "Let's check on Hugo, and then I'll come back. Is that all right with you, Miss Sophie?"

The girl nodded.

Lady Cooper led Callie out of the room, but Oscar

found himself lingering. The girl had caught him in her eyes again. So he walked up to the bed.

He didn't say anything; he just smiled a little at her. He hoped the smile said all the things he couldn't find words for, like *I hope you feel better* and *I am trying to get someone to help you* and *I'm sorry*. Though what he was sorry for, he was not quite sure.

The girl took him in with her eyes. They only seemed to grow wider, and suddenly Oscar saw the nightmare flickering there again. Her hand went to his arm, and she pulled him down toward her.

"Monster?" she whispered.

Oscar shook his head. "No. Not anymore."

The girl exhaled and sank into the bed. But the nightmares still lingered.

"It's all right," Oscar said. "It's—"

It's what? He couldn't guarantee another monster wouldn't come and he couldn't guarantee the spells that bound her wouldn't start failing again and he couldn't guarantee there would be no more nightmares. He couldn't even tell her what the nightmares might be made of.

So he reached into his pocket and pulled out the small wooden cat. The girl's eyes widened, and some sparkle replaced the dark things there.

The figure hummed warmly in his hand. He ran one

finger down the cat's back and then squeezed it a little so he could take the feeling with him. Then he placed the cat gently in Sophie's hand.

For me? Sophie's eyes said.

"For you. She'll keep you—well, she can't keep you safe. But she will keep you company. And she's nice to have when things aren't safe. You just squeeze her in your hand—yes, like that."

The girl looked up at Oscar. *Thank you.*

You're welcome.

"Her name is Block," Oscar added. In case that wasn't obvious.

He gave her a small little smile. And she bit her lip and then smiled softly back. And though the spells that writhed within her skin and blood and bones were uncertain and unknowable, Oscar and Callie would do everything they could to give her the life she was supposed to have. A human life. With red shoes and swishing skirts and all the fuzzy blank things ahead.

She was made of wood, but she was a real girl now.